A TOUCH OF DESTINY

OF FATE AND FURY BOOK 1

SCYLLA KAIROS

Siren Song Books

DEDICATION

Nana, you're the reason this book exists. Thank you for instilling a love of reading and writing in me at a young age and encouraging my creativity as I grew up. Now, please don't read this book!

CONTENT WARNING

A Touch of Destiny includes triggers such as a scene of domestic violence and attempted spousal murder, severe panic disorder and panic attacks, and mentions of vomiting (does not go into detail). Child death (not shown but mentioned). An implication of rape, violence, and scars. A Touch of Destiny is the first of a polyromance series, and there are mentions of partner jealousy and brief sexual content that will grow in intensity over the series. There are also several training scenes depicting physical and magical attacks.

CONTENTS

1. Ascension Day   1

2. A Grandmother's Love   12

3. All You Need is Love   16

4. Family Isn't Always Blood   23

5. A Turbulent History   29

6. Hearts of Ice   39

7. Going Through Changes   47

8. Sensory Overload   53

9. Always on Display   61

10. A Whole New World   70

11. Carriage Rides and Designer Dresses   75

12. Secret Plans   84

13. The Key to a Girl's Heart   89

14. Dancing the Night Away One Way or Another   93

15. Fight, Flight, Or...   100

16. New School, New Me   102

17. Just Kidding, Same Me   105

18. Lessons   112

19. For Life — 120

20. The Crimson-Haired Faerie — 122

21. What the Fuck was That? — 129

22. First Day of School — 134

23. Nothing Like a Little Ass Kicking — 141

24. Undeclared — 146

25. The Beginning — 156

26. Secrets Exposed — 160

27. All About that Bond — 165

28. Scorch Marks and Straitjackets — 169

29. Balancing Act — 177

30. The Heart Wants What the Heart Wants — 185

31. Magic Training, and Sparring, Oh My! — 191

32. So Many Things to Tell Her — 193

33. Misunderstandings — 198

34. Territorial — 205

35. Insatiable — 213

36. Go Easy on Me — 219

37. Jack-in-the-Pulpit Might Be the Culprit — 224

38. Something to Lose — 230

39. Raging Hormones — 236

40. It's About Time — 245

41. Beltane Bonds — 247

42.	Healing	256
43.	Holding Back	263
44.	Oceanic Views	272
45.	Core Memories	279
46.	Explosion	287
47.	Unlocked	295
48.	Morning Sickness Woes	301
49.	The Journey Begins	304
Acknowledgements		311
About the Author		313

Chapter One

ASCENSION DAY
One Twenty-Seven

I t was a beautiful day. The kind of day anyone would hope to experience on their last day on Earth. I walked down Dahlia Lane for the last time, just like I had a hundred times before.

An icy grip tightened around my chest when I spotted a human across the quiet street, his eyes locked on me. He lifted his iPhone, and the shutter click of the camera set my teeth on edge. I whirled away, heart racing, and darted into the nearest shop. All I wanted to do was run a few errands for my mom without a fucking human tourist getting in my face. I should've known that'd be impossible on Ascension Day.

I gulped down several deep breaths inside the shop, trying to quell the rising panic. On a normal day, I struggled to be away from my safe spaces and people. Home, work, and the woods were my sanctuaries. But that day, I'd ventured out because it was my last day there forever, and I wanted to make sure my mom would be cared for when I was gone. I drew in another calming breath and groaned when the spicy scents of cinnamon, clove, nutmeg, and vanilla hit my nose.

"Hello, One Twenty-Seven."

The shop owner's gravelly voice grated on my already overstimulated nerves. I jumped back, then shivered when my back pressed against the cool brick wall. Of all the shops on Dalia Lane I could've stepped into, it had to be *hers*.

"Morning, Acanthe," I murmured, staring at the spotless wood floor, my mind whirling with my options. Leave the store and take my chances with the humans or face the scariest matriarch of the Silver Bay coven. A heartbeat passed, then another.

"What brings you in?" Acanthe asked, breaking the silence.

I raised my gaze to meet hers and stepped further into the shop. Acanthe might be terrifying, but she was predictable. Humans never were.

"Sorry, I was trying to get away from the humans," I said, gesturing out the window at the man who'd crossed the street and now lurked outside the shop, phone in hand, seemingly waiting for me to exit.

"Ascension Day tourists," Acanthe said, glancing at him. "Pay them no mind."

I snorted. Easy for her to say. She was one of the most powerful witches in the Midwest. She'd have no problem fending off a horde of humans if they mobbed her. But me, a Magicborn who hadn't ascended yet? Well, I was physically no different from the humans currently lurking outside the shop. But apparently, our lack of ability was of no concern to the matriarchs. After all, there were laws that forbade harming us, but that didn't make it any less stressful to be followed and harassed by gaggles of trifling humans.

Humans called Magicborn blessed. They practically worshiped us. They took any opportunity to get near us, to touch us as if our magic would wear off of us and onto them. It was exhausting and terrifying, and there was no way to hide from them because we were forced by the coven matriarchs, Magicborn faction monarchs, and the human government to wear uniforms in varying colors that told the world our status. They said it was for our safety to ensure everyone knew we were Magicborn and not to be harmed. The man outside knew what I was because of the uniform and color I wore, all black, signifying my ascent that night.

"Hiding here won't help you," Acanthe said from behind the counter. "You can't take anything from Earth to Ilthyrium after Ascension. So,"—she brandished a deck of tarot cards from thin air—"unless you want your cards read, there's nothing I can help you with."

I cringed. The last thing I wanted was for Acanthe to read my cards. I had no desire for the witch to reveal any premonitions about my future. As an infant, my adoptive mother, Lillian, had brought me to her as was commanded. All Magicborn were to visit a tarot reader before they reached the age of one and have their future foretold. The premonition Acanthe gave of my future supposedly caused her to black out. She'd refused to speak on it ever since, except to the head matriarch of the coven. However, anytime I was in town, I'd catch the two of them staring at me with knowing smiles.

Acanthe stepped around the counter toward me. Her long, ebony hair wrapped tightly around her body, undulating with a sinuous grace. Thick strands of silver and copper highlights were woven throughout, and they wriggled and writhed unnaturally, as though each one was alive.

I was about to refuse her offer when Acanthe's eyes rolled back into her skull until only the whites of her eyes were visible. I nervously stepped toward the door to leave the shop and Acanthe behind.

When Acanthe spoke again, her voice transformed. Her usual gravelly cadence gave way to a sinister tone. "Destiny has touched you. You'll bring death and destruction to your enemies and freedom to the enslaved."

Nope, absolutely not. I scrambled backward toward the door, wincing when my shoulder blades slammed into the solid oak. I grappled for the handle, my eyes on Acanthe. I nearly sobbed with relief when my hand found the handle. The door flew open, pulling me out with it.

I stumbled. My feet floundered for purchase as I tried to figure out what the hell had happened. Somehow, my belt loop had snagged on the handle. I hung there for a moment, trying to yank my pants loose from the handle, while Acanthe advanced toward me, eyes still rolled up in her skull. I had no idea how she could see me, but that wasn't stopping her. I gave one hard final yank, and my belt loop ripped, sending me hurtling down the steps in front of Acanthe's shop.

"Oomph!" I plowed into someone so sturdy that I bounced off and lost my balance. My arms flailed desperately, reaching out for anything to stop my descent. I grasped a hand, which yanked on mine and pulled me up so forcefully that I face-planted into a very nice yet unmistakably female chest.

My face burned with embarrassment as I found my footing and took a small step back. "I'm so sorry," I muttered, my eyes locked on the concrete below, wishing I could vanish into its depths.

"Perhaps," an amused voice said, "watching where you're going will help you avoid these moments in the future." The voice had a unique blend of rough and melodic undertones. It also carried the smooth cadence only ascended Magicborn possessed. My head whipped up to look at the crimson-haired woman before me.

Her sharply pointed ears were pierced with little gold rings and displayed for all the humans to see precisely what she was. Not a woman, a female faerie.

She was dressed head to toe in all black, except for the polished silver insignia of a pair of crossed daggers on each shoulder of her jacket, which labeled her as a member of the fae Guard. A large sword, its hilt intricately decorated, hung behind her right shoulder. Her belt held an array of lethal-looking daggers, and... my hands.

I must have grabbed her waist when I fell forward.

I tried to yank my arms back, but the faerie gripped me tightly above each elbow. I glanced down at her hands, then back up at her face. She dropped my arms as though I'd burned her and wiped her hands on her pants.

I glanced at the insignia, searching for her rank. An intricately designed N wearing a crown sat between the crossed daggers. My cheeks blazed, and I darted a few paces away from her. I fisted my hand over my heart and bowed. She was an elite Queen's Guard.

I cleared my throat. "I'm sorry. I didn't see you there," I said.

I bowed before the guard, awaiting her permission to move on, silently cursing my clumsiness.

You weren't supposed to get in their way or touch them. It was strictly taboo to touch any member of the guard without express permission. And you definitely weren't supposed to plant your face in their chest—no matter how nice of a chest it was—*fuck*.

"Rise," the fae female said, simultaneously interrupting my spiral and releasing me from my bowed position. She cocked her head to the left. "Are you alright?" she asked, not unkindly.

I bobbed my head, afraid I'd embarrass myself further if I opened my mouth.

The faerie smirked, "Pay attention to where you're going." Then she stepped aside.

"I will," I said, as she strode away.

From behind me, murmurs and mutterings grew louder. I spun around and found myself surrounded by humans whispering to each other and snapping photos of the whole debacle.

My stomach churned. I hated even the smallest of attention and now there I was, center stage in the spotlight, providing prime entertainment. I looked at the ground, silently begging the sidewalk to open up and swallow me whole.

Sadly, the sidewalk refused to gobble me up and save me from further embarrassment, so fleeing was the only option. I spun, only to collide with another person. A much more solid someone this time.

"Whoa," a male voice said, his rough, firm hands catching me before I tumbled backward for the second time. At least this time, I didn't face plant into his chest. Peals of laughter rang out around me. Every nerve in my body screamed. I'd had enough. The sensation of ants crawling across my overly tight skin was all I could think about. I yanked out of the male's grasp, my body aching and my skin feeling like it was on fire.

"Sorry," I mumbled, not looking up to see who the voice's owner was. I didn't care who I'd crashed into and whether or not he might be important. Queasiness turned into full-blown nausea, and I thought I might be sick right there on the street. I swallowed back the bile rising in my throat, moved around him, and raced away.

I was dying to return to the safety of home to my mother, but there were errands I needed to take care of, so instead of fleeing home, I ducked around a corner into an alley to catch my breath. The stench of day-old food left in the sunlight greeted me when I sucked in a deep breath.

I gagged, and a wave of heat rushed over me, followed by chills. My heart's pace changed from a trot to a gallop.

Goddess, please, not here. Not now, I silently begged. But, as usual, the goddess ignored me.

I gasped, struggling to take a deep breath.

Tears streamed down my face as I clutched my aching chest, battling the rising tide of fear. But it was too late. There was nothing I could do. But that didn't stop me from trying the tricks that usually distracted me. I snapped my fingers, listening to the click of my middle finger hitting the soft pad at the base of my thumb. Nothing. I dug my nails into my palm, hoping the pain would ground me. Still nothing. The anxiety built. I fought it with every ounce of strength, resisting the tidal wave of dread until it finally crashed down on me, overwhelming me in its grip.

I bent at the waist, dry heaving and gasping for breath. I rarely threw up when the panic came. But my emetophobia made the ordeal a million times worse, especially since my anxiety almost always manifested physically, and most frequently it was stomach upset. My heart thundered in my chest, and for a second, I worried it would burst from my ribcage. The mildly rational part of my brain, still half-functioning, reminded me it was ridiculous.

The world closed in around me. My vision narrowed to tiny pinpricks. I was heading toward oblivion, which sounded cooler than saying I might pass out from hyperventilating because my brain liked to invent life-and-death panic over everyday crap like walking down the street. I needed to get a grip. "You're okay. You're okay. You're safe," I chanted, trying to quell the feelings roiling inside me by convincing my brain that there was no imminent danger.

A pair of scuffed white sneakers appeared in the tiny pinpricks of space I could still see.

"Breathe."

The soft female voice was a life raft in the ocean I was drowning in. I reached out to grab her. Contact. I needed contact. That would ground me.

I glanced up at my girlfriend's face hovering right above me. Fifty-Five grabbed my hand, and the pinprick in my vision widened as I clung to her.

"If I...could...don't you think...I would," I said between gasps.

"You can, babe. Sit with me," she said, grabbing my other hand and pulling me down to sit in the dirty alleyway.

Usually, I'd never because ew, but I was too far gone to care, so I allowed myself to collapse into a heap, even though I knew I'd regret it later. I tried to curl up in a ball to wait out the wave, but Fifty-Five stopped me.

"No," she said, tugging my arms and pulling me up. "Sit up and breathe with me."

Fifty-Five sat cross-legged across from me, and I mimicked her position while trying to pull air into my tight lungs and fight the nausea threatening to drown me.

Fifty-Five placed my hand on her stomach. "Breathe with me."

It took all my strength to focus on the rise and fall of Fifty-Five's stomach as she drew in several deep belly breaths. I slowly recognized the pattern. Inhale deeply with your belly for five seconds, hold for five seconds, exhale for five seconds, repeat. I closed my eyes and mimicked the technique, and the tightness in my chest slowly eased.

"Name five things you can see," she said, squeezing my hands.

I glanced around the alley and rattled off. "Pavement, trashcan, car, paper, you," I said, my gaze landing on her.

"Four things you can feel," she prodded.

I took another deep breath and said, "Your hands, gravel, the air, my hair."

Before she could give me the next thing, I rattled off three things I could hear—my breathing, kids running and screaming, the leaves rustling in the trees.

"Almost there," Fifty-Five said. "Two things you can smell."

I inhaled and wrinkled my nose. "Trash and..." I paused, inhaling deeply again, trying to catch a scent other than the stench of rotting food. "Your perfume," I said, leaning closer to her and inhaling in again. The crisp scent of her lilac perfume flooded my senses. It reminded me of spring, my favorite season, and our sanctuary in the woods.

"One thing you can taste?"

I opened my eyes. "You," I whispered. I leaned forward and gently pressed my lips to hers. She broke the kiss almost immediately.

My eyes widened, and I remembered where we were, and I quickly glanced around, checking to see if anyone saw us—saw me—kiss her. Magicborn weren't allowed to date or have sex before we ascended. So, we'd hidden our love, maintaining the facade of friendship for years.

"Breathe," Fifty-Five said. "No one saw."

My chest stopped constricting under the weight of my fear. I smiled and looked at Fifty-Five. "How did you find me?" I asked.

"I was down the block and saw everything," she said, brushing a strand of her long blonde hair out of her face and tucking it behind her ear.

I sighed, dropping my head in my hands. "You saw everything?"

"Yep. I did. I'm impressed, honestly. How did you crash into a faerie guard?"

I shrugged and held up my hands. "Hello, have you met me?"

Fifty-Five's laughter filled the space between us. "I guess *you* would be capable of that. At least you crashed into a cute guy right after," she said. "Not that you noticed."

I rolled my eyes. Fifty-Five would notice a cute guy, but me—not so much. I'd only ever had eyes for one person, and she was sitting with me. "Sorry, I didn't notice. I was too busy humiliating myself."

"At least you did it spectacularly." Fifty-Five reached out to caress my face.

"Yay me." I leaned into her caress for a split second before pulling away.

Fifty-Five dropped her hand and leaned back, bracing herself with her arms behind her back. "What are you doing on the Lane? I figured you'd avoid this place on Ascension Day."

"I wanted to say goodbye to the Lane and Rosalyn, and I had to run an errand for mom."

Fifty-Five studied me for a moment. "Wanna go to the spot?" she asked.

"Absolutely," I said. "But I have to take care of something first."

"Okay, what's first?"

"Rosalyn's," I said. It was a small grocery store named after its owner. Rosalyn was the closest thing I had to a grandmother.

"Let's go." Fifty-Five stood, extended her hand to me, and pulled me up beside her.

I pulled my cell out of my back pocket and opened the camera to check my face. My eyeliner was mildly smudged, but at least my face didn't have that splotchy I've-been-crying look.

Fifty-Five stepped in and ran the pad of her thumb under my eye. "There. You're perfect."

A shudder ran through my body at her closeness and warmth, but I shoved the feelings down for the moment. There would be time for intimacy later, when we were away from prying eyes. My heart picked up its pace again, not from fear this time, but anticipation as I lost myself in the thoughts of her hands and lips on my body.

"Shall we?" she said, interrupting my spicy thoughts.

I gave her a thumbs up, not trusting myself to speak. Fifty-Five looped her arm through mine, and I marveled at the touch. I'd never been fond of people touching me, but I'd always found Fifty-Five's touch soothing and exciting. I tightened my grip on her arm, and we stepped back out onto the bustling street of Dahlia Lane.

Chapter Two
A GRANDMOTHER'S LOVE
One Twenty-Seven

We stepped inside the shop, and Fifty-Five released my arm to pick up a grocery basket. "I'm gonna grab a couple of things. I'll meet you out front when you're ready," she said.

"Okay," I said, scanning the shop until I spotted Rosalyn at the counter looking over receipts.

When Rosalyn looked up, she dropped the receipts and hurried around the counter to pull me into a comforting hug.

I hugged her back. "Good morning, Grandma Ros." I pulled back, smiling at the short, round woman before me.

"Good morning, sweetheart," Rosalyn replied. Her glasses slipped down the bridge of her nose, and she plucked them off her face and set them atop her head, nestling them in her salt and pepper hair. "What brings you here, my girl?"

"Would you make a delivery after the ceremony?" I said. "To my mom." I continued when Rosalyn raised an eyebrow at me. "I doubt she'll be up to making herself meals over the next few days, and I think a basket of her favorites will help."

"Of course, sweetheart. Don't worry. I'll keep an eye on her and make sure she's taking care of herself."

"Thank you." I rolled my neck, releasing some of the tension in my shoulders. A slow, sad smile crossed my face as I gazed around the small shop. The rows were clean and organized, as always. Each aisle was meticulously cared for and well stocked to ensure the residents of Dahlia Lane had what they needed when they needed it.

I was relieved my mom would be cared for when I was gone, but even so, a wave of sadness flooded me when I glanced around the shop, trying to memorize each detail.

Since Rosalyn had no one to help her run the shop, my mom stepped in and helped when she could. I'd spent much of my childhood here, and once I reached thirteen, the legal age to work, I spent my summers stocking shelves. There were photos of the lane before anything was built and black-and-white photos of the lane as it grew.

An array of photos lined the wall above the check-out counter that told the shop's story. The story began with the Dain family standing in front of the shop when it was built and called Dain's Grocer, and carried on through the generations until the last photo that featured Rosalyn alone.

The males of the Dain family said to hell with the Lane when the coven took over, despite most of the women born into their family being witches. When it came time for Rosalyn's generation to take over, the shop was offered to Rosalyn's eldest brother, who refused, so Rosalyn took over the shop and rechristened it Rosalyn's.

Rosalyn had always been there for me when things were bad at home. But after the Ascension Ceremony tonight, I wouldn't be able to run to her when things got scary or hard. I wouldn't be able to seek comfort from her anymore. I was losing everything, and nothing, not even the promise of magic and new family made up for that.

Rosalyn pulled me into another tight hug. I towered over the older woman, but I felt small in Rosalyn's embrace. Her embrace brought me back to when I was little, and I'd crawl into her lap, and she'd read to me until I fell asleep on her chest just like I imagined a biological grandmother would. "I'll miss you, my girl. You'll always be in my heart."

"And you in mine," I said, tightening my grip before releasing her. I pivoted and walked away so Rosalyn couldn't see the tears falling down my face.

I exited the shop, wiping away the tears spilling down my cheeks. I stepped onto the sidewalk and leaned against the uneven brick wall of Rosalyn's small shop to wait for Fifty-Five. I took one last look around Dahlia Lane, doing my best to commit it to memory.

The sweet scents of cinnamon and yeast wafting from the bakery, mixed with the sounds of the click-clacking of passerby's shoes against the cobblestone. The brilliant gold and red fall leaves rustling on the small trees, which provided minimal shade from the warm autumn sun. Children's laughter as they raced down the street toward the ice cream shop, which featured outrageous flavors like pepperoni pizza and mac and cheese.

"I'm going to miss it here," Fifty-Five said from behind me, startling me. "Whoops, sorry. Didn't mean to scare you."

"I zoned out," I said.

"I figured," Fifty-Five said, chuckling. "You ready to go? Or was there something else you needed to do on the Lane?"

I took one last look around before turning back to Fifty-Five. "I'm ready."

She held up a wicker picnic basket. "I got food. Let's go. The staring is wearing on me." She gestured across the street to a group of humans staring at us.

I'd been so lost in thought I'd completely forgotten about them. A chill inched down my spine.

"On you? Lover of attention and the spotlight?" I quipped, raising my hand to her forehead, playfully checking for a fever and trying to push down the anxiety threading its way through my body.

Fifty-Five rolled her eyes dramatically. "Can you believe it?" She giggled and looped her arm through mine, quelling my anxious feelings.

"Come on, One Twenty-Seven, I want to be alone with you." Her voice turned husky and intimate, and I practically melted.

"I want to be alone with you too," I whispered. "I've wanted to do something with you all day."

"Oh?" Fifty-Five replied, looking up at me, her brilliant blue eyes shining lustfully. She bit her lip in the way she knew drove me crazy, and I moaned out loud.

"Let's go," I said, slipping my arm through hers. We started off down the lane together.

I wanted to drag her out of town as fast as I could, but we took our time, so we didn't draw attention to ourselves. To the outside world, we appeared to be best friends out for a stroll, but to each other, we were everything.

Chapter Three

ALL YOU NEED IS LOVE
One Twenty-Seven

Fifty-Five and I walked arm in arm toward the outskirts of town and into the woods. I paused inside the tree line, closed my eyes, and took in the earthy smell of the white pine trees, the spicy, fruity scent of the prairie wild roses, and the dirt beneath my feet. Robins flitted through the trees, their sweet songs filled the air, and the fall breeze rustled through the towering trees, sending a cascade of leaves plummeting to the ground. Even the scent of the decaying fallen leaves filled me with an unbridled joy. I enjoyed many things, but nature was near the top of the list. It was where I felt the most at home—the most at peace.

I glanced at Fifty-Five to find her doing the same.

Fifty-Five must have felt me staring, because she opened her eyes a second later and met mine. "I love the scent of the woods. All the life that tangles through it mesmerizes me. There's something so relaxing once you step over the border and into the woods. Something magical."

"I feel it, too." I squeezed her hand before I leaned in and stole a quick kiss.

Her soft lips greeted mine eagerly.

Desire pooled in my belly, and I pulled away from the kiss before either of us could deepen it and lose ourselves in each other. We'd been together for three years and intimate for the last two, and still, our desire for each other was always a lit match, ready to set us ablaze at any moment.

I tugged her hand, leading the way to a large ancient red maple that rose beside a stream. The tree had hollowed over the years, creating a cozy nook that overlooked the river. It was the perfect place to relax, read a book, or share a picnic with someone.

I clambered over a giant branch, but my foot caught on a knot in the tree bark. I barely caught myself and cursed my clumsiness as I dropped into the alcove, turning to help Fifty-Five into it, but she'd already gracefully scaled the tree and landed with a soft thump beside me.

I rolled my eyes. "Show off," I muttered, and she smirked.

I reached into the tree's hollow, pulled out a weatherproof bag, preloaded with a soft cotton blanket. I laid it out on the ground and flopped onto it. Fifty-Five immediately followed suit and opened the picnic basket she brought. She pulled out sandwiches, fresh fruit, and veggies, along with a bottle of wine and two plastic cups.

She handed me a sandwich, opened the baggies of fruits and veggies, and then popped open the wine, my favorite fruity red. I extended my cup. Fifty-Five filled it with the sweet-smelling wine before pouring some for herself, then she raised her plastic cup and said, "To us, may we always endure no matter where we end up."

I swallowed the lump in my throat and raised my cup. There was no guarantee we'd survive ascension, let alone ascend into the same Magicborn faction. Our relationship wouldn't survive if we didn't end up in the same faction.

Unable to speak, I nodded, clinked my cup against hers, and took a long drink. I held the wine in my mouth, letting the sweet, acidic drink caress my tongue. I swallowed and looked down at the sandwich—roast beef—another one of my favorites. "Thank you for bringing lunch," I said.

"You're welcome. I figured we were due for one last picnic."

We sat together in comfortable silence, eating lunch and drinking wine. Lucky for us, being Magicborn made our alcohol tolerance high since our bodies metabolized alcohol faster than we could drink it. We were encouraged by the coven matriarchs to partake in drinking wine during the Wiccan holidays once we turned sixteen, so there was little chance we'd get a slight buzz, let alone get drunk off one bottle of human wine, even if witches brewed it.

Fifty-Five lay against my chest momentarily before lifting her head and looking me in the eye. I was captivated by the deep ocean blue of her eyes. Then she leaned in and brushed her lips against mine. I deepened the kiss, pulling her to me. We lay there kissing for a couple of minutes, ramping up each other's desire, when Fifty-Five pulled back, panting, eyes glittering. It never took long for us to reach the need-you-now point.

Fifty-Five sat up and pulled her shirt over her head before moving on to her pants and signaling me to do the same. I obliged. Within seconds, I was lost in the feel of her body against mine, and I reveled in the way our bodies moved together as we found our rhythm. Our lovemaking was like wildfire consuming every piece of us until we had nothing left. At least until the next match was struck, and we were ignited again. We could never get enough of each other. Fifty-Five's appetite was endless, but so was mine.

The last few rays of sunlight shone through the fall leaves, creating an illusion that the leaves were on fire all around us.

"I'm going to miss this," Fifty-Five said, placing her head on my sweaty, heaving chest as I caught my breath after we'd found our release for the last time.

"Me too," I said.

Fifty-Five stayed quiet for several moments before speaking again. "Are you anxious about tonight?"

"A little, yeah, I'm still afraid of how much it's going to hurt," I said, wrapping my arms tighter around her.

"Me too. But we don't have a choice."

"No, we don't. What are you hoping you'll ascend to?" I asked. We'd spoken about it many times in the last few years, dreaming about which faction we might ascend to. We each had our favorite ideas. She wanted to ascend to a faction that could shapeshift between human and their faction form—a dragon or lycan was always among her top choices. I wanted something steadier, something that remained in the same form as much as possible, like a faerie or a vampire. But now that we were so close to ascension, I wondered if she'd changed her mind.

"I don't know. I still think a dragon would be neat. I'd like to fly," Fifty-Five said. My stomach twisted at the thought. I was terrified of heights, and flying didn't appeal to me at all.

"How about you?"

"I'd rather not change." I caressed her shoulder with my thumb. "So, I haven't thought about it much beyond what I've told you before. I guess I hope I become whatever you become, even if I have to fly, so I don't have to be alone, and we don't have to be separated."

"You'll be okay even if we transition differently. We'll have to find a way to be together even if we ascend into different factions," Fifty-Five said.

Was she trying to convince me or herself?

"I doubt we could make that work," I whispered.

"We could try. Hey, look," Fifty-Five said, pointing up at the sky. "The sun is setting."

We sat up and Fifty-Five settled between my legs and leaned into my chest. I wrapped the blanket around our naked bodies and watched the last vestiges of the sun set over the stream. Brilliant oranges, pinks, and purples slow-danced across the sky and drifted into night's dark embrace.

That was it—my last sunset as a human.

"Thank you for today. I wouldn't have had this day go any other way than this," she said, still looking up at the sky. I glanced down at Fifty-Five and saw a tear rolling down her cheek.

"You're welcome, and me too," I said. Stretching my tense muscles, I stood and shimmied back into my leggings and hoodie. I wrapped my arms around myself tightly, briskly rubbing my arms, trying to dispel the biting chill of the evening air that nipped at me. The cold enveloped me like a veil, and gentle shivers danced along my spine as I sought warmth in my embrace. "We need to get home and start getting ready," I said, my teeth chattering.

Fifty-Five agreed and slipped into her own clothes. "If I don't have another chance to say goodbye, I want you to know that I've cherished our relationship. I love you, and no matter where life takes me, that will *always* be true."

She leaned toward me and brushed her lips over mine in the briefest and lightest of touches. I fought against the torch relit in my body. Fought against the urge to have her one last time.

Fifty-Five climbed out of the alcove, leaving me alone to collect myself. She always seemed to know exactly what I needed.

I slung the waterproof bag over my shoulder. It was time to bring it home. I'd never be back. I glanced once more around the dimly lit surroundings. "Goodbye," I whispered, my voice cracking on the word. Then I clambered over the tree root and landed on the other side next to Fifty-Five. I took her hand, and we set off back toward town.

My thoughts whirled with the possibilities that ascension would bring tonight. No matter what change was coming. I hated change, but it was inevitable. As much as I hoped I'd ascend with Fifty-Five, it was wishful thinking, and, as a rule, I refused to allow myself to get too hopeful. Life was cruel, and I was a realist or a pessimist (depending on who you asked). I knew the odds were low that we'd be lucky enough to be together in Ilthyrium. So, I turned my focus instead to what was coming. A transformation that might end my life permanently, and if it didn't, it would change it irrevocably.

We continued the trip out of the woods and through the town in comfortable silence, simply enjoying each other's company. I walked Fifty-Five to her house, and as we approached, the sound of laughter reached our ears. Fifty-Five paused, taking in the small, green one-story house before us. We could see her family inside through the big bay window, laughing together as they gathered around the dinner table. Her younger step-siblings, her adoptive mother, and her father each sat in their place and looked at Fifty-Five's empty chair. None of them dug into the food.

I turned to Fifty-Five, and for the second time that day, I saw tears in her eyes.

"I'm going to miss them so much. How am I supposed to leave them?" she asked.

I didn't have an answer. I found myself thankful that it was just me and Mom. It would be easier for me to leave one person behind than the four Fifty-Five was leaving behind. I pulled her into a quick hug and let her go.

As she opened the door, her five-year-old brother Ben whooped, leaping up from his chair and throwing himself into her arms. I left Fifty-Five at her house and made my way home while imagining a life where we could be together without the complications of magic getting in the way, where we could stay with our families instead of leaving them behind.

Chapter Four

FAMILY ISN'T ALWAYS BLOOD
One Twenty-Seven

I stood outside our quaint two-story blue cottage with weathered white shutters and peeling paint. The house was a little on the worn side, but both the house and the grounds it stood on were meticulously cared for, and the property was well-loved. It had been in Mom's family for generations.

A gentle breeze rustled the leaves of the nearby oak tree, and the memories flowed unbidden. Beautiful memories of picnics on the living room floor with my mother and terrible memories of my mother being beaten and nearly strangled by my adoptive father, warred for space in my already crowded mind.

I yanked myself out of that memory before I could fall too deep, refusing to allow memories of him to taint my final moments with my mother. I reached the final step that brought me to the porch, and one last memory fell into my mind, knocking the breath out of me.

"Hey, sweetie, I need to talk to you."

I'm immediately on guard. Is Elik coming back? Has something happened to Grandma Ros?

"What is it?" My voice cracks as I swallow back anxious tears.

Mom sits on the edge of my neatly made bed, staring silently at the wall. Panic rises within me. It's going to be something terrible.

"The coven gives each family the option of how they want to handle this. You can either learn from school or you can learn it from me, and I wanted to be the one to talk to you about it," she says.

I relax a fraction. If it has to do with something the school will tell us, and other people are learning it, it can't be that bad.

"You know you're Magicborn," Mom continued, reaching out and taking my small hand in hers. "And you know you're adopted. But we haven't ever discussed what happens when you reach adulthood. Have you ever noticed that there aren't any Magicborn that live here as adults? They're here only once a year on Samhain?

Honestly, I hadn't noticed. I've been too busy dreaming up imaginary worlds to be concerned with what adults were doing—except for Elik. But now he's a distant memory, so I rarely think of him anymore. Well, at least I try not to think of him. Mom's staring at me, waiting for an answer, so I shake my head.

"Okay, well, I'll get straight to the point. On the Samhain, after your eighteenth birthday, there will be an Ascension Ceremony, which you'll go through. I don't know much about it. I've never attended, but I know that the reigning monarchs of Ilthyrium will be there, and you'll undergo a change."

"A change?"

"You'll transform into one of the magical factions and no longer be human. And after you'll leave Earth forever."

"Which faction will I change into?" I ask. My voice comes out high-pitched and squeaky, betraying the anxiety I desperately want to hide.

"No one knows, love. You could be any of the six magical factions that inhabit Ilthyrium."

"What if I don't want to go? What if I want to stay here?" My lower lip quivers, tears threatening to spill. "What if I don't want to change?" I whimper. I gasp for breath as the panic attack races toward me.

"Sometimes we have a choice, and sometimes we don't, my dear, and in this, we don't have a choice."

Great wracking sobs leave my body. My mother scoops me up in her arms and holds me tightly as I cry harder than I've ever cried in my life. When I'm spent, I pull back and look up at my mother to find her face wet with tears as well.

"I'll always love you. You're my daughter. That will never change."

The memory faded as quickly as it came as I climbed the porch steps. I purposely stepped on the creaky step as I'd done so many times before. A signal I'd worked out with my mother years ago, and still something done out of habit. Out of self-preservation, perhaps. The skills we learn to survive unstable situations stay with us for life.

"Eve? Sweetie, is that you?"

Warmth spread through my body, and I couldn't help but break into a grin at the sweet nickname my mother had lovingly chosen for me.

Magicborn are called by the number of their birth order. When the first Magicborn is born each year and delivered to one of the covens, it is named One, the next is named Two, and so on. And the pattern refreshes each year. Occasionally, it could get confusing when two Magicborn with the same number name were in the same place, but with the uniforms, we were easily identifiable by year as well, and anyone speaking to us would clarify which year they were speaking to. I was the one hundred and twenty-seventh Magicborn to be delivered, so my name was One Twenty-Seven. The act of naming Magicborn individuals was reserved for their Ascension, during which the monarch of their faction would gift them with their official name.

Despite the societal norms, my mom insisted on calling me Eve. I loved her for it. It made me feel cherished, not like a commodity to add to the ranks of whatever magical faction I ascended.

"Yeah, Mom, it's me,"

The familiar creak of the front screen door greeted me as I opened it and stepped into my childhood home for the last time. A shudder passed through me as I brushed a worn spot in the paint on the door frame in the shape of my finger—a mark of my time as a human that would stay as a reminder long after I was gone—on my way through. It was one of my mother's silly superstitions—to leave evil at the door. A tear escaped my eye. This would be the last time I'd ever cross the threshold. The last time I'd ever leave anything outside my mother's door.

Goddess, I hope nothing I've left at her door will ever find its way inside.

"I was beginning to think you wouldn't come home before the ceremony," Mom said, coming around the corner while drying her sudsy hands on a red dish towel.

"I could never leave without saying goodbye." A lump formed in my throat. I didn't tell her I'd considered it. Leaving without saying goodbye may have been easier, but I couldn't do it.

I stared at my mother, trying to memorize everything about her: the wrinkles around her eyes, the few silver strands in her deep brown hair, her all-knowing deep brown eyes, and the scar that ran below the hairline where Elik had broken a bottle across her head during one of their fights. I held her gaze, and she held mine. Neither of us was willing to make the move that would bring us to our goodbyes.

We'd been through a lot together. Lillian and Elik were married before I'd ever come into the picture, and Elik, beat the ever-loving crap out of her nearly every day until he almost killed her. I'd stepped between them, and he'd turned his fists on me. The coven arrived swiftly when the alarm within my blood triggered, and they removed him from the coven territory. Elik hadn't been heard from since, but knowing he was out there somewhere always had me worried about Mom and if she'd be okay once I was gone.

"I'm going to miss you," we said simultaneously, our laughter tinged with underlying sobs. Laugh instead of cry. That was what we always did. Whenever things got hard, my mom always pushed me to find something funny for us to giggle about. That day, it was a lot harder than usual.

Her love for me had been unwavering. But after tonight, she'd be left with only memories of me. She'd be at the Ascension Ceremony, but I wouldn't have a chance to talk to her, so I had to say my goodbyes to her before.

I collapsed in her arms as she collapsed into mine. Our tears fell in earnest down our cheeks as we sank to the floor. How do you say good-bye to your protector? The one person who loves you wholeheartedly without conditions?

We stayed there huddled on the floor, the cold seeping through our clothes until the distant toll of bells broke the silence.

"I love you, Eve. I'll love you until I die," Mother said, stroking my cheek.

"I love you too," I replied, though I couldn't make the same promise—not that I didn't want to—in truth, I didn't know if I'd even remember her after I ascended, and if I did remembered her, I'd long outlive her, and the memories would fade as time passed. But for now, at that moment, I could say I loved her.

"Be brave, daughter."

I stood and squared my shoulders. I looked down at her one last time, inhaling the familiar scent of her orange blossom perfume, knowing it would be the last time I'd smell it. I offered her a gentle, sympathetic smile. That moment marked the end of our time together.

"I will be thanks to you." My throat burned as I took in the ordinary cream-colored walls, the large, welcoming, worn sofa I'd spent my teen years lounging around and watching movies with Mom. I contemplated making my way upstairs to my bedroom, where I'd find a spotless room, meticulously cared for because I hated disorganization, but I knew if I walked up those steps, I'd throw myself on the bed and never leave, so instead, I spun on my heel without another word and walked out the door for the last time.

Chapter Five

A TURBULENT HISTORY
One Twenty-Seven

Following the unpleasant preparations for the Ascension Ceremony—which included a significant amount of time spent in the bathroom cleansing our digestive systems—my fellow Magicborn and I proceeded to the massive outdoor theater. Its magic didn't seem like it belonged in the world of humanity.

The theater was nestled deep within the woods of Silver Bay, where no human would stumble upon it accidentally. Cloaking spells hid it throughout the year, so if any wayward hiker came across it, they'd be redirected, and their memory wiped of the few seconds they came into contact with the theater. Select humans were allowed in the theater once a year to witness an Ascension Ceremony and get a glimpse of the Magicborn monarchs.

A somber hush fell over the ascending Magicborn as we walked single file, the soft rustling of the fallen leaves, damp with the evening dew, carpeting the ground beneath our feet, filled the air. We weren't permitted to speak. We were expected to focus on the task ahead. It would take every ounce of strength we had to survive.

The Magicborn from other covens were interspersed among the Silver Bay Magicborn according to birth number, but I saw a few Magicborn I knew. The ascendant in front of me offered a small smile as we halted just outside the arena doors.

Two acolytes stood on either side of the massive doors. Each held a basket. The acolyte to the left waited as we gathered by the doors, and once we settled, announced. "When you pass these doors, you'll be entering your new life. As such, the last piece of your human lives will be collected. This is your final chance to send one last text to your families."

I looked down at the phone in my hands. I'd been surprised when they'd told us to take it with us, but here was the reason why. I opened the text messages app, selected my mother's name, and paused. I'd already said my goodbyes. It felt almost cruel to have us do this. *I don't even know what to say.* Then it came to me. I hurriedly added a second contact to the text. Rosalyn.

I love you both so much. Take care of each other. I typed out as a soft drumbeat began within the arena, and the acolytes pushed the doors open, motioning us forward. I hit send as the line began. I checked to ensure the text went through before I powered off my phone for the last time and gently set it in the basket.

We entered the arena and climbed the stairs to take our places. A sense of reverence and awe overwhelmed me. The front of each step was adorned with intricate carvings of the history of the Magicborn inlaid with pure gold. The black marble was cool against my bare feet, and I was thankful the evening was warm.

The stage was surrounded by raised seating. The benches were made of rich mahogany, and each step was adorned with a tall carved candle, making the inlaid golden veins glimmer and dance. The candles cast a warm, inviting glow over the arena and offered enough illumination to see each other's faces against the darkness.

A door opened below, and the Magicborn monarchs took their places on the steps across from us. The werewolves, mermaids, and dragons were in their human bodies while the faeries, vampires, and pixies were in their fae, vampire, and pixie bodies. Each faction sat in their section with spaces for new ascendants. The theater hummed with magic, and I couldn't help but feel grateful and a little terrified to be a part of such a magnificent spectacle.

To the right, the crones of the thirteen covens were seated. Seeing them gathered in one place was a rare sight, and one I'd never seen before since Magicborn children weren't allowed to see an Ascension Ceremony before their own. Typically, the crones stayed with their covens scattered across what was once known as the United States. But every Samhain, the crones came together to perform their conversion magic, which they could only do when the veil was the thinnest between worlds because of the immense drain on their powers. It made the death and rebirth easier.

Directly below us were the parents of the ascending Magicborn and the humans who won that year's lottery to witness Ascension. It would be the only one they would be allowed to witness, as each human could only win the lottery once.

I wished for the thousandth time that I didn't have to ascend. I wished remaining human was a choice. My eyes landed on a set of brown eyes, glistening with unshed tears, staring back at me. I gave my mom a shaky smile and glanced away, afraid I'd lose it if I stared too long.

Matriarch Sylvaine, the leader of the Silver Bay witch coven, made her way across the stage to stand behind the podium. Energy radiated around her, creating a glow-like effect which illuminated her.

"Good evening, everyone, and Happy Samhain," Matriarch Sylvaine's magically enhanced voice boomed through the arena, disrupting my thoughts. "Tonight, we honor our beloved dead and celebrate those who'll shed their humanity and move into their next lives in their true form with their new faction and family." Matriarch Sylvaine turned to face the Magicborn monarchs. "I welcome our special guests—the leaders of the Ilthyrium realms, who'll soon take the newly ascended to their lands to live their new lives." She turned to address our parents next. "And I welcome the special individuals who've raised these children as their own for eighteen years. They've opened their homes, fed and clothed these children, and have loved them as their own. Thank you." The Magicborn monarchs stood up on the other side of the auditorium, fisted their hands over their hearts, and bowed their heads toward the parents, recognizing the depth of their sacrifice.

Finally, Matriarch Sylvaine turned to the humans, who won the lottery. "Lastly, I welcome the winners of this year's lottery. Please be respectful as we go through the ceremony. No pictures or videos may be taken, and we ask that if you are sensitive to witnessing individuals in agony, you leave now. This won't be pretty, nor will it be easy. Ascension is gruesome." The matriarch waited for several moments to see if anyone would leave. When no one did, she nodded her approval.

"Excellent. There are a few technical details to address before I begin the story. First, expect a light show. As each Magicborn steps into the circle, it will light up in the color of their new faction. When you arrived tonight, you were provided a handout with what each color represents, so you can refer to it as needed. Furthermore, each Magicborn who ascends tonight will die. Some will be reborn and some will not. If you do not wish to see death, I ask again that you leave now. This is your final chance." Nobody moved. "Very well. Let's begin."

The Matriarch cleared her throat.

"A millennium ago, the Magicborn factions warred to the brink of extinction. As they fought to the death, destroying each other, an unknown faction started training children and placing them on the battlefield to compensate for the lost numbers. Instead of condemning the actions of placing children on the front lines, the other factions, blinded by their hatred for one another, also began placing their children on the battlefield. Within a year, hundreds of thousands of Magicborn children were murdered in war. With the death toll rising and the Magicborn factions sending younger and younger children onto the battlefield, something had to be done." The matriarch's voice rang out strong and clear as she gripped the edges of the podium and continued her tale.

"One year after the Magicborn began sending their children into combat, a child was born to a faerie couple and appeared healthy and normal, but moments after birth, the child changed drastically. The fae features disappeared, and the child became noticeably human. At first, the fae thought it was a fluke, but then it happened again and again. And not just to the fae.

"It happened within all the Magicborn factions. These human children were in danger in many of the Ilthyrium realms. Those born in the mermaid realm, Oxlis, drowned within moments of birth. The vampires in Erastrith struggled with their bloodlust around the human infants. Pixies couldn't care for their offspring because the small stature of the pixies made it impossible to lift the human children. They could change their size to resemble that of a human for brief spurts, but nothing long enough to care for a human infant. Draconian Magicborn children couldn't survive in the harsh climates of Nivothia, and lycan cubs were abandoned each night as their parents answered the moon's call and transformed.

"For the first time in a hundred years, the Magicborn monarchs put aside their differences because they were facing extinction as their offspring were no longer magical, but human. As the Magicborn convened and argued about what to do, the Goddess Alecto entered their meeting with the only plausible solution. The human children needed to reside in the human realm on Earth.

"Her solution was met with hostility and disdain. But as time passed, more Magicborn children died. The factions were unwilling to allow their children to be raised in another realm. However, they finally decided that the witches of Earth could carry the responsibility of raising their children. Alecto assured them that each faction's children would be well cared for by the witches."

The silence in the theater was absolute as the Matriarch continued her story. I sat at the edge of my seat, clutching it with both hands as I listened to the history I'd been dying to learn for years. Finally, I was getting the answers of how and why I was here. I glanced around at my peers. Similar emotions played across each of their faces. Tranquility at finally knowing our story and trepidation at what was to come.

"Without the children to replenish the battlefield, the wars in Ilthyrium ceased, but for the Magicborn children who came to Earth, their battles were only beginning."

Matriarch Sylvaine looked up to where we were sitting, high above everyone else. "Word got out that Magicborn children lived among humans, and chaos ensued. Humans sought out the Magicborn children. Some wished to worship them, others wished to harm them because of the risk they posed. Churches began teaching their congregations that the Magicborn were the offspring of demons and needed to be purged from the Earth. These teachings resulted in attacks on the children and the coven members who cared for them.

"As Magicborn children were attacked, the Magicborn factions of Ilthyrium found a common enemy: Earth. Under the imminent threat of annihilation, the World Government quickly imposed a set of stringent laws on their religions and deities to protect the children. Both from attacks and from being worshiped as gods.

"On the Samhain after the first group of children's eighteenth birthday, everything changed. One by one, in the order of their birth, each child experienced several moments of agony where their body underwent a transformation. None of them were able to transition fully, but after a careful examination, it was clear that each was transforming into the form of one of the six Magicborn factions. Though in this situation, the process killed each of them, and once again, the Magicborn in Ilthyrium threatened the humans of Earth, although they had nothing to do with these deaths for once.

"The Matriarchs were at a loss. Alecto appeared to each matriarch in a dream and told them exactly what they needed to do to help the Magicborn through the Ascension process. Thus, the Ascension Ceremony was born." Matriarch Sylvaine's words rang out over the hushed crowd, enraptured by her story. Many of us were hearing the story for the first time. Each human in the crowd looked shocked.

"At the first Ascension Ceremony, there were a few hiccups as the witches worked to balance their power, and more Magicborn died than ascended, and those who survived did not ascend to the faction of their birth. The witches thought that they'd made mistakes in performing the transformation magic. The next year, more Magicborn children survived the process, but again none returned to the faction of their birth. In the third year, further adjustments were made, and nearly all the Magicborn children survived the change. Still, none of them ascended to their birth faction.

"The monarchs accused the witches of doing it intentionally, and the witches argued that it wasn't them. Only when all hell was about to break loose did Alecto once again appear before the witches and the Magicborn, telling them that the children would never return to their faction. That was the second part of the curse. To keep the factions from continuing their war, no child would ever return to the faction of their birth.

"This was a devastating blow to the Magicborn. Knowing they would never see their children again caused many Magicborn to refuse to procreate, leading to extinction concerns again, so each monarch decreed all factions must produce children to Earth every year until the curse could be broken. And thus, the Ascension Ceremony continued, and the Magicborn stopped tracking their human children to ease their grief.

Now, you know everything we know. Let's begin the Ascensions. Blessed be children."

Matriarch Sylvaine took a moment to look at us before she leaned forward, bracing herself against the sturdy podium, and called the first Magicborn forward to ascend.

Each Magicborn went through Ascension one by one chronologically. I stretched my neck to one side, then the other, and rolled my shoulders, trying to ease the tension there.

The flimsy paper gown I wore hung barely below my bottom and was open on the sides. The only thing stopping the shift from revealing my body to the community was the small, equally fragile paper straps tied together on each side. One wrong move and everyone would see everything. Not that it mattered. When it was my turn to ascend, my gown would be shredded, and everyone would see me naked anyway. Still, I'd wanted to maintain some dignity while I still could.

"Magicborn Fifty-Five from Silver Bay. You are called to ascend. Come forward and be reborn." The Matriarch's voice boomed through the arena, and I stood straighter.

Fifty-Five walked down the stairs with her head held high, but I saw the nervousness in the tense way she held her body as she made her way to the center of the stage, where we all had a perfect view. She hesitated briefly before stepping onto the glowing sphere in the dais's center. Two acolytes collected the shackles from the floor and clasped them around her wrists while another acolyte slipped adhesive heart monitor stickers under her gown. The shackles were a necessary evil. It kept us contained, unable to flee while the covens worked their excruciating transformation magic. The heart monitors would announce when her heart stopped beating and when it started again.

Once Fifty-Five was safely shackled to the floor, the sphere around her spun, pulsating, and flashing colors. The pulsating stopped abruptly, and a brilliant purple and gold light illuminated her. An expectant hush fell over the theater.

I glanced down at the card provided to see what faction had purple and gold lights, because those colors hadn't appeared yet. "Faerie," I whispered.

Fifty-Five's screams of agony filled the air, and she fell to her hands and knees. She gagged and retched, crying out, begging for the suffering to stop. She curled in on herself like she was trying to hold herself together. I cringed as the unmistakable sound of bones cracking and tendons snapping filled the arena. Queasiness washed over me as the girl I loved bent and twisted at odd angles and broke over and over.

I drew slow, deep breaths through my nose and blew them out through my mouth. Don't be sick. Not here, not now. Be strong for her.

I clenched my fists and winced as my nails dug into the soft flesh of my palms.

Do something! Stop this, save her.

I gripped the edge of my seat and my back stiffened as I pushed against the overwhelming urge to rush down there. She had to go through this, and I had to trust that she'd survive. My heart twisted in my chest, aching at my inability to rescue her from this agony as her sobs filled the amphitheater.

I glanced around the room, searching for something, anything, to focus on that wasn't my best friend's impending death. My gaze landed on Fifty-Five's adoptive mother, Charlotte, who was clutching her husband. Her face was stark white, and tears streamed down her cheeks as she watched her oldest child in excruciating pain. I looked away, unable to comprehend the pain etched across their faces. It had to be even greater than my pain and fear.

Fifty-Five's screaming came to an abrupt halt, and the heart monitor flatlined.

"She is dead," Matriarch Sylvaine's voice shook with the announcement.

Chapter Six

HEARTS OF ICE
One Twenty-Seven

My heart shattered. Logically, this was to be expected. I clutched my chest against the ache that settled there. Tears rolled down my face unbidden as I stared at the prone form of my girlfriend.

"Stay strong," whispered One Twenty-Six. She grabbed my hand and gave it a comforting squeeze, keeping her eyes trained on the scene below.

Charlotte's sobs cleaved through the air, and Matriarch Sylvaine's knuckles went white as she gripped the edges of the podium. Perhaps the same podium they used during our high school graduation ceremony not so long ago.

"Her human life is no more." The Matriarch continued. Her tone was gentler for Charlotte than for all the other grieving parents and perhaps softer for herself as well because not only was Charlotte losing her adoptive daughter, but the Matriarch was losing her adoptive granddaughter. She directed her gaze down to her sobbing daughter. "Now, her true-life force will pass through the veil and enter her."

There was still hope.

I clutched One Twenty-Six for support. My lungs burned as I fought to remember to breathe. I stared at Fifty-Five, willing her heart to beat again.

The theater was utterly silent as we waited for a heartbeat to sound through the speakers.

Thump, thump.

The sweet sound of a heart taking its first beat, then a second, rang through the theater.

Get up. Get up. Get up.

Fifty-Five winced as she clambered to her feet.

I heaved a sigh. She made it through. She's okay. My body turned to jelly. I released One Twenty-Six. My hands shook as the vestiges of adrenaline faded from my body. I slumped and drew several deep breaths. I shook out my hands, hoping to stop them from shaking.

Focus on something else, damn it! I snapped my gaze back toward Fifty-five and examined the changes in her body.

Fifty-Five's delicate gracefulness was still there, but she was more muscular now. Her ears were sharply pointed, and her jaw was more angular and defined. She looked at her hands and the rest of her body, then looked out at the crowd and unleashed a roar of ecstasy.

Thunderous applause filled the theater. The gorgeous golden-skinned fae queen slowly approached the sphere. Fifty-Five crouched to meet the stranger defensively. The fae queen held her hand up and spoke gently. I strained to hear the queen's words with my human ears.

The fae queen gestured to the two fae behind her, and they brought forward a robe that the queen draped around Fifty-Five's shoulders.

"Welcome home, Lianna Hirovonen," the queen announced so all could hear.

Lianna. The name fit her, and I couldn't help but stare, entranced by her beauty. Cheers erupted again, and the crowd chanted her new name thrice. The weight sitting heavily on my chest dissipated as the crowd chanted Lianna one last time.

She'd always been pretty, but now she was radiant—ethereal. Her long blonde hair had come loose from its braid and hung to her waist, shimmering in the moonlight. There was a lightness in her step, and the way she held herself screamed regal. The candlelight accentuated her curves and the glow of her skin.

Lianna focused on the seats reserved for the fae, and she nonchalantly, almost coldly, walked down the steps. She didn't hesitate or linger to look out into the crowd at her parents, who were openly weeping. I couldn't tell if they were happy or sad tears, but if I had to guess, I'd say it was a mixture of both. Lianna took her seat, and Matriarch Sylvaine, pride in her voice, called the next Magicborn to the stage. The ceremony continued.

I stole glances at Lianna as the ceremony continued. During one of my looks, Lianna caught me staring at her and gave me a huge grin.

It's amazing! she mouthed.

I grinned at her and returned my attention to the stage as a small, frail girl, number Sixty-Two from Humphrey's Peak coven, made her way up to the dais. It was clear she was ill as she struggled to make her way up the tall steps, and when the acolytes shackled her to the floor, she collapsed under their weight, falling to her knees. The sound of a bone shattering filled the arena, and the girl winced but said nothing, as if she were used to breaking bones. Murmurs ran through the crowd, and dread hung in the air. I glanced down at the monarchs sitting near the stage. Every one of them wore a grim expression. My brow furrowed. That couldn't be good.

A wail tore from the girl on stage, and I turned my attention back to the dais, where the girl was bathed in light, the deepest forest greens and rich, earthy browns of the lycan clan. She was to be a wolf. Her body contorted and her back arched before it snapped. Her cracking bones and pitiful whimpers twisted my heart. I didn't know the girl, but I wanted to rush down there, scoop her up in my arms, and run away with her to save her from what was to come. I clenched my fists, nails digging into my palms, trying to ground myself as the horror unfolded on the stage. I pleaded with the goddess to spare the girl.

Bloody tears streamed down Sixty-Two's face, pooling at her knees.

She won't make it. The voice in my head confirmed what I already knew, but that didn't make it easier to accept. She was someone's child. Someone loved her, and there was nothing we could do, despite all the magic we possessed, to save her.

A wet, rasping cough and a failing heartbeat were the only sounds that filled the silence as the girl's lungs filled with blood while she fought to fill them with air. She coughed again, and blood spattered on the floor before her.

More blood than one would think possible spilled from her eyes, her nose, her mouth, and her ears. She was half transformed when she collapsed entirely onto the floor, a gruesome, broken, twisted rag doll. Her body shuddered with her final breath, and then she was still. The long continuous beep of the monitors, signifying no heartbeat, told us she was gone.

Nobody moved, nobody breathed until a scream sounded from the Humphrey Peak coven's section of parents. More screams filled the theater. Not the screams of the Magicborn as they underwent their Ascension. No, these screams tore at my soul. It was so distinct that anyone within a mile radius knew what it meant. It was the sound of a mother losing her child.

Matriarch Sylvaine trudged across the dais and kneeled beside the girl, feeling for a pulse despite the machines already telling us she was gone. She did it for the mother weeping in the room. She shook her head, and an acolyte turned off the monitor, the harsh tone immediately cut off.

Her voice, amplified with the power of her goddess, Matriarch Sylvaine said, "Magicborn Sixty-Two of the lycans is no more." She bowed her head, and a tear glistened on her cheek.

Chaos erupted as a shrieking woman rushed toward the dais. Her arms outstretched toward the mutilated, broken girl on the stage. Several acolytes caught her before she could reach her daughter and ushered her out, her shrieks echoing through the night.

A lithe brown-haired female rose. The lycan alpha gathered a black shroud in her arms, slowly made her way up the dais steps, and stood before the girl. Matriarch Sylvaine took several respectful steps back, giving the lycan monarch space.

"Welcome home, Amaris," the alpha's voice rang clear and strong through the crowd. The alpha kneeled beside the prone girl who'd never be a wolf. Would never run through the woods under the moonlight, never experience the joys of being healthy, and gently draped the shroud over the body before motioning for her to be collected.

Several acolytes reverently picked up Amaris's body, carrying it to another room to prepare her for burial so Amaris would be ready to return home to Ilthyrium to be laid to rest in Menefos, the lycan realm. Other acolytes cleaned the blood from the dais. As they finished, Matriarch Sylvaine stepped back to her podium and looked out at us. Several moments passed before she spoke, and then, as if nothing had happened, she called the next Magicborn forward.

The show must go on.

For the second time tonight, I heard words echoing in my head. Words that weren't my own. It was a voice I'd heard many times ever since I was little, but I could never tell whose voice it was and it always sounded as though it was coming from a long tunnel. But that night it had come through clearer than ever before.

I searched the crowd for anyone who might have sent the message. Seeing no likely owner, I turned to the dais and saw a male in the center of the sacred circle. Once again, the brilliant greens and browns of the lycan faction lit the surrounding sphere. He looked strong enough to withstand the change, but I averted my eyes, disassociating my way from the horror that had taken place on the stage.

My attention was drawn back to the stage several Magicborn later as another faerie ascended. A male named Koen. Jealousy ran through me. Jealousy because he would be where Lianna would be when there was still a possibility that I wouldn't be.

"Magicborn One Twenty-Six, please come to the stage," Matriarch Sylvaine's voice called out, interrupting my impending spiral. The Magicborn next to me gracefully made her way down the marble steps, and my body went cold, then hot, and my chest tightened. I'd be next. As One Twenty-Six passed Lianna's seat, I caught Lianna's eye, and she grinned at me and gave me a thumbs up.

Lianna mouthed, *You've got this!*

I shrugged, hoping she was right.

A piercing scream broke the spell, yanking my attention to the scene below to find Magicborn One Twenty-Six in the sphere's center. It was lit in a brilliant blue with muted black hues that rippled like the ocean. I grimaced, knowing these colors signified the ascension of a mermaid. Watching this change was far more brutal than watching a shift from human to faerie, vampire, or dragon. Everyone collectively held their breath, but for a different reason.

This time, we held our breath to see if the girl would survive. One Twenty-Six appeared healthy and had an okay chance of surviving. I sincerely hoped she wouldn't join those who'd already failed to make the change tonight and had died permanently.

The mermaid change was one of the most dangerous and extensive changes one could go through. Their physiology was forced to change at a much more intricate level to include nearly translucent skin. Their legs merged into a fin, and they grew thin, membranous wings. But the most dangerous part of their change was their hearts turning to ice. It was said to be one of the most painful and traumatic changes a Magicborn could undergo.

Please, please, please don't let me be a mermaid.

Below us, One Twenty-Six's legs slowly knit together, and her skin split open along her shoulder blades as wings emerged from her back.

Her legs fully knitted into a fin. Her fingers and nails grew into long, thick talons. With each change, One Twenty-Six released a tortured scream until she fell silent. The monitors emitted another flat-line tone. Matriarch Sylvaine announced that One Twenty-Six's human life was over.

It took a long time for the new mermaid's heart to beat, and when it did, there were long pauses between beats. Mermaid hearts didn't beat the same as human and other Magicborns. One beat for them was five to ten heartbeats for a human. Each beat crackled like ice breaking. After what felt like an eternity, she opened her eyes and sat up.

The ascended mermaid followed much of the same pattern as those before her—staring at her new webbed hands and her fin and twisting to see the translucent wings on her back. Then she looked at the crowd and unleashed an unearthly screech that had everyone covering their ears. Kaikala, the mermaid queen, strode forward in her human form, keeping a careful distance from her, and named the new mermaid Sereia.

Acolytes approached the stage, wheeling a large water-filled glass tank. Sereia hissed and swiped violently at a young acolyte who got too close. Sereia drew blood and flew into a frenzied state. She lashed out with her fin, gnashing her teeth. She yanked at her chains. Her gaze never once left the young acolyte's terrified face. Mermaids were known homicidal feeders who'd eat anything they could get their hands on.

Sereia had no self-control over her blood lust, and we all, humans, Magicborn, and witches alike, were seeing it firsthand as Sereia's enraged shrieks filled the theater.

It was seconds before the acolytes got her unchained, using the terrified, bleeding acolyte as a distraction. Sereia lunged for the injured acolyte, who screamed at the top of her lungs. The acolyte retreated and crashed to the floor when her ceremonial robes tangled around her feet. Sereia barreled toward the girl, using her hands and fin to propel herself forward. My heart thundered, positive I was about to watch an acolyte be eaten by Sereia when Queen Kaikala opened her mouth and sang.

A haunting melody filled the theater, stopping Sereia in her tracks. Sereia turned to her queen, malice gleaming gold in her eyes. She screeched in rage, but still, the queen sang, and the molten liquid gold gleaming in Sereia's gaze melted away. When her eyes were clear blue again, Sereia inched to the edge of the stage and toppled into the tank awaiting her. Only when the tank was closed and locked did the queen's song stop.

"Sheesh, that was intense," said One Twenty-Eight on my other side.

I agreed. Now that Sereia was in her tank, the ceremony would continue.

And it was my turn.

Chapter Seven

GOING THROUGH CHANGES
One Twenty-Seven

"One Twenty-Seven, come forward and ascend!" Matriarch Sylvaine's voice boomed through the theater as her gaze landed on me.

I froze. My limbs refused to follow the directions my brain shouted at them.

You need to move, I told my frozen limbs. My frantic gaze searched the room as I tried to regain control of my body. It landed on my mom, who was staring up at me. She gave me the tiniest nod of encouragement and mouthed, *I love you*. That was all the encouragement I needed. I moved into the aisle and down the cool marble steps toward the stage.

In my hurry, my foot slipped on the smooth marble, and I stumbled as I neared the final few steps. No one was close enough to catch me. I accepted my fate and braced for impact. A flash of red appeared in the corner of my eye, and then someone wrapped an arm around me and caught me.

I stared into the greenest eyes I'd ever seen. Flaming red hair filled my vision, and I held back a groan as the crimson-haired faerie guard rescued me for the second time that day. I gave a slight bow, and she released me now that I was steady. Without a word, she dashed back to her seat across the theater. She'd gotten to me in a fraction of a second from the opposite side of the theater. She gestured toward the dais when she caught me staring after her, and I remembered what I was supposed to be doing. I burned with embarrassment as I glanced around the theater and found everyone staring at me, waiting to continue.

I'm not ready.

I need more time.

I'm not finished yet.

Please don't make me do this!

I forced myself to take one step and another until I reached the edge of the glowing center of the stage, where my human life would end. I paused and glanced at my mom again. She smiled at me, proud tears shone in her eyes. *I can do this. I can do this. I can do this.* I took a deep breath, gathered my courage, and stepped inside.

Two acolytes shackled my wrists while another attached a heart monitor. The cold metal dug into my wrists. Their weight pulling me down. A shiver crawled up my spine as the chill seeped into my skin.

The sphere spun around me. I peered through the flashing lights, trying to find my mom's gaze so I could draw strength from the love I knew I'd see there. But it was impossible to see anything against the black spots popping in and out of my vision. Nausea rose, and I squeezed my eyes shut, battling rising queasiness.

Thank the Goddess they had us purge right before the ceremony. My toes began to tingle, then my feet, followed by my legs. The tingling dissipated when it reached the top of my head, and I gasped when ice flooded my veins. It was painful but tolerable. Every hair on my body rose when electricity raced through me, and confused whispers filled the room.

"What is she?" I heard someone say aloud.

What do they mean, what am I?

I opened my eyes and saw I was illuminated in a golden light with purple hues.

Faerie. I had only a moment to think before the pain began, and I could consider that I wasn't bathed in the right lights to be a faerie. I was drenched in a golden glow with purple hues rather than the traditional purple light with golden hues. There was no faction whose Ascension colors were golden with purple hues.

Fire blazed in my veins, blasting out the ice. My legs buckled, and I crashed to the ground as the change ripped through my body. The searing pain from my knees meeting the unforgiving marble floor consumed me. A scream tore from my throat as I burned from the inside out. I tried to curl into a ball as my bones shattered and reset. Each crack excruciating. Just when I thought I couldn't take any more agony, my heart tripped over itself, trying and failing to force blood through my body.

This is it.

My heart strained on the brink of breaking.

I took in a final breath.

My eyes closed.

My heart slowed. The outward physical changes were complete, but the inner changes remained. I thrashed helplessly as the pain consumed my spirit.

Except I wasn't thrashing. My body was lying on the floor, unmoving. But I was ablaze. I was caught in an undertow, flipping and floundering, trying to distinguish which direction was up. I struggled to find my bearings and put myself back together as I was violently ripped apart, shattered, and remade over and over. Then, a shift at my core, the essence of everything that made me *me* unraveled. Everything went silent. Then the long, high-pitched tone emitted from the monitor as my human heart stopped beating.

"She is dead," Matriarch Sylvaine's voice came through, clear and strong.

She's me. I'm dead. It was surreal. Unfathomable. They'd taught us what would happen. Tried to explain it, but there was no logic to this. To be physically dead but still here.

Someone in the crowd was wailing.

Mom!

Mom was crying.

I opened my mouth to reassure her, but the mouth attached to my body stayed closed and soundless.

Trapped. I'm trapped. But I couldn't dwell on it because my mom's heart was shattering for everyone to see and hear, and I couldn't do anything.

I'm okay, Mom. I'm coming. Don't cry. I begged silently, dragging myself through the water and clawing my way back to my body.

As I transitioned back into my physical form, the only thing I perceived was an overwhelming darkness and those heart-wrenching sobs. My mom had never cried like that before. Not when Elik almost killed her. Not when I'd almost been taken from her. Never.

I have to get back. I have to live. I shoved through the darkness. And surfaced.

I was only dead for a minute, maybe two, before my heart pumped once, then again.

My essence reshaped into something new, and little of the old me seemed to remain in the prone body on the ground. The fire cooled as I took my first breath, then another. I opened my eyes, squinting against the brightness. My stomach roiled as I battled not to embarrass myself by vomiting in front of these people.

You're okay. Everything's okay. I silently chanted as I typically did when feeling sick, resisting the emetophobia panic urging me to run away from here. Being shackled to the floor made escape impossible, and that realization raised my panic from a manageable five to an unmanageable fifty in the space of two heartbeats.

I fought for control, searching the crowd for Mom's familiar brown eyes. Instead of earthy brown eyes, my gaze landed on a set of eyes in the deepest shades of meadow green, and as suddenly as it came, my panic was blasted from my body. I shifted my gaze from the crimson-haired faerie to the crowd, then to myself.

Everything ached, but my stomach calmed, the pain subsided, and I did a mental inventory of my body. Strength and power coursed through me. I raised a hand to my head and ran my fingers over sharply pointed ears. I could hardly wait to get in front of a mirror to see what I looked like. I flinched as my long, sharp nails nicked my right ear. I pulled my hand away to see blood smeared on my fingers. The crowd thundered applause, and I remembered where I was.

I sat naked, waiting for someone to come and claim me, name me, and clothe me.

But no one approached. The applause faded, silence filling the amphitheater. I chewed my bottom lip, glancing at the coven matriarchs.

The matriarchs huddled together, whispering. Acanthe caught my eye, a knowing look crossing her face. Matriarch Sylvaine called Queen Nasryn forward. The gorgeous golden-skinned female who approached Lianna earlier approached the matriarchs and joined them in their hushed discussion. I could hear snippets of their words as I acclimated to my new fae ears.

"Strange colors." One matriarch muttered.

"Are we sure she's truly fae?" Another said.

"What say you, Queen Nasryn?" Matriarch Sylvaine asked.

The queen scrutinized me. With a nod to the matriarchs, she concluded, "She bears the unmistakable traits of the fae."

"She does," Acanthe said. Her tone left no room for argument.

The queen approached me. I whirled, crouching to meet the intruder defensively.

The queen held up her hands and spoke gently. "Hello, child. I am Queen Nasryn. I won't hurt you."

It was as though thousands of years of instinct slammed into me all at once. I straightened and bowed my head to acknowledge my queen like I'd been doing it for years.

"Welcome Home, Riona Vandeleur," the queen said.

The name felt right. Riona Vandeleur. That's me now. It was like I'd slipped into a perfect-fitting pair of shoes meant only for me.

"Thank you," I said. My voice rang out higher, smoother, and somehow more magical and not at all like my own.

Acolytes hurried forward and unlatched the shackles, freeing me. The queen draped a soft velvet cloak over me and motioned for me to follow her off the stage and into my new life.

I pulled the cape around my naked body, wishing for something more to cover myself with before I stepped off the stage. I caught sight of my mother beaming with pride, tears shining in her eyes. She gave me a huge grin and mouthed, *I love you*. I smiled back.

Chapter Eight

SENSORY OVERLOAD
Riona

As the ceremony progressed, I struggled to focus on the stage. The scent of sweat, blood, and death hung in the air, blending with the deep, pungent fragrance of decomposing leaves and damp earth from the nearby forest. Screams and groans as Magicborn ascended overwhelmed me, leaving me dizzy and disoriented as I tried to process them all.

The pillar candles, now nearly entirely burned out, flickered and sputtered, their flames struggling to stay alight. They cast dim, dancing lights over the stadium. The smoke in the air made breathing difficult and added to the already-heady atmosphere.

The crisp sound of brittle branches snapping in the distance, accompanied by the scurrying of creatures through the dense thicket and the rhythmic heartbeats of human, witch, and Magicborn alike, blended into a jarring symphony within my mind. When my soft velvet robe brushed against my ankles, I nearly jumped out of my seat. My heart thudded. Heat filled my cheeks. Within seconds, it was like my chest was caught in a vise that was squeezing air from my lungs second by second.

A hand reached out and gently clasped mine, interrupting my absent-minded finger tapping on the arm of my chair. The pale, smooth skin unmistakably belonged to Lianna. Mimicking her slow and deliberate breathing technique, I inhaled deeply, focusing on the rise and fall of my belly as my chest expanded. Air filled my lungs. I counted to five and then slowly exhaled. My panic lessened with each repetition of the process.

I looked at Lianna, but her eyes were trained on the stage as a Magicborn ascendant was bathed in orange and red hues. She tightened her grip on my hand and the weight of her hand in mine calmed the remnants of the storm. I turned to the scene before me as the newly ascended dragon rose.

Lianna sighed softly, and I squeezed her hand to comfort her. She'd wanted to be a dragon, and while I was thrilled we'd be together, I knew how disappointed she must be. She gave a slight squeeze back, and I returned my attention to the stage, marveling at the dragon's gorgeous red and black scales and mighty wings that furled behind it. The dragon was massive, at least twenty-five feet when it stood up straight. It barely fit in the amphitheater. An adult full-sized dragon would never fit.

Stretching their neck toward the night sky, the dragon roared, shattering the surrounding stillness. I winced, covering my sensitive ears as Lianna did the same beside me.

Throughout the theater, a final round of applause echoed. The dragon monarch made their way up to the stage, draped in a luxurious cloak of deepest black. A large dragon was on the back of the robe, meticulously stitched in green thread. I took my hands down from my ears and heard the dragon monarch say, "Welcome home, Indarrul, Life Taker." The monarch whispered something my new fae ears couldn't pick up, and the new dragon shrank back into their androgynous human form.

Dragons didn't have a general sex. They could be both, either, or neither at any moment, and it was entirely their choice. A robe was draped over Indarrul's shoulders, and their new monarch led them down the steps to their faction.

Matriarch Sylvaine slowly made her way to center stage. She no longer projected the powerful and regal image she'd possessed earlier. Her posture was hunched, making her look several years older. I glanced at the rest of the coven matriarchs and found each similarly weakened—all except Acanthe, who, if anything, looked brighter, stronger, and perhaps even younger.

"Let's take a moment to honor those who couldn't ascend," Matriarch Sylvaine said.

The dead were brought from the burial preparation room; their bodies laid out on display. Each was wrapped in silk in the colors of their faction. There were five in total from three of the Magicborn factions. Mermaids in shades of deepest blue, lycans in the deep green and brown of their forest home, and vampires in black silks adorned with deep burgundy designs. Five Magicborn children were lost that night. To some. It wasn't a large number, but with the Magicborn races dwindling, the number felt significant. A list magically generated above the matriarch's head, which listed the number of each Magicborn and the race they'd have been if they'd made it through.

Matriarch Sylvaine stood over each fallen Magicborn and recited their monarch-bestowed names and parting words of their faction. "Morgan, Ondine, and Maren, mermaid faction, may the waters be peaceful on your final journey to the deep," she said before continuing to the next. "Amaris, lycan faction, may the pale moon shine brightly upon your travels. Ciaran, vampire faction, may the wings of Nyx carry you swiftly to her warm embrace."

A hauntingly beautiful song of mourning filled the air as the mermaids wailed for their fallen sisters. Everyone in the amphitheater covered their ears—everyone except me.

I glanced around the theater at everyone covering their ears and wincing. The mermaid's song was haunting and beautiful. Leaning toward Lianna, I attempted to pull her hand away from her ear. Wincing, she complied.

"What is it?"

"Why's everyone covering their ears? Their song sounds incredible. Sad. but beautiful." I whispered.

Lianna looked at me like I'd lost my mind. "You're kidding, right? It sounds like nails on a chalkboard except way worse." Lianna whispered back, placing her hands back over her ears.

I glanced around the theater again as the song continued. Every person except the mermaids and me had their ears covered. Out of the corner of my eye, Queen Nasryn, ears covered, stared at me, her face filled with curiosity.

Then the vampires and wolves uncovered their ears and joined the call, sending up their songs to their fallen. The song changed as the arena was filled with the mourning song honoring the dead, my voice, as though it had a mind of its own, took up the song. It was the only thing that ascending Magicborn were taught before the ceremony because we would inevitably need to sing it before the night ended. Our section's melody was lyrical and ethereal. As we all sang together, the weight of the shared sorrow enveloped us like a heavy fog. Each note flowed effortlessly into the next, weaving through the poignant lyrics, linking us by an invisible thread of grief.

As if guided by an unseen conductor, our voices fell silent in unison, and the vibrant amphitheater was enveloped in stillness. The echoes of our melodies gradually faded into the twilight, leaving only a tranquil hush that settled over the crowd like a soft blanket.

Matriarch Sylvaine's eyes shone with unshed tears, and she looked out at the crowd. "This concludes this year's Ascension Ceremony. To our human guests, thank you for joining us. Please follow Acolytes Kyva and Ahri out. They'll lead you back to your belongings and vehicles."

Matriarch Sylvaine waited for the humans to take their leave. "Parents, thank you for your attendance. To the parents who lost their children to Thanatos, the goddess of death, tonight, our hearts are with you, and we carry the burden with you. To the parents whose children ascended, rejoice that your children are off to begin the next journey of their lives. Thank you for caring for these children. Please follow acolytes Raya and Citra to the Dahlia Hall for the Samhain celebration."

My mother caught my eye and waved. She was smiling, but she looked exhausted, and I could see the sorrow she tried to hide. *I love you*, I mouthed, raising my hand to wave before she was swept into the crowd.

As the last parents trickled out of the theater, Matriarch Sylvaine turned to address the newly ascended Magicborn. "Your lives are just beginning. Remember what you've learned during your time among humans and witches and take it with you as you embark on the next leg of your journey. Thank you. Blessed be all. Until next year." Matriarch Sylvaine hobbled off stage and staggered down the stairs, where her acolytes awaited her. One took her arm, steadying her.

A portal opened on the dais. Brilliant prismatic colors emanated from it, lighting up the theatre. Queen Nasryn motioned for us to remain seated as members of each faction of Magicborn rose from their seats, collected the bodies of their fallen, and reverently carried them through the portal, one by one.

Only when the last group of Magicborn pallbearers entered the portal did Queen Nasryn rise. Her guards followed suit, including the red-haired faerie I'd crashed into earlier today. I blushed, remembering the feeling of my face pressing into her chest. She glanced at me, a smirk spreading across her face as though she knew exactly what I was thinking, and I immediately returned my attention to Queen Nasryn, awaiting instruction.

Queen Nasryn turned to the three of us and beckoned us to rise. "Are you ready?" she asked.

"Yes," Lianna answered us all, but what else was she supposed to say?

No thanks, we'd rather stay here. Of course, that was all I wanted to say. I didn't want to leave. The urge to run back to my mother overwhelmed me. Goddess, I missed her already.

"Excellent," Queen Nasryn said, stepping up to the portal. She stood beside it, waiting for Lianna, Koen, and me to join her.

As I ascended the steps to the portal, a prickling sensation crawled up my spine as if I were being watched. I turned to find Acanthe studying me. She was motionless, but her eyes locked on mine. I shivered, chills running through me, goose bumps rose on my arms, and every tiny hair on my neck stood. Something about her seemed different. Otherworldly. It was like I'd never seen the real her before that moment, as if a shroud had been pulled off and I was seeing the true her for the first time.

Living darkness encircled her, undulating and writhing in unsettling patterns. I rubbed my eyes, trying to clear my vision, positive my new eyes were playing tricks on me. But she was still staring at me when I opened my eyes again. The air around her pulsated with a dark power. She grinned, her sharply pointed teeth gleaming in the candlelight, and her eyes flashed. I knew deep down there was so much more to Acanthe than the shop owner and coven member she'd made herself out to be. I turned away, anxious to get away from her, and Queen Nasryn gestured for me to enter the portal.

I took a small, cautious step into the portal. It shimmered with warmth. It was as though I was walking through a forest on the perfect summer day. The sun shone through the treetops. The soft, mossy ground cradled my feet with every step I took. The air was crisp and clear, similar to the fresh spring air after rainfall—sharp and clarity-inducing.

I appeared to have entered an endless hallway. I stepped forward, and Lianna and Koen entered the portal hallway behind me, followed by Queen Nasryn.

"Welcome to the Hall of Realms. This is a place between worlds. Each portal leads to another realm. This is the only way to travel to the different realms of Ilthyrium." She smiled and swept past me as her guards exited the portal.

The Hall of Realms shimmered in shades of silver, the walls giving off a prismatic, rainbow effect. Like any hallway, several doorways lined the walls. However, unlike 'normal' doors, each was an open archway in a different color. The first door on the right swirled with blues and blacks, and I intuited that it would take me to Oxlis, the mermaid realm. Across from Oxlis, the portal was pitch black, which must have led to the vampire realm, Erastrith. A fiery red and orange portal that would take me to Nivothia, the dragon realm, sat next to the vampire realm. There seemed to be no pattern to how the doorways were aligned. The hallway and doorways stretched as far as the eye could see.

"How far does the hallway go?" I asked.

"To Oblivion," Queen Nasryn answered, stopping in front of a beautiful purple and gold-colored portal just past the portal to Nivothia.

She turned to us. "Here we are. Welcome to Vakrass," she said before stepping into the swirling purple and gold portal.

Her retinue followed her, but the crimson-haired faerie stayed behind, presumably to make sure we got into Vakrass safely. Lianna took my hand. We stepped into the portal together with Koen following and the guard bringing up the rear.

Peace settled upon me like a gentle blanket. It was like being engulfed in my mom's hugs. It was the feeling of home. I stepped out of the portal and into an opulent throne room.

My feet sank into the plush cream carpet beneath my feet, and for a split second, I worried about my filthy bare feet soiling the carpet, but my filth was forgotten as I took in the opulence of the throne room. Ornate gold chandeliers were filled with hundreds of candles and cast a calm glow over the room. Gold swirls blended into the white marble walls, and an elaborate, gilded throne sat atop a dais at the end of the room. Fae filled the throne room. I shrank back, ready to run, but Lianna grabbed my hand and held me steady. We faced the room together.

Chapter Nine

ALWAYS ON DISPLAY
Riona

Queen Nasryn walked through the crowd and sat on her throne. She looked out over the faeries gathered and then motioned at the three of us to join her. Lianna stepped forward, tugging me behind her. Once we joined her, Queen Nasryn stood.

"I'm pleased to introduce you to our three newest ascendants, Lianna Hirovonen, Riona Vandeleur, and Koen Trevarthen," she said, addressing the room. "As always, they'll stay at the palace until they leave for Vakmore Academy. Please make them feel at home.

I overheard several faeries commenting on how there were only three of us, but I didn't have time to wonder what that had to do with anything.

Queen Nasryn continued, "It is unusual for an uneven number to ascend. However, they'll have to make the best of it. I believe we will see some interesting outcomes from this group."

The queen turned away from them and faced us. "These," she said, gesturing at the group of faeries below us, "are the caretakers of the palace. Each of you will be assigned an attendant while you're here. They'll show you to your rooms. There you'll find clothing and everything you need for the evening.

"Tomorrow, you'll be brought into the market to purchase new clothing for Vakmore and the Ascension Ball, where you'll be officially inducted into fae society. You'll leave for Vakmore Academy the day after the ball, so you'll have a couple of days to settle in before your begin classes."

She started to turn away, but Lianna interrupted her, asking the question that'd been whirling in my mind. "Queen Nasryn, a question, if I may?" Lianna didn't wait for a response. "You stated it's unusual for an uneven number to ascend, but why is it unusual?"

"Most Magicborn fae usually ascend in pairs, and each pair typically becomes bondmates. Only in exceedingly rare cases do they not become bondmates." Queen Nasryn flashed a look over her shoulder at the crimson-haired guard behind her. "We've never run into an uneven number of newly ascended. Your group is an anomaly, so we are all understandably interested in what that might mean for us and you all as well. After you've spent some time training as a unit and passed your first-year graduation trials, you'll come back to the palace for the bonding ceremony, which takes place on Beltane in your second year."

"What's a bondmate?" Lianna asked, clasping her hands in front of her.

"There are two types of bonds. Unitbonds and bondmates. Unitbonds are formed during ascension. You go through school with them, and you work as a unit. You're in sync with them wholly. Bondmates are mated partners. Once you're mated, the bond can only be broken by death. However, unitbonds are more easily broken when there is no further need for the unit. Unitbonds can also be remade if the cause of the break is something other than death."

"I see," Lianna said. She glanced at me and grinned, and I smiled back. Then her gaze flitted past me to where Koen stood, and her cheeks flushed.

I frowned, watching the two of them share a look, and immediately checked my jealousy. Lianna and I'd agreed long ago that she could take lovers if she felt so inclined. I knew she loved me, and she'd tell me when there was something to tell.

My mind whirled with more questions about bondmates than before. What happened to those who should've had a bondmate, but one died during the Ascension Ceremony? Or what if someone didn't make it through their trials? Then what? I glanced at Koen. What if two fae ascend, and they hate each other? If only Koen and I'd ascended together, there was no way I'd have ever bonded with him.

A flurry of activity pulled my attention as three fae, one male and two females, pushed their way through the crowd.

"Ah, perfect," Queen Nasryn said. "These are your attendants. They'll help you with everything. Your attendants will get you settled. Now, if you'll excuse me, it's been a long day, and I'm going to retire."

"Hello, I'm Juniper," said the slight female on the left of the attendants. She had silky black hair and full pink lips and carried herself stiffly like she was afraid she might wrinkle her clothing if she so much as bent at the waist. "I'm here for Riona. Which one of you would that be?"

All three of us were silent until Lianna nudged me, and I remembered I was Riona.

"Me," I squeaked, then I cleared my throat. "I'm Riona."

"Follow me. I'll show you your rooms."

"What about Lianna? Can we share a room?" I asked, looking back. I didn't want to be alone.

"I'm afraid not," Juniper replied, her brow furrowing as she looked between Lianna and me. "Queen Nasryn wishes everyone to have their own room. Now, come along."

I threw Lianna a panicked look, wishing she'd pipe up and demand we be allowed to share. Instead, she gave me a thumbs up and mouthed, *You've got this*, before I followed Juniper down the exquisite hallway of the castle, away from the throne room. Juniper's kitten-heeled shoes clicked against the natural stone floors as we made our way toward what I assumed were the bedrooms. Each door we passed was rich mahogany and ornately carved.

One door we walked past had a large open book carved into it. I halted.

"Is this a library?" I asked, pointing at the door I stood before.

Juniper stopped ahead of me and looked at the door I was pointing and dipped her head. "This way, please," she said, gesturing for me to follow her.

I was dying for a tour of the castle, specifically the library, but I followed Juniper silently, wary of disturbing the eerie silence within the castle walls. The hallway was impossibly long and seemed to never end. I was about to ask Juniper if we should stop for food and water when she stopped, pulled out a ring filled with old-fashioned skeleton keys, and selected one. She inserted the key, and when she turned it, the loud click seemed to ricochet through the silent hallway as the door popped open.

"Here you are," she said, stepping aside.

I gasped. It was huge. The main room I entered was a sitting room with dark oak floors. A cream-colored sofa and two matching armchairs sat before a roaring fire set in obsidian stone. The walls were a neutral shade of cream with an accent wall in an espresso brown. Off of the sitting room to the right of the door was a small kitchenette. An ice chest sat on one side between a layout of marble counters, and a sink sat on the other side. A sturdy, small oak table that would sit two or three people around it sat in the center of the kitchenette.

"This is your sitting room. Your bathroom is through that door," Juniper said, gesturing to a door on the opposite side of the room. "There's also an entrance to the bathroom in your bedroom, which is through that door there," Juniper said, gesturing to another door on the other side of the wall. "Tomorrow, you'll go to the marketplace to visit the tailor to get all the clothing you need. Charis will accompany the three of you, so you don't get lost. Think of her as an unofficial tour guide. Money has been added to your accounts to get you started." She added when I opened my mouth to protest that I didn't have any money.

"You'll remain in your quarters while you're a guest here," she continued as she bustled about the room, fluffing couch cushions and tidying the small kitchenette. "Morning and midday meals will be brought to you, and you can dine alone or with your unit. That's up to you. Dinner is served with Queen Nasryn. You aren't to wander the castle alone. You'll be escorted to all meals. You may be tempted to disregard these boundaries, but remember, this is the queen's home, and she has a right to privacy, royalty or not. There are unfortunate consequences for not respecting those boundaries. Understand?" she asked, hands on her hips when I said nothing.

"I'll stay in my rooms," I said, staring around the immense space, wondering what I'd do all day. "Juniper?" I blurted before I could second-guess myself.

"Yes," Juniper prodded, glancing at me.

"Could someone take me to the library so I could find a book or something to keep me busy while I'm here?"

Juniper hesitated. "I'll speak to Her Majesty about it, but don't get your hopes up. Queen Nasryn is private, and the library is her sanctuary."

"Thank you," I said.

"Good. Let's get you ready for bed," she said, ushering me into my bedroom. On the beautiful four-poster bed hung gauzy chiffon curtains. On the bed lay a set of gold satin pajamas.

Upon seeing the bed, a wave of exhaustion settled over me, and suddenly, I was dying to crawl into those satin sheets and sleep for days. I didn't have time to admire or dive headfirst into those satin sheets though because Juniper rushed me past it and into the bathroom, where she filled the tub with water and sweet-smelling bubbles, gestured for me to enter, and left the room. I slipped off the velvet Ascension robe, let it fall to the floor in a puddle, and climbed into the scalding water.

Thank the Goddess for magic.

Vakrass was powered by fae who wielded elemental magic, but I didn't know how much power they could wield and if they could ever get my baths as hot as I liked them at home. I shouldn't have worried.

I sighed, sinking into the tub. The stiffness in my joints and muscles melted away as I lingered until the water chilled to lukewarm.

"Knock, knock," Juniper said as she bustled back into the bathroom. "Let's wash that hair."

I groaned. I dreaded hair wash day. My curls made the process exhausting, but under Juniper's skilled hands, my hair was washed in no time. Juniper held a towel up for me. I paused. Hundreds of people had already seen me naked tonight, but that didn't mean I liked it or wanted to add one more stranger to that list.

"Would you turn around, please?"

"That would make it difficult for me to dry you off. But I'll avert my gaze," she said, looking away from me, pointedly.

I stood and tried to cover myself, but as I took in the high sides of the claw-foot tub, I dispensed with modesty and placed both hands on the side of the tub, bracing myself so I wouldn't fall as I exited the tub. Juniper wrapped the warm towel around me and dried me before ushering me back into my bedroom, then left me to dress.

Ten minutes later, I was dressed in gold satin pajamas, sitting at the vanity as Juniper worked a comb through my tangled, unruly curls. I stifled a yawn. It had been a long day.

"A snack will be up shortly," she said, running curl cream through my hair before stepping back to examine me. "All right, you're all set. Once you eat, you can head to bed. You look exhausted."

"I am exhausted," I said through another yawn. It felt as though I'd been awake for days instead of just one.

We returned to the sitting room, and Juniper bid me goodnight. I plopped onto the couch to wait for my food.

I didn't have to wait long before a knock sounded at the door.

"Just a moment." I moved more quickly than I meant to, still not fully accustomed to my fae body, and my foot slid into the coffee table leg, stubbing my big toe. I grabbed my foot, hopping around the space as blistering pain ricocheted through my foot. "Ow, ow, ow!" I exclaimed, setting my foot down and gingerly putting weight on it. At least my toe didn't appear to be broken.

Another knock sounded at the door. "Miss, are you all right?" a male voice called from the other side.

"Yes, yes," I said, then opened the door.

I stepped aside as a male swept into the room, wheeling a fancy dinner cart. A rich, spicy aroma filled the air, and my stomach growled loudly.

The male evaluated me momentarily before focusing on the covered platters on the tray.

"Hello, I've brought you some broth and bread," he said as he took the lids off the dishes.

"Broth and bread?" My vision turned scarlet around the edges. I'd expected more when he'd rolled that fancy cart into the room. Broth and bread felt like a slap in the face. Here I was in this vast, gorgeous palace, and the most they served their guests on their first night was broth and bread?

I clenched my fists. I considered ripping the male's throat out, but before I could act on it, the rage passed. The red haze that had filled my vision moments before dissipated.

What the fuck was that?

"It's your first night as fae," the male explained, oblivious that I was ready to tear his throat out seconds before. "Most new ascendants can't handle eating on their first night despite their hunger. Also, try not to devour your food. You'll regret it." He took a small step back and collected the remaining food from the tray to place it on the table. "I'll leave you to it."

"Thank you," I said as he finished laying out the food.

He looked over the table one last time, straightening the spoon so it lay perfectly next to the bowl of broth. "When you're done, place the tray outside the door."

The male left, and I sat down at the table, picked up my spoon, and dove into my broth while tearing chunks of bread off between bites of my broth. Within moments, I discovered what the male was talking about when my stomach churned.

My spoon clattered against the ceramic bowl, and I swiftly rose. Overwhelming nausea consumed me. I left the meal on the table and grabbed the blanket that hung over the back of the sofa and curled up before the fire. I stared into the fire, pushing away thoughts of how I felt and focusing on anything that would distract me. My thoughts turned to Mom. Goddess, I missed her so much already,

I reached into my back pocket to grab my cell phone to text her, only to remember I no longer had a cell phone. They didn't work here. I'd given it up before the ceremony, leaving it for the next family who needed a cell phone for their Magicborn adoptee.

The ache in my chest became unbearable as I fought the overwhelming feeling of being utterly alone. I miss you, mommy.

Tears slipped unbidden down my cheek. I wondered if she missed me as much as I missed her. I hoped she hadn't fallen into the depression she was prone to. The depression left behind by the PTSD she suffered through because of Elik's abuse. An ache grew in my chest, and I pulled the blanket closer, trying to push away the sadness that came with knowing I'd never see her again. I wished Lianna were here with me instead of somewhere else in the castle, in her room. Loneliness and isolation weren't something I did well.

Chapter Ten
A WHOLE NEW WORLD
Riona

I woke to the sun streaming in the window and a fae female starting a new fire in my fireplace. I bolted upright, trying to figure out where I was before everything from the day before came flooding back.

"Good morning, Riona. I didn't mean to wake you." Juniper stood and wiped the soot from her hands onto her apron before she moved away from the now roaring fire.

I rubbed the sleep from my eyes. "I didn't mean to fall asleep on the couch. I guess I was more tired than I thought."

"Most new ascendants fall asleep on the couch after transformation. It takes a lot out of a fae."

She bustled into the kitchenette and started pulling lids off of dishes. The delicious aromas of fresh-baked bread and raspberry jam filled the room, along with the bitter scent of freshly brewed coffee. "Once you've finished breakfast, get dressed, and Charis will be along to take you to the market."

I rose and stretched. "Thank you, Juniper," I said

"Juni," she responded, folding the blankets I'd used and laying them back over the couch. "I prefer to be called Juni."

"Okay, cool. How long have you been here, Juni?" I asked. I didn't want to come across as rude as I fished for her age.

"Here at the palace? Or here in Vakrass? Juni asked, seeing through my question.

I looked down, avoiding her eyes. "Sorry," I muttered, embarrassed.

"Don't worry about it. Every new fae asks. I ascended fifty-seven years ago. My bondmate is a soldier, so he's away training a lot. Soldier's bondmates are given jobs in the palace as compensation for our mates being gone so much. It also helps to be close to the healers when we start feeling the negative effects of the distance."

I started to ask what she meant by negative effects, and why we needed soldiers when we weren't fighting wars anymore, when she glanced at the clock above the fireplace. "Oh my, you need to hurry. Charis will be here soon." She gestured toward my food, and I could tell the conversation was over.

"Thank you, Juni," I said, choosing the path of least resistance to avoid any potential conflict.

I grabbed a slice of piping hot, barely toasted bread, slathered butter over it, then smothered it in raspberry jam. I hesitated before taking a bite, remembering how horrible I'd felt after eating last night. However, Juniper was watching me, so I took a tentative bite. The tart flavor of raspberry flooded my mouth, and I took another bite, famished. I slowed to ensure there weren't any ill effects, but after a few test bites, everything felt fine, so I hurried through my breakfast as Juni puttered around the room, tidying up an already tidy room.

"Once you're done eating, you'll need to dress. Would you like me to lay something out for you, or would you like to do it yourself?" Juniper asked from across the room.

"I can do it," I said around a mouthful of eggs.

"There's a wardrobe in your bedroom filled with clothing. You should find something in your size there. If you can't, yell."

I took a quick swig of orange juice and then wiped my hands on a napkin. "That was delicious," I said.

"I'll let the cook know you approve," Juniper said, smiling.

In my room, I found an entire wardrobe with clothing of all sizes—dresses, tunics and trousers, jeans, and leggings. I opted for a pair of black leggings and a black T-shirt. I completed the look with a purple flannel and a pair of black ankle boots. The familiar clothing was a welcome reminder of home.

Juniper ushered another female into my bathroom as I worked a comb through my hair. "Riona, this is Charis. She'll be taking you to the market today," Juni said.

"Great," I said as I grappled with my unruly hair.

I was about to give up and try to wrestle it into a messy bun or ponytail when Charis stepped in. "Would you like help?" she asked.

I eyed the female, who looked close to my age. I was reasonably sure this female was on the younger side because of her brightly colored blue and purple hair and her punk rock clothing that was so different from everything else I'd seen in Vakrass–not that I'd seen much.

"I'd love some help," I said with a laugh. "It's been a while since my hair was this crazy, but I guess ascending from human to fae, traveling through a portal, falling asleep on a couch with wet hair, and doing no nighttime hair routine will do that to it."

Charis chuckled, reaching for the comb in my hand.

"I'll leave you to it then, Juniper said, leaving the bedroom. I heard the clatter of dishes, then the door shutting behind Juni. Charis and I were alone.

I peered at her in the mirror as Charis untangled my rebellious curls. Her black T-shirt and ripped black jeans contrasted sharply against her porcelain skin.

"You can ask," she said, catching my eye in the mirror.

I averted my eyes. "Sorry," I mumbled. "I never would've expected a faerie to be dressed like that or have cool-colored hair, like you do."

"You'd be surprised, honestly, but I only ascended a couple of years ago, so I'm a lot newer and less inclined to follow tradition and expectations."

I instantly liked and envied her. She reminded me of Lianna with her carefree spirit. I wished I could be so unworried.

I sat there as she continued gently working through my curls when a thought occurred to me. "You said you ascended two years ago, but I don't remember seeing you in Silver Bay?"

"You wouldn't. I was with the Humphreys Peak coven, so I only came to Silver Bay for ascension."

I paused momentarily before asking the question that'd been burning in my mind since Queen Nasryn first brought it up. "Is it really strange that only three of us ascended to fae?"

"It's pretty strange. Some factions see more ascendants than others for a variety of reasons. Mermaids are frequently the most common because many mermaids don't make it through ascension. And even though they're immortal, there used to be a lot of infighting among them, and they'd kill each other off. It's their nature.

Charis focused on a difficult snarl in my hair.

"But things are changing." The knot released. "When Kaikala became the new mermaid queen. She created a law prohibiting murder between mermaids. Anyone or anything else is fair game, though.

"I'm surprised Queen Kaikala has survived this long. Mermaids aren't harmonious creatures given their hearts of ice. Killing is what they do, and they're good at it. Other factions, like ours, are also practically immortal. We die of old age or in battle, but old age to us is thousands of years, so we don't get as many ascensions," she explained, pulling my hair back into a ponytail.

"I didn't know that's how it works," I said.

"The faction leaders and coven matriarchs are all pretty tight-lipped about any useful information," she said, checking out her hair in the mirror. She pulled out a tube of black lipstick and smeared it over her lips before offering it to me.

"No thanks," I said, pulling out my basic cherry lip balm that I'd found in a bin of unopened toiletries on the bathroom sink. "Presentable?" I asked.

"Perfect. Let's go," she said.

Chapter Eleven

CARRIAGE RIDES AND DESIGNER DRESSES

Riona

Charis and I were bundled in expensive warm coats, waiting for Lianna and Koen at a palace entrance. It may have been fall, but it was freezing in the mountains where the palace was, especially near the windows and doors or pretty much any location that didn't have a fireplace.

"It'll be warmer at the market," Charis said through chattering teeth. I wasn't sure if she was trying to reassure me or herself.

"I'd think you'd be used to it," I said, eyeing the petite faerie. "You know, since you live here all the time."

"The cold shouldn't bother me so much. I grew up in the mountains, but I've always been cold, no matter where I live. Once summer's over and the temperature drops, I freeze. It sucks."

I smiled, trying to look engaged in the conversation. To me, cold was cold, and I hated small talk.

"Hi!" Lianna's cheerful voice rang out, saving me from having to pretend any longer. I glanced to the top of the stairway where she was cloaked in a cobalt thigh-length trench coat similar to my crimson one, but hers enhanced her clear blue eyes. She was dressed in jeans and flats, and a pale pink knit sweater. Her long blonde hair hung in ringlets down to her waist.

Lianna bounded down the steps to us, something I could never do as a human and probably not something I could do as fae either. I was still waiting for that ethereal grace to kick in. She sidled up to me and moved to give me a peck, but I pulled back before she did since we weren't alone. She took a quick step back, leaving plenty of space between the two of us.

I glanced at Charis to see if she'd noticed, but she was busy staring at her shoes, clearly pretending like she hadn't seen anything.

"Good morning." Lianna's cheerful voice echoed off the walls, ash she buttoned her coat and tied the sash around her waist.

I groaned. Even transitioning from human to fae couldn't cure her of being a morning person.

"Morning," I said. I pulled her into a quick "friendly" hug. "I missed you," I whispered before I pulled away.

"Hello, ladies," Koen's smooth baritone voice called above us.

I turned to see him making his way down the steps as if he owned them. His long blondish-brown hair was pulled into a low ponytail, and he was wearing a T-shirt that showed every single abdominal muscle. A fae male trailed him in the standard black uniform that Charis had changed into before leading me down here, and I assumed he must be Koen's attendant.

"Riona, Lianna, this is Tristan," Charis said as the males joined us.

I smiled at Tristan before I rolled my eyes at Koen. "It's a little cold for a T-shirt," I told him.

Koen smirked. "Aw, it's sweet you're worried, Riona. It shows you care. Don't worry, I run hot," he said in what I think was supposed to be a seductive tone.

I resisted the urge to roll my eyes a second time and settled for shrugging. "Well, don't expect us to save you when you start freezing to death."

Koen's face broke into a sly smirk. "I think I'll be okay." He shot a cocky grin at Lianna and added, "But if things look dire, I'm sure Lianna wouldn't mind cuddling up to me and sharing her body heat."

A red haze clouded my vision, and every muscle within me coiled, ready to strike Koen and tear that smirk right off his face.

"Alright," Charis said, cutting through the tension and positioning herself between us as though expecting my next move. "Let's get going, shall we? I believe the carriage pulled up."

My heart skipped a beat as I felt a hand slide into mine and a wave of warmth ran through my body. Lianna squeezed my hand, grounding me back to the present moment. Despite not being a fan of PDA and also not being able to show our affection on Earth, I'd always loved Lianna's hand in mine. I pushed down the irritability and pulled my hand out of hers. I still didn't know the rules here, so a friendly squeeze was all I'd allow in front of others.

Charis opened the door and shivered violently as the blustery wind blew inside. She beckoned us out the door, and we rushed into the frigid air toward the ebony carriage with gold etchings and trim. The gold carvings formed trees with a ton of tiny leaves forming the treetops. The carriage was detailed down to the swirls in the tree trunks and the indents in the leaves.

The driver leaped down and opened the carriage door, holding his hand out to us. I took it and carefully stepped into the carriage to avoid any mishaps. The carriage's interior was plush with red and gold cushions and pillows. I sank into the softness. Lianna hopped in and sat beside me. Once the five of us were inside, the driver shut the door, and we were off.

An hour later, we arrived at the bustling marketplace. The decadent aromas of fresh-baked loaves of bread and sweets mixed with the hearty scents of salted meats roasting on spits engulfed me. I inhaled, and out of the corner of my eye, I saw Koen and Lianna doing the same. I peeked out the carriage window, curious to get my first good look at the market.

The marketplace was packed. Fae scurried back and forth between vendors. Some carried packages while chatting with their companions. But as our gilded carriage drove into the center of the square, the flurry of activity came to a sudden halt, and, almost as one, everyone turned to gawk at the carriage.

"Almost feels like home," Lianna quipped. "Except there aren't any children."

I wanted to answer her, but my mouth had gone dry. It did feel like home, especially because Acanthe was grinning at me across the way.

"Lianna," I hissed, "Look," I said, pointing to where I'd seen Acanthe.

"Riona, it's rude to point," Lianna semi-scolded.

"Acanthe's over there!" I hissed.

Lianna looked toward where I was pointing before turning back to me. Her eyes filled with concern. "Acanthe's not there, Riona. Are you okay?"

I looked out the window again, and the woman standing where Acanthe had been only moments before looked nothing like Acanthe. I craned my neck, searching the crowd for Acanthe's writhing black hair, but she was nowhere to be found.

"She was there," I said.

"Riona," Lianna whispered. "Why would Acanthe be here? She's a witch. She'd never cross over to Ilthyrium. Perhaps you saw someone who reminded you of her. I did say this place feels like home."

She was right. There was no reason for Acanthe to be there.

I'd never known of a witch willingly crossing into Ilthyrium. They weren't welcome, even though they cared for the Magicborn and had magic in their blood. Magicborn had always seen them as less and didn't want to have anything to do with them beyond allowing them to safeguard their children on Earth, and that included having them come into their world.

"Sure," I said, "Maybe you're right." I tried to push away the image of Acanthe there in Vakrass Market—a place she shouldn't be—staring at me, but I couldn't shake the feeling in my gut that something was off.

We all stepped out of the carriage, and as it drove away, the onlookers gawked for several moments before Charis called out to them all. "Yes, yes, how exciting the new ascendants are here! Go about your business. We have things to do."

With that, she returned to us and gestured at the entire market. "Welcome to Vakrass market."

I found myself homesick for Dahlia Lane. The marketplace of Vakrass was nothing like the marketplace in Silver Bay, but something felt familiar and comforting. However, I couldn't quite put my finger on what it was.

Fae combed the streets, stopping at various vendors, which was the first difference. While there weren't actual shops, there were several vendors set up like a street fair selling their various wares. The second difference was the complete and utter lack of modern technology. On Earth, humans were glued to their cell phones and devices, and shops were lit with modern electricity. In Vakrass, there wasn't a device in sight, and faeries traveled in groups of two or more, chatting and laughing as they went.

A hand slipped into mine again. I looked down at it before looking into Lianna's eyes. "I know," she said, giving my hand a quick squeeze before letting go.

I reached out to take her hand back before considering where we were. I dropped my hand before Lianna even realized it was there. I didn't want to draw even more attention to us. Not because I was ashamed of her, but because I hated being in the spotlight and because I still didn't know what the rules for our relationship were.

"Wander around and check it out," Charis said. "Tristan and I will stay close."

Koen meandered off, and Tristan followed him. Lianna and I wandered the stalls, eyeing the wares. Clothing, food, and weaponry seemed to be the prevalent items available. Charis followed us.

As we worked our way through the clothing vendors, an enormous building in the distance with a tower reaching toward the sky caught my eye. "What's that?" I asked, turning to Charis and pointing at the building behind me.

"That's the library."

"It looks huge!"

"It is. The Vakrass library holds every book ever written in all of Ilthyrium and Earth."

"Why?"

Charis looked confused. "Why what?"

"Why are they here in Vakrass? Why are they not housed somewhere else?"

"Humans can't preserve them like we do. We couldn't keep them in Oxlis because it's underwater. Most of Nivothia burns, so that wouldn't be a suitable option. Erastrith is unbearable to visit because it is always dark, and nobody wishes to try to read there. Not to mention, the vamps have a penchant for devouring Magicborn blood at an alarming rate anytime an unprotected enters, so they wouldn't provide complete, unfettered access. The pixie buildings of Airestia are much too small, as are its citizens, and everyone knows the Lycans are overgrown puppies who'd either urinate on them or use them as chew toys.

"So, Vakrass was the most reasonable place to house them. We alone have the climate to ensure the survival of the books, but we also are the only ones able to treat them with the respect they deserve and understand them fully. Out of Ilthyrium, we have the most rounded education."

"So, do all Magicborn and humans have access to the library here?" Lianna asked.

"Of course, they have to submit a request for a visit and their intent, and they are provided with an escort at all times, but the Vakrass Library is open to all," Charis said.

"That makes sense," I said, staring at the massive building. I was dying to get inside. Libraries held a soft spot in my heart, thanks to Rosalyn. Rosalyn had taken it upon herself to help me fall in love with reading. Whenever I ended up at her home, I curled up in her lap, lay my head on her chest, and listened to her read me stories. As I got older, she'd bring me to the library to help choose the books she'd read to me, or rather, I'd read to her after she taught me.

Books were my escape from anxiety. They were my escape from Elik. I could do anything, be anybody when I read a book. "Can we go there?" I asked.

"I'm afraid we won't have time for that today," Charis said, dashing my hopes. "But if you look off in the distance, behind the library, you can see Vakmore Academy. That's where you'll spend the next three years."

I glanced into the distance, noticing an imposing castle that appeared to be even larger than Queen Nasryn's palace. It was gothic and old, set back in the hillside, shrouded in cloud cover. "We spend three years there?" I asked Charis, looking back at the female.

"Yep. At the end of your first year, you'll face your graduation trials before you move into your second year, where you'll spend your time honing your intrinsic ability."

"What about you?" I asked, turning away from the Academy and library to face Charis. "You said you only ascended two years ago. Shouldn't you be entering your third year at the Academy?"

Charis blushed and dropped her gaze to the ground.

"I'm sorry," I blurted. "I meant no offense."

Charis peeked up at me. "It's alright. I failed my first-year trials, so they stuck me in the palace as an attendant. Maybe to make an example of me, who knows? All I know is my job is pretty damn easy, so..." Charis trailed off with a shrug.

"Are you bonded?" Lianna asked.

"No. Um... my partner died in our first-year trials, so we never had the chance to be bonded. It's also why I failed."

"Oh," Lianna said, shuffling from foot to foot, looking between me and Charis as though she didn't know how to respond.

"I'm sorry," Lianna said after several long minutes of awkward silence.

Charis shrugged again, clearly wanting to be done with the conversation.

"Let's walk, shall we?" I cut in and walked away because I didn't know what else to do.

Charis trailed behind Lianna and me as we strolled from stall to stall, taking in the sights of the beautiful rugs the weavers displayed and the exotic cloth the tailors worked with.

We were walking by a sewist vendor when an ankle-length amethyst chiffon dress with sections of sheer lace panels in the bodice caught my eye.

"Oh, my goddess, Lianna, I have to have that dress," I said, pointing at it.

"It's perfect for you," Lianna gushed.

Charis followed my gaze. "Ah yes, that's Edyn's. She's one of my favorites. Her work's extraordinary. We can get you fitted. It will be perfect for the ball tomorrow night!"

Chapter Twelve

SECRET PLANS
Lianna

The ride back to the palace was as jarring and uncomfortable as the descent, particularly with a full stomach. Still, I didn't mind. The irregular jolts of the carriage provided an unexpected thrill when each bump sent me crashing against Riona. It was a blessing in disguise because it gave me the perfect opportunity to draw closer to her without risking her boundaries.

Riona's hands were clasped in her lap, her posture rigid and reserved. I couldn't help but admire her grace, even in discomfort. The way her hair tumbled over her shoulders in her long ponytail, and how the warm glow of the afternoon light highlighted her features. I ached to reach out, to take her delicate hand in mine and feel the warmth of her skin against my palm, but closing the distance felt insurmountable. Longing swelled within me, and each brush against her was a reminder of how much I craved her.

I'd planned to sneak out the night before to find her and ensure we were still us. Instead, I succumbed to a deep sleep, and then it was all rush, rush, rush to get ready to go to the market.

Now, uncertainty wrapped around me like ivy climbing an ancient tree. She'd been distant today with not even a hint of wanting or needing to be alone with me. I was desperate for her love and attention, and I feared the silence between us hanging like a fragile thread waiting to snap.

Was she angry I hadn't come to her last night? Had she expected me to? Last night, she'd asked if we could share a room, but when Juniper told her no, she'd looked at me like she wanted me to argue, and I hadn't. Why hadn't I?

I peeked at Koen out of the corner of my eye. He was why. Or perhaps my attraction to him was why. I didn't want him to know about my relationship status yet. Not until I'd figured out what was in my head and heart regarding him. But, looking at Riona's stiff posture and her coolness toward me, perhaps I'd misstepped. I needed to figure out how to make it up to her.

"You'll have dinner with Queen Nasryn tonight, but the afternoon is yours," Charis said, answering a question I'd missed. "Remember to be respectful and avoid wandering around."

I grumbled inwardly, already feeling the weight of boredom pressing down on me like an oppressive blanket. I stole a glance at Riona, and a small, mischievous smile tugged at the corners of my mouth. Screw the rules.

I knew what I wanted to do with my day. I could almost see the spark of excitement in Riona's eyes as I imagined her exploring the endless rows of books in the library. The bumpy ride back to the palace became a whirlwind of scheming and plotting, each bump fueling my determination to sneak Riona into that enchanted library, where adventure and knowledge awaited us.

The moment we stepped foot into the palace, Koen and Tristan walked off together, and I put my plan into action. I didn't know where Riona's room was, so my entire plan was hinging on Charis, taking her to her room first. Luck was on my side.

Charis led the way down the hall with a couple of males trailing behind us, carrying some of our packages. Charis stopped before a door that was not mine, and Riona walked inside, not saying a word to me. The male carrying her packages stepped inside also and stepped out a moment later, closing the door behind him.

"Thank you," Charis said. The male shot her a thumbs up and walked back the way we'd come before continuing toward my room.

I counted the doors between mine and Riona's, ensuring that when I went searching for her room, I'd get the right one.

"Here we are!" Charis said at my door. "Do you need anything?"

"No thanks," I said, eager to get my plan underway. I wanted to spend my afternoon with Riona, and that meant getting rid of Charis.

"Alright. I'll leave you to your afternoon," Charis said as she and the male who'd carried my packages left.

I waited five minutes before I opened my door and popped my head out to make sure they were gone. I hurried to Riona's room and knocked on her door. I breathed a sigh of relief when Riona's voice called out, "Come in."

I eased open the door and slipped inside. Riona was sitting on the couch, wrapped up in a blanket, staring into the fire before she looked up and saw me. A grin spread across her face, and I hurried to her and pulled her into my arms, inhaling the lavender scent of her shampoo.

"I missed you," I said into her hair.

"I saw you like ten minutes ago, silly," she whispered. But she wrapped her arms around me and squeezed.

"I meant that I missed touching you. Today was torture."

"Same," Riona said, pulling back. "I'm glad you're here."

I looked around her room, which was decorated so differently than mine. Mine was all blues and sandy browns. It reminded me of the ocean, but hers was done in earthy browns and creams.

"So," I said, pulling my attention away from the decor. "Want to hang out?"

"Absolutely. I'm afraid there's not much to do in here though."

"Oh, I've no intention of hanging out here. I have a surprise for you. Do you trust me?"

Riona hesitated. "Why do I have a feeling you're about to suggest breaking the rules?"

My grin stretched across my entire face. "Because you know me well."

"Lianna..."

"Follow my lead," I said, grabbing her hand. I wasn't about to let her talk me out of it.

I stuck my head out the door once again to make sure nobody was out there before pulling her out the door with me and down the hall toward the library. I stopped at the library doors and listened for voices. When I was sure nobody was coming, I eased the door open.

Riona gasped.

The library was massive. Much bigger than I thought it would be. Books were stacked on shelves from the floor to the high vaulted ceiling.

"I don't even know where to start," Riona whispered, and let out a nervous giggle. "We aren't even supposed to be in here. What if we get caught?"

I shrugged. "Then we play dumb. Who cares, Riona? Live a little. I know you're dying to check out this library." I could see the wistfulness in her eyes as she took in the hundreds of rows of books.

"Fine, you win," she said, pulling on my hand and leading me away from the door and into the stacks.

She led me halfway down a row before whirling around and pulling me tight into her arms. "Thank you!" she whispered, brushing her lips against mine

Chapter Thirteen

THE KEY TO A GIRL'S HEART
Riona

The scent of aged parchment and polished wood enveloped me, creating an atmosphere rich with history. Lianna's hand slipped from mine, and I hesitated, feeling lost amidst the array of books that beckoned to be explored. I groaned, unsure where to start.

I moved away from the heavy history tomes and on to the next row. The self-help section was filled with colorful covers, promising transformation of all kinds, but I passed them. Next came the cookbooks, stacked with mouthwatering images and intricate recipes, yet they didn't capture my interest either.

After wandering through several more rows, a thrill of anticipation surged through me as I stumbled upon what I'd been searching for—the fiction section, a magical realm in itself bursting with imagination and emotion. The romance novels beckoned me, their covers adorned with whimsical designs that hinted at the passionate stories within.

I browsed through the books, fingertips dancing over the spines. I spotted a sapphic fae romance that drew me in. After a bit more searching, I discovered a promising, vibrant, and inviting polyamorous romance. With both books in hand, I began making my way back to Lianna. But a faint whispering caught my attention—two people were sharing secrets in hushed tones, their voices weaving through the quiet sanctuary of the library.

Cursing under my breath, I pressed my back against the cold, hard shelf, my heart pounding in my chest. I held my breath, praying they wouldn't come this way and discover my hiding spot.

"I don't care. I want her in training immediately," a familiar female voice echoed.

"Without the blood test, you'd be putting her at serious risk," countered an unfamiliar feminine voice, sharp and tinged with caution.

A tense silence loomed before the familiar voice rose again with more urgency. "We are all at risk every day. And you know what's at stake for me if this doesn't happen now."

"Of course I know," the unfamiliar voice hissed, barely concealing their frustration. "But that doesn't change the fact that there are processes to follow and safety measures that need to be put in place."

"I don't care about the processes! I want results!" The familiar voice's demand sliced through the air like a knife.

"I won't risk the wrath of those in power for you. Like it or not, they're the ones with the real influence." Tension crackled palpably.

"For now," the familiar voice replied. "And I'll remember this."

A shiver ran down my spine in the shadows of the hallway. I felt the weight of their conversation—a dark secret swirling around hidden agendas. My heart thundered so loudly I feared they would hear it and come to investigate who was listening in on their extremely private conversation.

I ducked back the way I came as I sought to distance myself from the alarming words in the thick air behind me. Whatever sinister drama was unfolding behind those closed doors was not something I wanted to be tangled in, especially not right after my arrival in Vakrass. It would be better to forget the ominous conversation and pretend I'd never heard it.

Lianna leaned against the towering stacks of ancient books right where I'd left her, oblivious to the storm brewing within these walls.

I seized her hand. "We have to go. Now," I whispered.

Lianna's eyes widened as she read the urgency on my face. Her gaze darted back toward the shadows from which I'd emerged. Her bravado faded, and the color drained from her cheeks.

The sound of voices grew louder along with the sound of footsteps approaching. Lianna's grip on my hand tightened, and we bolted toward the exit, pushing the door open a crack to slip outside as quietly as shadows.

"Hurry," I urged.

We raced back to my room, the door creaking as I burst inside, pulling Lianna behind me and slamming it shut with a heavy thud. The room was a haven, a barrier against the chaos.

Lianna erupted into giggles, her laughter a stark contrast to the tension. "That was close," she said, eyes sparkling with adrenaline.

I remained silent. The echoes of the library conversation haunted me.

Lianna tilted her head. "What's wrong?"

"Nothing," I replied as though my words could brush away the unease. "Look," I said, lifting the two books I'd snatched from the shelves. "I brought some reading material—sapphic for me and poly for you." I tossed her the book I'd selected for her, its cover adorned with vibrant colors and captivating artwork of three fae, two women and a male, wrapped in a passionate embrace.

She glanced at the back cover and shot me a wide grin. "Okay, this sounds excellent. Readathon?"

"Absolutely." We settled on the couch, and I spread a warm, cozy blanket over us, creating a cocoon of comfort. We lost ourselves in the romantic escapades of the books we read until Charis collected us for dinner with the queen.

Chapter Fourteen

DANCING THE NIGHT AWAY ONE WAY OR ANOTHER

Riona

The next evening, I paced outside the ballroom doors dressed in the decadent purple lace and chiffon dress I'd found at the market. I cursed myself for arriving so early. I hadn't meant to beat Koen and Lianna downstairs, and now I was by myself, which I was notoriously bad at. I was tempted to sit on the floor and run through some meditations when someone cleared their throat behind me.

I whirled and found Lianna. She was gorgeous in a floor-length sapphire gown that shimmered as she walked. The bodice featured an illusion corset, giving people a glimpse of her pale skin beneath. The dress clung to her hips and flared out at the knees. Her long blonde hair was pulled up and styled in a sleek bun and sparkled like her dress.

"You look beautiful," I blurted, and my cheeks burned at my awkwardness. I was horrible at expressing myself in moments like this. As a child, I was so socially awkward that the coven was concerned about my academic development, but I flourished in my classes and schoolwork—in part because of Rosalyn's determination to teach me to read—it was communicating with people that I struggled with.

Lianna looked me up and down twice. There was a gleam in her eye that hadn't been there before, one that made me want to reach out and touch her. I clasped my hands behind my back before I did anything stupid, like pinning her against the wall and having my way with her right there in the hallway. Yesterday had been torture after the library. I was sitting on the couch reading romance novels and waiting for her to make a move to let me know we were still us, but she didn't make a move, so I was left confused and frustrated all night.

"Thank you, Riona," Lianna said. "So do you." She whispered the last words, her voice filled with longing and need.

I peeked at her again and swore the world became a little clearer and a little brighter. I peered at her, searching for signs that she felt it too, but I just smiled at her when I saw none.

What's happening to me?

"We all know I look amazing," Koen said, interrupting my thoughts.

He leaned against the wall behind us, and I wondered how long he'd been there. Based on the way he was looking between us, my guess was too long. He sauntered up to us and draped an arm around us.

"Damn, you girls sure are lucky you get to compete for my affections."

Lianna's laughter echoed while I frowned and squirmed away from his embrace. Something about him rubbed me the wrong way. Maybe it was the way he looked at Lianna, or perhaps it was because Lianna laughed at his unfunny jokes that were always about himself—either way, I wasn't a fan, and I certainly didn't like him touching me.

Charis emerged from down the hallw, dressed in her uniform, footsteps echoing against the polished marble floor. "The ceremony will begin in moments. First, you'll be introduced to Vakrass society, and then the ball will begin immediately. Enjoy it. Tonight is in celebration of you all."

She appraised us and then said, "Line up. Lianna, first, then Riona, then Koen."

We lined up, and she bent to fix Lianna's train and then mine. "Once those doors open," she explained, "Lianna will lead the way down the aisle. Riona, you'll follow when Lianna is halfway there. And Koen, you'll join when Riona is halfway down. Any questions?"

The three of us shook our heads. The huge double doors to the throne room creaked as they swung open. Charis scuttled out of view, and Lianna's shoulders rose and fell once before she stepped forward.

I was mesmerized by how her dress flowed around her. It shimmered like waves lapping at the beach.

"Go," Koen hissed when I missed my cue to walk.

I jumped a little and took a couple of quick steps forward, nearly losing my balance but righting myself as I came through the doors into the throne room. Hundreds of eyes turned to me, and I faltered.

Oh no, oh no, oh no. Come on, legs move.

I sucked in a breath, feeling the constriction of my corset, and then exhaled forcefully, imagining that with each breath out, my anxiety was dissipating into the air. I reached the midway point as Lianna reached the dais base and turned back to face me. I focused on reaching Lianna at the end of the eternally long aisle. Lianna gave me a small smile and a slight bob of her head that said, *you can do this.*

I glanced behind her and met the startling green eyes of that crimson-haired faerie. She stood to the right of Queen Nasryn's throne, her hand resting on the hilt of her sword that was strapped at her hip instead of over her shoulder. Her meadow-green eyes assessed me for the briefest of moments before they flicked back to the crowd. I ascended the platform and positioned myself next to Lianna.

Queen Nasryn commanded the space. She was adorned in a striking one-shouldered black Grecian-style gown embellished with a lavish band of beading that scattered shimmering reflections across the dimly lit chamber. With its three menacing points, her crown was a sinister, twisted symbol of authority. She exuded the commanding presence of an ancient and formidable monarch, ruling with unyielding strength.

Koen came up beside me, and Queen Nasryn glanced down at the three of us for a moment before turning her gaze to the crowd behind us.

"Welcome. Tonight, we thank the goddess for bringing us three new members. Join me in welcoming Lianna Hirovonen," she said, then held her hand out to Lianna.

Lianna took Queen Nasryn's hand and walked up the steps to stand beside her. Thunderous applause filled the throne room.

Queen Nasryn held up her hand, and the applause cut off.

"Riona Vandeleur," Queen Nasryn said, then held her hand out to me.

I took it, and as gracefully as I could, ascended the steps and stood beside Lianna. More applause rang out.

"And Koen Trevarthen." Queen Nasryn held her hand out to Koen, and he sauntered up the steps, without a care in the world.

I worked to keep the grimace off my face. Queen Nasryn stepped in front of us and said, "They only make us stronger."

The crowd eagerly chanted her words, sending a wave of unease through my gut. But as quickly as it appeared, it dissipated before I could understand it.

Queen Nasryn held up a hand, silencing the crowd. She snapped her fingers, and the fireplace and candles blazed to life. Where the candles had offered a soft glow before, they now magically lit the room.

I stared out into the crowd of impeccably-dressed fae. Some females were dressed in long ball gowns while others were dressed in short cocktail dresses. The males were relatively uniform in dress in extravagant tuxedos. However, they weren't only in the traditional black. They wore every color imaginable. Some had even incorporated random trinkets. A locket in hair, a feather in a pocket, a pocket watch as a necklace. Ordinary things worn in unique ways.

Music began playing, and they parted every which way, clearing the ballroom floor. They stared at us expectantly. My mouth went bone dry. What do they want? Why are they all staring at us?

Koen stepped in front of Lianna and me.

"We're supposed to dance," he said.

He held out a hand to each of us. Lianna took one, but I shook my head.

I didn't want to be touched by him again.

Koen shrugged, but Lianna allowed him to lead her onto the dance floor. A surge of jealousy welled in me at the sight of Lianna in Koen's arms, but I pushed it down. I didn't own her, and she could dance with Koen if she liked.

They swept elegantly around the dance floor, and mutters of approval blanketed the crowd. Yet, each moment Lianna was in Koen's arms, my thoughts turned darker and angrier.

"They look good together, don't they?" Queen Nasryn said. "I believe they'll be bonded when the time comes."

I glowered at the queen, and my fury turned into an inferno.

"Maybe. Maybe not," I said through gritted teeth. With those words, I gathered my courage, suppressed my rage, and walked down the steps to where Koen and Lianna danced.

I would reclaim what was mine, no matter how archaic it felt to think the words, I'd been avoiding the truth, and the truth was Lianna was mine. I wanted everyone to know it, regardless of whatever "rules" there might be here. I especially wanted the queen and Koen, who appeared smitten as he spun my girl around the dance floor, to know.

"May I cut in?" I said, interrupting them.

"Absolutely." Koen grinned, moving to take my hand.

"Oh—um, no. I'm going to dance with her," I said, stepping out of his reach and cocking my head in Lianna's direction. "Is that alright with you?" I asked Lianna.

Koen scowled at me, but Lianna's eyes lit up.

"Yes," she said, breathlessly. "I've been waiting for you."

I reached for her, and Koen stepped forward like he was about to argue. Lianna stepped into my arms, and I swept her away from him without another look.

We danced around the room, and I felt graceful for the first time in my life. With Lianna in my arms, I was on top of the world, and nothing could bring me down. I looked down at her to find she was looking up at me.

"You're so beautiful," she said. "I know I said it earlier, but it bears repeating. Are we..." She grew quiet. Lianna was rarely at a loss for words, and unlike me, she wasn't socially awkward. She cleared her throat and asked, "Are we still us?"

Our dancing slowed as we stared at each other. "Do you still want us to be us?" I asked, though all I wanted to do was say, I'm yours and you're mine.

She didn't hesitate. "Yes, Riona, that's what I want. Is it what you want?"

My heart burst with untethered joy. Everything I'd ever wanted was before me. I leaned down, pressing my lips to hers in answer. I'd heard everything I needed to hear. Her body against mine sent my heart racing, igniting a fire in my core.

The room filled with a cacophony of wild cheers and exuberant whoops, and I recoiled from Lianna and a fierce blush spread across my cheeks as I remembered we were in the center of the dance floor surrounded by strangers, and a fierce blush spread across my cheeks. I took another step back and glanced around the crowd. My gaze landed on Koen, who was directing a murderous glare at me.

A shiver ran down my spine. It was clear he wanted Lianna, but I hadn't realized how much. Seeing the malice in his eyes, I knew I'd made an enemy. An enemy that I'd live in close contact with for the next three years. But when I saw Queen Nasryn's cold, calculating stare, my stomach twisted, bile rose, and a single word clamored in my mind.

Flee.

Chapter Fifteen

FIGHT, FLIGHT, OR...

Lianna

Riona dashed down the ornate hallway, her footsteps reverberating off the stone floors like an urgent drumbeat. She pulled me along, the fabric of my long dress tangling with every hurried step. The tall heels I wore threatened a broken ankle with each misstep. My lungs burned trying to keep up with Riona in my skin-tight dress.

I was still trying to piece together the frantic energy surrounding us. Gasping, I finally mustered enough strength to say, "What's going on, Riona?"

Riona halted in front of her bedroom door. Its surface gleamed in the dim light. She glanced at me for a moment, then with a quiet creak, she pushed the door open and gestured for me to enter. Her wild eyes spoke volumes.

Surprised by the weight of her fear, I stepped inside.

"What the fuck was that?" I asked, my chest heaving. Her face had gone white. "What is it? What's the matter?"

She rubbed her face, smearing her eyeliner. "I don't know!" she wailed. "I had this horrible feeling, an overwhelming urge to flee, so I did. Now I feel stupid."

"You're not stupid," I said, forcing my voice to be calm and reassuring. Riona was trembling so hard she could barely stand upright. I scanned the room, taking in the cozy ambiance, before guiding her toward the couch in front of the crackling fireplace. I tugged her onto the soft couch cushions and wrapped her in my arms. She laid her head on my chest while I focused on my breathing, so she'd take my cue and breathe with me when she was ready. It was second nature to me now. I'd been guiding her through breathing techniques for years. It was the method that worked the best for her.

Within a few moments, her breathing steadied, and the shuddering ceased. She sat up, her eyes meeting mine.

"What the fuck *was* that?" I asked again, tamping down my irritation.

"I'm so sorry for pulling you away from the ball, Lianna. That was unfair of me. I couldn't bear to leave you behind if there was danger, which obviously there wasn't, but…"

I sighed. It was an irrational reaction to no visible danger. I'd grown used to her random fight or flight—mostly flight—urges to go with it, but I was a little annoyed that I hadn't gotten to stay for the rest of the dance. The damage was done, though, and there was no way I was going to go back and try to save face after that exit. I glanced at Riona, and desire coursed through my body. Might as well make the most of it. "Well," I said, arching my eyebrows. "Since we are alone and everyone is at the ball, why don't we…" I left the innuendo and offer open.

"Oh goddess, yes, please," Riona said, rising and pulling me up beside her. She dragged me farther into her bedroom and pushed me onto the bed. She climbed on top of me, dress and all, kissing me with a fervor that took my breath away.

She pulled back, her eyes searching mine as a soft smile played on her lips. "I'm so glad we are here together," she whispered. Then she leaned down again, capturing my lips in a tender kiss.

So am I.

Chapter Sixteen

NEW SCHOOL, NEW ME
Riona

The afternoon after our embarrassing exit from the ball, Charis delivered Koen, Lianna, and me to the front doors of Vakmore Academy, where we'd spend the next three years learning about our abilities and what would be expected of us.

Since the coven matriarchs never knew which factions Magicborn children would ascend to, they were prohibited by the Magicborn monarchs from teaching us anything useful about the factions except for the mourning song we sang for the lost Magicborn at the Ascension Ceremony. But on the ride there, Charis explained that during our time at Vakmore, we'd learn Vakrasi, the fae language, how to wield our magic, the physiology of our bodies, combat, medicine, and the history of the fae lands.

I couldn't have cared less. All I wanted was to find a small cabin tucked away in the middle of the woods, curl up, and be alone with Lianna for the rest of my life.

But I had no say over it, so I stood with Lianna and Koen outside the enormous double doors of Vakmore Academy and waited to be let inside.

The stone building was ancient and breathtaking. I tried to see the tops of the towers, but they rose so high that the tips of them hid in the clouds.

The colossal steel double doors opened with a groan, and a tall female with tawny skin, deep brown eyes, and graying black hair greeted us.

"Welcome to Vakmore Academy. I'm headmistress Thea Oldfield. You may call me Thea."

"Hello," we said in unison.

"Charis, thank you for delivering them here." Thea turned to us. "Come inside. I'll show you to your rooms."

Charis waved at Thea before turning to me. "Good luck!" she said.

I smiled. "Goodbye, Charis, and thank you."

Charis grinned back and hurried to the waiting carriage.

We entered, and I couldn't help but stare at the ceiling. It appeared to be miles above our heads. Intricately crafted black steel sconces hung on the walls, each filled with a burning candle, lighting the antechamber with a soft glow. A wide staircase was set several steps inside the doors, and the walls were covered in photos set in ornately carved wood frames.

"Come now, you'll have plenty of time to gawk later," Thea said, snapping her fingers. "I don't have all day."

We caught up to Thea as she walked up the opulent staircase.

"Riona and Lianna, you'll be rooming together. Koen, you'll be in a room next to them. You'll do everything as a unit: eat, sleep, and train. You'll have all the same classes until you declare an area of expertise. At that point, you'll start taking classes in that specialty."

I missed a step and stumbled forward. I clutched the banister, righting myself.

Expertise? I might have to take classes by myself? My palms grew clammy, and I wiped them on my pants. Lianna shot me a look that said it didn't go unnoticed, and her concerned glance flooded me with ease.

"The specialties are broken into five major categories," Thea continued, oblivious to my inner meltdown. "They're magic, combat, agriculture, construction, and medicine. Each class has subclasses as well. All classes are influenced by magic."

We reached the top of the staircase, and she led us down a long hallway, continuing her spiel. "Your classes will start in three days. You have a few days to settle in, get used to Vakmore, and learn your way around. I've assigned unit five to show you around for the first week, but you'll be alone after that. Don't expect them to be friendly. Units are not allowed to mingle with other units. You're not here to make friends, you're here to learn the ways of the fae and learn to work within your unit."

She stopped in front of a door about halfway down the hall and pulled out a ring of skeleton keys that reminded me of Juniper's set at Queen Nasryn's palace. Thea selected one and slid it into the door's lock. It clicked open. Then she took the key and held it between her hands. When she opened her hands, there were two additional keys. "Riona and Lianna, this is your room." She placed the original key onto her keyring before holding the new ones out to us. "Here are your keys until you learn to lock your doors properly."

"Properly?" Lianna asked.

"With magic, of course," she replied.

Lianna rolled her eyes. "Of course. How silly of me."

I brushed my hair out of my face and examined the key again.

"Koen will be next door," Thea said, ignoring Lianna's disrespect. She gestured to the door next to ours. "Settle in and get ready for dinner. I'll send unit five down to bring you to the dining hall."

"Thank you, Headmistress," Lianna said sweetly. "Bye Koen,"

It was my turn to roll my eyes as she grabbed my hand and pulled me into our room.

Chapter Seventeen

JUST KIDDING, SAME ME
Riona

"Can you believe we're finally here?" Lianna squealed the moment we were alone.

I glared at her. I was exhausted, and I couldn't fathom getting ready for dinner, let alone dealing with people. Plus, Lianna's mouth and attitude seemed likely to get us into trouble. I sighed. How would I keep her safe when she made it so hard? At least it didn't sound like there would be much interaction between us and other units. Maybe that would make it easier.

I looked up, and Lianna stared at me, waiting for a response. "It's great," I said. My shoulders slumped and my body felt cumbersome.

"Oh, come on, it's exciting," she gushed, dropping onto one of the beds. The springs creaked, and the noise grated on my nerves, violently jarring me.

"No!" I snapped, reaching my breaking point. I glanced wildly around the room, seeking an escape, and saw it on the other side of the bedroom. I dashed across the room and into the bathroom, shutting the door behind me. I winced when it slammed shut, shaking the mirror above the sink.

Heat consumed me. I grabbed a washcloth off the hook, soaked it in cold water, and set it against the back of my neck, trying to cool my rising body temperature. I'd kill for an ice pack.

"Ri? Are you okay?" Lianna's voice was muffled through the bathroom door.

Ri? Did she call me Ri? I liked it.

"Can I come in, please?" she asked.

"Uh—I'll—um..." I stuttered, trying to form the words to tell her I'd be right out, but they wouldn't come. Instead, I slid onto the floor in front of the sink, holding the soaking-wet cloth to the back of my neck. Cold water dripped down my back, soaking my shirt, further setting every nerve it came into contact with on edge. I put the cloth on my knee and yanked my shirt over my head, banging my elbow in the process.

"Ouch! Shit!" I rubbed my elbow, trying to ease the throbbing ache as the washcloth soaked through my jeans. A sob hitched in my chest, and I ripped the cloth off my knee. It was no longer cold. I shrieked and whipped the cloth across the room. The splat it made when it hit the wall was gratifying. I buried my face in my knees as sobs wracked my body.

"Ri? Come on, if you don't answer me, I'm going to come in."

I couldn't answer her. My panic attack was here in full force, and there was no backing down from it. I hated how overstimulation could instantly cause a panic attack. Tears cascaded down my cheeks, and I grabbed my shirt off the floor and shoved it against my mouth, trying to muffle my cries. When the panic was at its worst, I couldn't keep them quiet. I was dangerously close to that.

The door opened and closed. I wanted to look up at her and tell her to go away, but I couldn't. The words wouldn't come, and the thoughts barely formed.

"Hey, hey, it's okay! I'm here," Lianna said, coming and sitting right before me. "I'm right here."

She grabbed my shirt, yanking it from my hands and mouth, and I threw my head back. My head hit the cupboard beneath the sink but not hard enough that it caused me a great deal of pain. Pity. Pain might have helped snap me out of it. Instead, it was embarrassing. A strangled sob worked its way out of my mouth.

"Look at me." Her voice was quiet but commanding.

I shook my head. "I—caa-can't."

"You can. And you will. Look at me now."

I lifted my gaze to meet her calm, sparkling blue eyes.

"I'm here with you," she said, taking my hands. "Right here with you. Breathe with me."

Once again, she led me through breathing exercises, like she had on Samhain, like she always had whenever she was present for one of my attacks, and like always, within five minutes, I was feeling so much better. I stared into her eyes, and I wanted to kiss her again. I leaned in to do so, but she pulled back.

I retreated, doubt clamoring in my head. I was naked from the waist up. Any other time, I wouldn't care, but the echoes of my panic were too near, and my vulnerability level was sky-high, especially after she pulled away from my kiss.

"Um, thanks. I feel better," I said, covering my breasts with my arm and cursing myself for not wearing a fucking bra. She averted her eyes and handed me my shirt, and I slipped it on. I cringed as the cold, wet material hit my skin.

"Don't worry, I didn't look." Lianna's voice pulled my thoughts away from the atrocious feeling of wet cloth clinging to my skin.

She winked and added. "Much."

I picked myself up off the bathroom floor and turned the faucet on to splash some cold water on my burning face. Lianna stood behind me, assessing me in the mirror.

"I'm fine," I said. "It's no big deal. They happen all the time. I'm fine."

She raised an eyebrow. "Are you trying to convince yourself or me?" she asked. "I didn't realize they happened this often," she continued, not waiting for an answer. "Maybe it was a bad idea to keep them a secret. My attendant at the palace told me that what we bring with us multiplies. For example, you had anxiety and panic attacks as a human. So, they won't go away here. They'll likely get worse." Her eyes filled with tears. "I should've never helped you hide your panic attacks from the coven. They could've helped you."

"They would've taken me from my mother." My words were flat and dull.

Immortality was looking bleaker by the second. I'd been holding on to a slim hope that my anxiety would get better with time, but it sounded like it wouldn't ever get better.

My panic attacks weren't a secret. I'd had them in front of my mom so many times. Mom never disclosed to the coven the toll the anxiety and panic attacks had taken on me after the ordeal with Elik. She'd pleaded with me to allow her to, but I'd held my ground and refused to give in. I figured they'd try to take me away from her again, and that thought terrified me more than living with the panic attacks. She'd planned to inform Matriarch Sylvaine until she'd had a run-in with Acanthe when she was on her way to the meeting with the matriarch. I don't know what Acanthe said, but my mom returned home without going to the appointment, and the subject never came up again after that. Then, when I'd had my first panic attack in front of Lianna, I'd sworn her to secrecy, and she'd agreed.

"We should never have hidden it," Lianna scolded.

"They would've taken me from my mother!" I screamed, my voice reverberating around the small bathroom.

Lianna flinched at my outburst. "You don't know for sure they would've taken you away," she muttered, looking away. "I'll leave you be. It'll be dinnertime soon, so prepare for that." She left the room, closing the door behind her.

Shame burned through me. I hadn't meant to shout at her. *Is it true what she said? Will my anxiety be worse here? I don't think I'll survive it if it gets worse.* My anxiety was terrible when I was a human, unbearable sometimes. I couldn't imagine it getting worse, but I knew there was truth to Lianna's words because I already felt it growing stronger. The magic in my blood was strengthening it—transforming it into a wild, uncontrollable beast—and I didn't know if I could cage it again if it ever escaped.

I looked into the mirror, and my deep brown eyes reflected back at me.

"I don't know if I'll survive this," I told the girl in the mirror. But she didn't respond, and I was left to my devices. I left the bathroom before I could fling myself back on the floor and give up. I'd never been a quitter, and I wasn't about to start now, even though that was all I wanted to do. I didn't want to go through three years of training. I just wanted a little cabin in the woods where I could live out my days with Lianna and not have to deal with anything. Maybe then my anxiety wouldn't be so bad.

A dry shirt flew at my head, and I snatched it before it smacked me in the face. I stared at the shirt in surprise. I'd never caught anything before. Were my reflexes finally kicking in? I turned around and slipped out of my soaked shirt and into the soft, dry one before turning back around. "Thanks."

Lianna opened her mouth when a sharp rap interrupted whatever she was about to say. Lianna gave me a quick once-over and pointed to a sweatshirt on one of the twin beds, then headed out of the bedroom and opened it.

I grabbed the white hoodie, threw it over my head, and went to the living room. Koen was in the doorway with four others. They all peered at Lianna and me.

"Hello," the tall olive-skinned female at the head of the group said. "We're unit five. I'm Amalie, the unit leader. This is Briggs, my second and my mate," she said, gesturing possessively to the tall, muscular male beside her. "Behind me are Nicodemus and Nissa. They're also mates. And, of course, you know Koen. Strange that there are only three of you."

"Yeah. I don't think that's ever happened here before. It will be interesting to see how you navigate that," Nissa chimed in.

Amalie shot her a look, and Nissa shut up. "We're here to take you to the dining room for dinner. Ready?"

"Sure are!" Lianna said. "Oh, I'm Lianna, by the way, and this is Riona."

"We know." Amalie spun on her heel, and her unit moved aside, allowing her passage down the hallway. "Let's go. We're hungry."

Briggs walked beside her. Nicodemus and Nissa gestured to Lianna and me to walk ahead of them. Koen walked behind us with Nicodemus and Nissa bringing up the rear, sandwiching us between the unit.

"So, what's it like here?" Lianna asked.

"It's the best program in Ilthyrium," Nissa said. "Of course, everyone thinks their school is the best, but Vakmore is."

Amalie stopped and turned to face the female. "Nissa," Amalie's voice was chiding.

"She asked a question, Amalie. It's not like we weren't new once. I was trying to be helpful."

"You know the rules: no fraternization. It's bad enough we got put on this stupid detail. It's below us." Amalie scoffed.

"Well, don't you think Thea assumed we'd talk to them since we're supposed to show them the ropes? It's not fraternization," Nissa argued.

"I'm the unit leader. You do as I say."

Amalie glared at Nissa, and I got the feeling Amalie wasn't challenged often. I glanced at Nissa appreciatively, trying to convey with my eyes that even though I just met her, I admired Nissa's attempt to stand up to her unit leader by answering Lianna.

I stared in disbelief as Amalie threw what could only be described as an adult tantrum right in the middle of the hall, and her unit didn't call her out or do anything to defend Nissa. Nissa fell silent and dropped her head in submission.

"Alrighty," Lianna said, breaking the awkward tension that descended on the group. "How about we go to the mess hall, and you all can go on your merry way?"

Amalie sneered at Lianna before spinning on her heel and walking back down the hall without another word.

Chapter Eighteen

LESSONS
Riona

When we got to the dining room, Lianna, Koen, and I stared in awe at the cozy dining room filled with about thirty students.

"We'll leave you to it," Amalie left us in the doorway to fend for ourselves.

"Helpful, isn't she?" Lianna quipped, glancing around the room.

"So helpful." Koen laughed, staring down at Lianna, his eyes bright with want.

A lump lodged itself in my throat. I stared at the room full of fae I'd have to walk through and eat in front of in abject horror. My stomach dropped and twisted violently.

"Ri, let's go," Lianna urged when she noticed I wasn't by her side.

"You guys go ahead. I'm not hungry," I lied, stepping backward. I'd go back to our room and hide.

Lianna grabbed my hand. "You have to eat sometime. Might as well be now, and I know you're hungry. You're always starving after a panic attack," she whispered so only I could hear her.

I hesitated.

"Koen and I have your back," she said as Koen came to stand beside us.

His gaze fixed on our joined hands. "What's happening?"

"Ri's nervous," Lianna told him.

I shot her a dark look. It was none of Koen's business, but she shrugged it off.

"It's just food…" Koen said, as if that made it easier.

I took another step backward toward the door, but Lianna wasn't letting me go back. She pulled me into the room. I tried to plant my feet, but Lianna shared a look with Koen. He took my other arm, trapping me between them, which made me feel a little better, even though I still didn't like Koen touching me.

They led us to the buffet line with me safely sandwiched between them. With each step, tension released from my body piece by piece, starting at my shoulders and working its way down until each muscle was relaxed. We gathered our food, found an empty table, and sat down.

"Vakmore's different from what I thought it would be," Lianna said, breaking the silence between us. "Colder, I guess. I didn't think they'd keep us so secluded, and everyone is stuck spending time with only their unit? What's that about?"

"I don't know," I said, returning my attention to the two of them.

"Me neither," Koen said, his eyes on a female a few tables away.

The female caught him staring at her and grimaced a second before the male beside her caught Koen staring. The male was next to our table in a flash, yanking Koen off his chair and holding him in the air by his neck.

"What are you staring at?" the male snarled.

Koen paled and tried to speak, but he squeezed Koen's throat tighter. Koen's eyes bulged. His color returned, and his skin turned a blotchy red. Koen clawed at the male's arms as he hung in the air, fighting desperately for another breath.

"Why the fuck were you staring at my mate?" the male demanded.

Lianna jumped up. "He didn't know!" she yelled, rushing to Koen's defense. "He's sorry. He won't do it again," Lianna said, making promises that Koen couldn't make for himself.

Suddenly, the female Koen had been checking out stood beside her mate. I hadn't even seen her move.

"I'm sure he didn't mean it," the female said. "Look at him. He's brand new. Put him down, Aithan. He's not worth getting expelled over."

I kept my mouth shut despite the overwhelming urge to blurt out that Thea had told us to keep to our unit. It was an urge that often got me into trouble, but I hated it when someone thought I didn't know something. Especially because I was a rule follower to my core.

Reason seemed to return to Aithan at his mate's words. All eyes were on our table as Aithan lowered Koen to the ground and pulled him nose to nose. "If I ever see you look at my mate like that again, I'll kill you," he said, then released Koen.

Koen stumbled backward, averting his gaze, his face red for a different reason. The female looked at us. "Who's supposed to be showing you the ropes, so this doesn't happen?" she asked.

"Amalie," Lianna answered quietly, eyeing the female before us.

"Of course, it's fucking Amalie," the female spat, spinning and searching the room until her gaze landed on the group staring from across the room. "Amalie, come here," the female commanded. To my surprise, Amalie hurried over.

"Yes, commander," she said.

Power whipped through the room, pulling the air from my lungs as though all the energy in the room was being consumed. The new female grew several inches to tower over Amalie. "One of your charges nearly lost his life. I suggest you stop slacking and educate them on how things run before we have to bury one of them."

"Yes, commander," Amalie mewled.

"You owe them an apology."

"Yes, commander," Amalie said before turning to us. "I'm sorry I didn't follow through on my duties." Her tone was stiff. She turned back to the other female and said, "Forgive me, commander. I'll execute my duties to the fullest extent of my abilities. I won't fail you again."

"See that you don't," the female said, shrinking back to her normal height. She spun on her heel and walked back to her table.

Amalie turned to us, resentment blazing in her eyes.

We shrank against her glare, and suddenly, it cleared as quickly as it set into her face. "Well, I suppose we should teach you the ins and outs of Vakmore Academy before you get yourselves killed and, more importantly, make me look bad in front of Xenryn again," Amalie said as the rest of her unit joined her.

"We'll start with her. Xenryn is the commanding officer of the third years, which is what we are. What she says goes. She also helps train newbies, so I'm sure you'll run into her again. Make sure you show her the respect she deserves."

The three of us nodded in understanding.

"Let's get a few things straight," Amalie said, gesturing to our table.

The seven of us sat and stared at each other, waiting for someone to speak.

"First things first," Amalie started, "there's no fraternization between units or classes, and that includes looking at them for longer than a second if they aren't speaking to you. You're first class because it's your first year. We are third class because we are in our third year. You move up as you advance in your years of study. If you ever get confused about what level someone is, look at their uniforms. It's pretty straightforward. White for first years, gray for second years, and black for third years."

I glanced around the room, it was a sea of gray and black. We were the smallest group by far in white. There were at least twelve second years dressed in gray and twenty third years dressed in black.

"Second, everyone in a unit is platonically bonded. It's the way the change happens. We come through as a unit, and the romantic bonds fall into place after the first year of training. Obviously, your group is different because there are three of you. We don't know what this means, so don't ask. With me so far?"

We looked at each other and nodded. Queen Nasryn had already explained this on our first night in Vakmore.

There was no way I'd romantically bond with Koen, but I could see myself bonding with Lianna.

"Are same-sex bonds a thing here?" I surprised myself by asking aloud.

"Of course. They're rare, but they happen. Typically, when two females or two males ascend, and only if they were already romantically inclined to same-sex relationships," Amalie said, rolling her eyes as if it was the dumbest question she'd ever been asked. I sat back, determined not to say another word.

"Now, if I may continue—"

"That was a fine question to ask," Lianna said, coming to my rescue. "We don't know anything about being fae or what is and isn't allowed. That isn't our fault. I'm sure you had questions like us."

"You're right. Now, can we please move on?" Amalie said impatiently. "Just because you three don't have classes yet doesn't mean we don't."

Lianna gestured for her to continue.

"Like I said, everyone is bonded and territorial over their bondmate, so don't try anything. Even looking at a bondmate is worthy of a challenge, as Koen here demonstrated for us so beautifully."

"Got it," Koen said. "What else?"

"Next week, you'll start classes. It will be the smallest group we've had in a long time. Usually, at least four ascend. But as a general rule, there are typically eight who ascend to make at least two units of four. Our year was rather large. Twenty of us ascended, so there are five units, but the second years have twelve ascendants, three units.

"We train as a unit and are pitted against our unit to help us learn and strategize how to fight together. It helps us become attuned to what moves our unit members will make next so we can be in sync." She paused.

"Once we master fighting against each other, we fight the other unit or units that ascended in our year. That'll be different for your unit, and I'm sure the instructors will explain how that will go down when the time comes.

"As you get stronger, you'll be pitted against upper-level students and work as a team. However, you'll likely be fighting upper-level students earlier because of the one-unit issue, and your trials will differ from what we experienced. Your classes, however, will still be the same. You'll be trained in magic, combat, and the healing arts. You'll also have Vakrass and Ilthyrium history classes and Vakrasi lessons to learn the language most commonly spoken here."

Bells chimed. "You'll have to wait for the rest. Nicodemus and Nissa will escort you to your room. Stay in your rooms and try not to cause trouble," Amalie demanded.

"Wouldn't want to make you look bad." Lianna smirked.

Amalie's hand flashed out, cracking across her face.

The dining room fell silent, and every head turned toward our table.

"Watch how you speak to your superiors, Hirovonen. You're not at the top of the food chain here, as you may have been as a human. You're a first-year. You're a bug, and we have no problem squashing you under our pretty little boots." Amalie sneered.

Lianna put a hand to her cheek. Animalistic rage burned inside of me. I stalked to Amalie, grabbed her face, and glared into her eyes. At first, she struggled, but after a moment, she stopped and went limp as I gazed into her eyes.

"Let me be fucking clear when I say if you *ever* touch her again, I *will* kill you. You may be a higher class and have more experience, but I'll find a way. I promise." I released her.

Amalie's squadron released their breath in a whoosh like I'd been withholding the air from their lungs as I held Amalie's face. Amalie looked at Briggs. He shook his head.

When I knew they wouldn't do anything, I returned to the other side of the table. Amalie and Briggs left, though the rage in Amalie's eyes was impossible to miss. I might pay for that later, but it was worth it. A couple of whoops and cheers went up. I blushed furiously and ducked my head, peeking at Lianna from the corner of my eye.

Lianna's mouth was agape. She looked at me like she'd never seen me before.

"Well, that was...bracing," Nissa said. "I've never seen anyone stand up to Amalie, except for Xenryn, but she has the power to do that, so it's not a huge deal when that happens. Nobody else in our year ever stands up to her, let alone any other years. Congratulations. You painted a target on your back. She may have hated you before, on principle, but now she hates you on a personal level." Nissa's eyes were pitying.

Great, what had I gotten myself into?

The adrenaline was wearing off, and the realization of what I'd done flooded me.

Nissa and Nicodemus—who went by Nico—brought us to our rooms and told us to stay there. They'd collect us in the morning.

"What classes do you have at night?" Koen asked, looking out the large window across from our rooms at the darkened sky.

"Astronomy. It's hard to study the stars in the daylight," Nico said with a wink, and they left the three of us alone.

"I can't believe you threatened Amalie!" Lianna exclaimed.

"Are you okay?" I turned to her, brushing a strand of her hair back behind her ear. I gently took her chin in my hand to get a better look at her cheek. There was a large hand-shaped welt on her face. She'd have a bruise eventually, but right now, it looked red and angry.

"I'm fine. I can't believe you did that. You went from having panic attacks to threatening upper-level students. What's that about? I've never seen you act like that before. It was awesome."

"I don't know," I said. I didn't want her to know how I'd felt when Amalie's hand cracked across her face. I wasn't ready for her to know something was changing in me. I wasn't even sure what it was, but I was starting to feel increasingly territorial over Lianna, which worried me. Plus, the more I thought about what I'd done, the more anxiety filled my body and mind.

"Can we drop it, please?" I asked, my voice raspy.

Lianna must have heard my struggle. "Yeah, we can drop it. For now." she turned to Koen. "I think we are going to head to bed. Good night," she said.

Without waiting for a response, she grabbed my arm and pulled me into the room.

Chapter Nineteen

FOR LIFE
Lianna

My mind reeled from the show Riona had put on downstairs in my defense. It was a welcome change being rescued instead of being the rescuer.

I liked assertive Riona. Riona flopped onto the couch, and I took the opportunity to explore our space now that I didn't have to focus on calming Riona.

The entryway opened into a cozy kitchenette and living area. The living space exuded tasteful minimalism, with a plush, inviting emerald couch against one wall. Two sturdy wood desks sat side by side opposite the couch beneath a large picture window that framed a breathtaking view of the sprawling woods of Vakrass behind the castle. Sunlight streamed through the glass, casting gentle patterns on the floor.

In the bedroom, two twin beds caught my eye. They stood on either side of the spacious room, their brightly colored bedding contrasting against the soft, neutral tones of the walls. This arrangement had to change. I crouched and ran my fingers along the sturdy legs of the beds to confirm they weren't bolted to the floor.

Returning to the living room, I found Riona nestled on the couch, her legs tucked beneath her as she flipped through an old book. I approached her, my heart racing with anticipation. Why was I nervous? We've been together for years. It's the logical next step.

"Hey, Ri." My voice barely above a whisper. "Do you want to share a bed?" The question tumbled out before I could second-guess myself.

Her face lit up, and a bright smile spread across her face. "Absolutely! Want help moving the beds?" she asked.

"Yeah," I replied, relieved she was on board with my plan.

We spent the next several hours transforming our bedroom, moving furniture until it was right for both of us. Each piece was carefully placed to create a cozy, inviting atmosphere that felt like our little sanctuary. When we finally collapsed onto our shared bed, we were exhausted, our bodies weary but our hearts full. I'd never felt so content in my life.

Chapter Twenty

THE CRIMSON-HAIRED FAERIE
Riona

The following day, Lianna and I woke to a knock at our door. When we didn't answer it fast enough, they began banging.

"Alright, alright. I'm coming. Keep your shirt on," Lianna called.

I groaned and debated pulling her back into bed to have my way with her when I saw what she was wearing. Another bang on the front door shoved the idea from my mind. Instead, I eyed Lianna as she hurried to the door. Her shorts were so short that half her ass was hanging out, and fuck it was a nice ass.

I rolled out of bed and headed to the bathroom. I didn't care who was at the door this early in the morning until Lianna knocked on the bathroom door and said, "We need to be ready in five minutes, Ri,"

I opened the door, still brushing my teeth, to find Lianna pulling on her jeans and a sweatshirt. Goddess, she looked good in everything.

"Ready for what?" I asked around the sudsy toothpaste filling my mouth.

"Huh?" Lianna asked, her nose wrinkled in confusion.

I spat the wad of toothpaste in the sink, rinsing it down the drain, and tried again. "Ready for what?"

"Apparently, Amalie wants to show us around this morning so she 'doesn't have to waste her entire day on pathetic first years.' Her words, not mine," Lianna said. She grabbed her hairbrush and ran it through her hair.

I groaned at the mess of curls on top of my head. "This," I said, pointing at it, "will take longer than five minutes."

Lianna shrugged. "Ponytail?"

I sighed. My unruly curls rarely enjoyed being shoved into a ponytail, but it didn't look like I had any other option. I opened my drawer and made sure everything was in its place before I selected two thick hair ties and my hairbrush to brush the top of my hair back. The little hairs sprang out again.

I groaned.

I didn't have time. I wet my hairbrush and found some gel in my pack of stuff I bought at the market before returning to my hair. I had to be unlucky enough to have these unruly curls. Lianna, engrossed in applying her eyeshadow, didn't notice my jealous gaze as I admired her straight hair.

In the bedroom, Lianna laid out clothes for me. "I figured I'd help since you have like thirty seconds left to get dressed," she said.

"Thanks," I said. I looked over at what she'd set out and groaned. A pair of white leggings, white socks, and a white sweater with the school emblem blazoned above the breast were not at all my typical go-to outfit. I slipped into the leggings and pulled the sweater over my head, careful not to mess up my hair. *How the hell will I keep this clean?*

"You're late," Amalie said, when we exited moments later.

"Sorry, maybe if we'd had more than five minutes' notice, we wouldn't have been," Lianna said.

"We're getting breakfast and then taking you on a tour of the school," Amalie said.

Amalie and Briggs led the way while Nissa and Nico took up the rear, flanking us.

After a quick breakfast of scrambled eggs and toast, we headed down to the classrooms. The hallway was a long corridor with several doors. Each Door displayed numbers one through three, each with a corresponding class name. The first section of doors had a one above them, while the sets after that had a two above them, and the doors at the end of the hall each had a three.

"First-year students should only use doors labeled with a one. The gym is different. It's a combined class, so we all share the gym during the same hour." Amalie said.

Amalie opened the door of the classroom nearest to us, labeled *Vakrasi 1.* "This is your Vakrasi class. You're expected to be fluent by the end of your first year."

"It's easier than it sounds," Nissa piped up at the look that Lianna, Koen, and I shared. "Because we speak it almost exclusively once we learn it. And our teachers also teach in it, so you pick it up quickly."

"The teachers teach in Vakrasi? How will we learn everything if we don't know the language yet?" Lianna asked.

"They teach in English and Vakrasi. It's supposed to be immersive." Nissa explained.

"Doesn't that make the classes longer? Saying everything twice." Koen said, brushing his hair out of his face, then shoving his hands into his pockets.

"At first, yes, but after the first couple months, you pick everything up quickly and then you don't have to worry about it anymore. Then they switch to solely Vakrasi. If you ever don't understand something they say, tell them. If they find it is taking too long to get through the material, they use English and recommend everyone spend some time working on their vocabulary. If you don't keep up, you might get left behind or kicked out of school."

"Are you finished, Nissa?" Amalie interrupted.

Nissa ducked her head, tears welling in her eyes.

Lianna and I glared at Amalie.

"At least Nissa is helpful and explains things. You should be glad because us knowing things makes you look good," Lianna said.

Amalie ignored Lianna. "Let's go down to the gym so you can see it," Amalie said, leading us toward another staircase at the end of the hall.

When we reached the gym, I gasped. It was *massive*.

There was a pool and workout equipment. There was also an array of weaponry—bows, swords, daggers, and so much more. "This is where we have sparring class," Amalie said.

"Damn," Koen said, looking around the room. "This might be my favorite room."

"Of course it is." Amalie sighed. "Nobody's surprised by that. It's literally the favorite room of most of the males here."

"And why is that an issue?" a cool, smooth voice said from behind the seven of us, and we all turned. I flushed when I saw the female was the one I'd crashed into on Ascension Day. I ducked, praying she wouldn't recognize me.

"Oh, n-no issue," Amalie stuttered. "Sorry, Sorcha," she said, backing away.

I eyed the new faerie warily before glancing back at Amalie.

"You're Sorcha Rietveld?" Koen asked, his voice filled with awe.

The crimson-haired female turned her gaze on him. He shrank back.

"I am," she said.

"This is Koen's first year," Amalie said, forgetting her earlier hesitation and looking to get on the good side of the guard. Sorcha glared at Amalie, and the air around Sorcha crackled. The hair on my arms stood. Who the hell was she?

"I know who he is. I was there when he ascended." Sorcha said.

Amalie bowed her head. "My apologies, Sorcha, I wasn't thinking," she whispered and stepped back.

"Clearly," Sorcha said, glaring at Amalie for another moment before she turned back toward us and assessed us silently. "So, this is what the goddess saw fit to bless us with this year?"

Koen puffed up his chest, trying to look bigger. I finally glanced up, and her gaze landed on mine. My head swam as her dark, stormy green eyes held mine prisoner as if she were trying to see into the depths of my soul.

"Pity," she said. Sorcha swept out of the main gym and into a nearby office without another word. The third years released a sigh.

"Never talk to Sorcha without her permission. She could kill you without a moment's hesitation if you displeased her."

"She seemed pretty displeased as it was, and she didn't cut us down here and now," I said with more bravery than I felt. I didn't know what had happened between us in that stare or why I felt the need to defend her.

"If she were truly displeased, you'd know it. She may have been disappointed with the goddess's selection, but she'd never go against the goddess's choices or decisions," Nico explained.

I was surprised to hear him explain anything. Thus far, he'd seemed to be along for the ride most of the time.

"That was *the* Sorcha Rietveld," Koen said, awestruck, staring after her with hero-worship eyes. "I thought she was a Queen's Guard. What's she doing here?"

Amalie huffed. "She's a Queen's Guard, but she's also one of the most elite warriors in Ilthyrium. She teaches at Vakrass when the queen isn't traveling. Can we move on?" Amalie said.

"Yes," said Nissa, trying to keep the peace.

Amalie led us to the doors on the opposite side of the gym, and as I was about to step out behind Lianna, a prickling sensation alerted me to someone's eyes on me. I turned and found Sorcha staring at me from her office. Her eyes flashed, and I collapsed on the ground in a heap as my world went dark.

"Ri? Ri, wake up." The voice came from a long, dark tunnel, and I tried to work my way to the end to find the voice and answer.

"What the hell happened?" a male voice I knew said from above.

"I don't know. One minute, she was walking out behind me, and the next, she was on the ground, out cold," Lianna said. I recognized her voice. I knew her. "Lia," I croaked as I slowly opened my eyes. My skull was on fire. "Ouch!" I felt like it was going to explode.

"Perhaps you should bring your friend to the infirmary," a cool, concerned female voice said.

I searched for the voice's owner and found Sorcha Rietveld staring at me. Her face had gone pale, though her tone was the same as earlier. Something had spooked her. When she saw me look up at her, she averted her gaze.

"Get her out of here and to the infirmary, now!" Sorcha demanded, rushing back to her office and slamming the door behind her.

"That was odd," Briggs said. "I've never seen Sorcha act like that."

"Does it matter?" Lianna snapped. "You heard her. Get Riona to the infirmary. Amalie, maybe you could close your mouth and show us where that is."

Amalie stared at Lianna. Shock crossed her delicate features before she moved into action. "Follow me," she said.

I was lifted into muscular arms and looked up to see Koen holding me against him. I flinched away, but he pulled me tighter against him. His arms were like vises. Unbreakable.

"Don't worry," he said. "I won't drop you. You're not the first damsel in distress I've had to carry to an infirmary."

I rolled my eyes, desperately trying to hide my discomfort at being in his arms. Goddess, he's so cocky. It was infuriating.

Thank the goddess, I'd never liked men. For a second, I felt a flash of pity for Lianna. Being bisexual and having to deal with men like Koen must've been such a chore. Laughter bubbled within me, and Lianna shot me a concerned look. "I'm sorry you like boys," I said.

Lianna blushed bright red and said nothing.

"At least you like girls too. So you still have me, even when boys are idiots." Lia shot daggers at me. Then she seemingly assessed Koen. I clamped a hand over my mouth so I'd shut the hell up.

Chapter Twenty-One

WHAT THE FUCK WAS THAT?

Riona

We climbed the steps to the main floor and headed toward the west wing of the school, which held the infirmary. When we arrived, Koen set me on a bed and moved out of the way of a kind-looking female who reminded me of a much younger version of Rosalyn.

"What do we have here?" she asked.

"She passed out. We don't know why," Lianna answered.

The woman looked down at me. *Hello, my name is Ophelia. Will you allow me entrance?*

Is she speaking telepathically? I thought.

Yes. Now, will you grant me access? By aligning my senses with yours, I can better help you discover what went wrong.

"You want to read my mind?" I asked aloud.

I don't need to read your mind. I prefer to request access telepathically because it is total consent. You can't lie telepathically, even if you might want to.

I hesitated. Someone rooting around in my mind was terrifying. I didn't want anyone seeing what went on in my childhood. I didn't want the pity or the questions, and I didn't want to open myself up that much to someone I just met.

"Can't I give verbal consent today? I don't know how to open my mind, and I don't feel comfortable doing so to a stranger," I said.

I understand. I'll take verbal consent today. But I've a feeling you and I will see a lot of each other.

"Alright," I said, ignoring the last part of her sentence. "I give consent for you to treat me."

"Alright, if anything is painful, let me know, and I'll stop immediately."

"Okay."

She looked at the rest of the group and said, "You all can go. When my exam is complete, I'll find someone to escort Riona back to her room."

Everyone turned to leave, except Lianna. "May I stay? Please?" she asked.

The woman looked at me. *Are you alright with that?*

I gave the okay, and the female turned back to Lianna, "You may stay, but please remain quiet while I perform my exam."

Lianna sat in a chair by the head of my bed. Ophelia rubbed her hands together before placing them on my head. A shot of warmth raced through my body and then cooled. She removed her hands.

"You can sit up," she said. "You're dehydrated, for starters. Something else happened, though I can't identify what it was. What happened before you fainted?"

"I saw Sorcha looking at me. That was the last thing I saw before I collapsed. A weird rush of heat went through my body like a shock first, though," I said. "Nothing else happened. I didn't even feel like I was going to faint. I was walking out one moment and waking up on the ground the next."

"Huh. Well, Sorcha has always had some effect on others. Usually, males, if I'm being honest, but I can't say they've ever been so overcome they've passed out," she said, winking. I had the distinct feeling that she was trying to make light of the situation. I also felt she was hiding something. I pushed the thought away, sure I was imagining things.

"So, am I good to go? I don't want to be stuck here when classes start in two days."

"You can go, but I want you to rest today and take it easy tomorrow. Don't go traipsing around the school."

"Okay," I said, looking at Lianna. "I guess you and Koen can go without me."

"Yeah, like that'll happen," she scoffed. "We're staying in and lying around tomorrow. We can read," she said, her eyes twinkling.

"I don't want to keep you from getting to check everything—"
She held a hand up, stopping me.

"I've seen enough, honestly. We'll figure it out together, after you're feeling better. Who cares if we have to learn after we start classes? It will be fine. I'm going to nurse my girlfriend back to health." Lianna winked at me.

Inwardly, I crooned at her use of the word *girlfriend*. I was relieved we could spend the day alone together in the comfort of our room. Maybe I'd get lucky, and she'd wear some more shorts that showed off her ass, and we could squeeze in some sexy time. I blushed as I remembered we weren't alone. I glanced at the female tending to me, and she seemed oblivious to my thoughts, thank the Goddess.

"You're all done here. Ensure you drink plenty of water. Like I said, you're quite dehydrated. I also want you to take meals in your room tonight and tomorrow. I'll let the kitchen know to deliver your tray to your room," she said.

"Trays, please," Lianna piped up from behind me. "I'm not leaving her."

"Trays," the healer clarified before looking back at me. "Riona, if you need anything, come see me."

"Thank you, Ophelia. I appreciate it."

I hopped off the table and wobbled a bit. Lianna caught me and threw a quizzical look at Ophelia. "Are you sure she's okay?"

"Like I said, she's dehydrated, so ensure she's pushing fluids. It will help with the weakness and lightheadedness she's experiencing."

"Alright," Lianna said.

We left the infirmary together, and when we were halfway down the steps on our way back to our dorm, Lianna looked at me, concern filling her ocean-blue eyes. "Are you sure you're okay?" she asked. "I'm picking up on something, but I can't tell what it is. Something has felt off since you met Sorcha."

"It's been a long week, you know."

"That's true," she said, taking the hint that I wanted to drop it.

When we returned to our room, Lianna rushed over to our bed and pulled the covers back. "Get into bed," she said.

I obliged because I was exhausted. She pulled the blankets up, tucking them around my chin, and I drifted off to sleep before she finished.

Gentle tapping on the door and voices woke me. The fragrant aroma of freshly baked bread and chicken alfredo permeated the air. I moaned, and my stomach let out a ravenous growl. Lianna thanked whoever delivered the food and carried two trays into our bedroom. She set one on her side of the bed. I sat up and accepted the other tray.

I groaned when the first bite touched my tongue. Rich garlicky flavor exploded in my mouth. There was something about fae food that was much better than any food I'd ever eaten. I devoured my food within minutes and was still starving.

"I might go down and get more food," I said. "I'm ravenous."

"You're in luck. They brought an extra tray. I left it in the kitchen. They said you might be hungry after Ophelia's exam. Evidently, the process is exhausting and can also speed up your metabolism for a little while. It's not permanent though." She went and grabbed another tray that she'd set on the small table at the end of the bed. She handed me the new tray and took the old one.

"Thanks, Lia," I whispered.

"Lia," she said, turning it over in her mouth. "I like it. It fits."

Once we'd finished, I was, once again, utterly exhausted. "I think I might go to bed now," I said. "I'm so tired."

"Go for it. I'm going to read," Lia said, holding up her current romance novel. Another polyromance novel we'd snuck from the palace library for before we'd left. "If you need anything, wake me up. Sweet dreams," she said.

"Goodnight," I said, yawning.

Chapter Twenty-Two

FIRST DAY OF SCHOOL
Riona

Two days later, we met Koen at breakfast. Lianna and I'd spent the entire day before curled up in bed reading smutty novels and acting out some of our favorite scenes. We hadn't seen Koen at all, so we caught him up on the events of the infirmary over pancakes and bacon before Nissa and Nico showed up and led us to our first class of the day, which was Fae Physiology. Amalie was, blissfully, nowhere to be found.

"Welcome to physiology, I'm Cyrus," the teacher, a neatly dressed fae male, said. "The first thing we're going to do today is draw your blood. We can learn a mountain of information from your blood, including what type of intrinsic you are. It also lets us know of any potential diseases you may be susceptible to and can help us make any medical decisions on your behalf if needed."

"What's an intrinsic?" Koen asked.

We determine your base ability. The magic that resonates the most within your blood. Combat, medical, agriculture, and construction are a few of them, but of course, there are more.

He pulled out a kit with a rather large-looking needle and several blood vials. "Who wants to go first?"

Koen stood. "I will," he said.

After Koen was finished, I went, then Lianna. Once we were done, Cyrus ran through the basics of fae physiology, which included increased eyesight and hearing, pointed ears, along with vulnerabilities like fire and iron.

After fae physiology was Vakrass History across the hall.

An ancient faerie lectured at the front of the class, writing on a worn blackboard. She slowly turned around upon our entrance. "Greetings," she said. "My name is Ora, and I teach Vakrass History." Every word took much longer to say than it should've, and she had a lisp on top of it. She might have been tall once, but now she was hunched, her wispy silver hair was coming loose from her bun, and her speckled glasses were threatening to fall off the bridge of her nose.

Ora shuffled her way over to them. "Please take a seat. We'll get started." She picked up a single textbook from a small stack of large textbooks on the corner of her desk and hobbled over to where Koen had taken his seat and placed it on his desk before traversing back to the desk to collect another book and set it on mine and Lianna's desks. By the time she'd completed that, we were twenty minutes into our forty-minute class, and she hadn't even begun teaching.

This is gonna suck.

It did indeed suck. We'd just opened our books to read when the bell rang for the end of class.

"Read chapters one through three in your textbook for tomorrow's lesson," Ora said as the three of us gathered our belongings and hurried out of her room, thankful to be free.

"I hope the rest of our classes aren't like that," Lianna said as soon as we were out of the room, and the door closed behind us.

"That was brutal. I don't think it's possible for her to talk any slower. Why does she even work here? She's gotta be at least a thousand. Why hasn't she retired?"

"Actually," Nissa said behind me, "she's two thousand two hundred and three. She's one of the oldest fae in Ilthyrium. She wrote the textbook she gave you, so study it well. She might be a slow speaker, but she's sharp as a tack when it comes to history, especially since she's lived through it."

"Good to know," Koen said, smiling at the female.

"Anyway, I'm here to bring you to the dining room for lunch," Nissa said, pointing toward the exit.

"Excellent, I'm starving," Koen said, even though we'd eaten breakfast a couple of hours before.

I wasn't hungry at all. "Why is lunch so early?" I asked.

"Because they want us to have plenty of time to let our food settle between lunch and novice sparring and combat techniques and novice magic training. You won't be doing a whole lot of action in your first week, but they like to get you into the habit of going several hours without meals before you spar so you don't yak on the gym floor. Supposedly, they used to do lunch right before those classes, and let's just say the custodian hated his job."

"That's disgusting," I said, trying not to think of a bunch of fae working out and puking.

"Agreed," Nissa said, leading us into the dining room.

"Hello, hello," chimed a cheery voice as we walked into our second-to-last and longest class of the day. The instructor was a slight female, her chestnut brown hair tied back into a tight ponytail. She wore a simple forest green jumpsuit, and her demeanor was friendly and open. "I'm Christina, and I'm your novice magic teacher."

The three of us took our seats. I was excited to jump into magic training because hello, who doesn't want to learn how to do magic?

"To start, we'll learn the basic principles of magic and magic generation. The first thing you need to know is that your magic comes from within you. The amount and strength of it can't be altered no matter how much you learn. Once it's unlocked, you have what you have.

"Magic is tied to your emotions. It can manifest when you least expect it and in surprising ways until you learn control, and often, students find the magic is trapped within them when they need it most, or they unwittingly use it when they least expect it.

"That being said, in dire situations, magic can be shared. The more intimate you are with someone, the more likely you'll be able to tap into their magic. With consent, of course. Often, bondmates share magic with each other, especially when those bonded have different magical strengths. Because unitmates are immediately platonically bonded, that means you three already have an ability to tap into each other's magic. This is why units are formed immediately upon ascension."

I listened as Christina broke down the magic that coursed through my veins. I glanced at Lianna out of the corner of my eye and saw she was also entirely focused on everything Christina was laying out for us.

It was the best hour-and-a-half class I'd ever taken. By the end, I was *excited* about the homework she assigned.

I entered the gym with Lianna and Koen flanking me, ready for our first sparring lesson. The gym was full of other students split into groups.

Sorcha was running a group of third years through a series of complicated-looking moves at the head of the gym. Their bodies were deadly weapons under her skillful guidance, and for some inexplicable reason, it sent a thrill through my veins.

Sorcha's nostrils flared, and her head snapped toward us, her intense gaze locking with mine like it had two days before. However, this time, she immediately broke eye contact, but a wave of dizziness still washed over me.

"Hello again, a familiar voice said in greeting."

I turned to find Xenryn and Aithan.

"Hello," Lianna said.

Koen wisely avoided eye contact with both, and I gave a small wave hello.

"Aithan will work with you as a group." Xenryn explained, "And when you're ready, I'll step in to teach you more advanced stuff, but that won't be for a while."

"Yes, commander," Koen said, still avoiding any eye contact.

"Great. We'll start over there," Aithan said, pointing to a corner on the opposite side of the room.

Xenryn moved away from us and back to the group she was working with. Aithan sat cross-legged on the mat and signaled for us to sit with him.

"We're going to work on simple meditation—"

"Meditation?" Koen interrupted. "That's it? Why aren't we learning to fight? Isn't this a sparring class?"

I groaned inwardly. *For the love of the goddess, shut up!* I glanced at Lia, and we shared an eye roll. At least she's as annoyed by him as I am.

"You can't fight if you can't breathe, Koen," Aithan said, staring him down, his animosity clear.

Koen snapped his mouth shut.

Once the expectations were laid out, Aithan led us through a series of stretches and deep breathing techniques before the bells chimed, signaling the end of classes.

"You did well today. I'll see you all tomorrow," Aithan said.

He walked over to Xenryn and Sorcha, and the three began a heated discussion. I longed to know what they were talking about. I don't know why it mattered, but it did. Suddenly, they all threw a look at me, and I had a feeling I knew what they were discussing, though I didn't know why they'd be discussing me.

"Earth to Riona," Lianna said, calling me back.

"Technically, we're not on Earth anymore," I said, grinning.

"Ilthyrium to Riona doesn't have quite the same ring. You know?"

"True. What's up?" I asked.

"Koen was asking if we wanted to study at the library. Can you believe how much homework we got on the first day?"

I couldn't. It was so much for the first day of class. I yawned. "We should do that. We need to learn Vakrasi first, so we aren't lost," I said, retrieving my bag from the doorway.

"I get why they want us to catch on right away, but how are we supposed to learn anything if we don't know the language they're teaching us? It's so dumb. Like, come on."

Amalie sauntered up. "Can you find your way back to your rooms now, or do you still need help?" Her words were kind, but her tone was snide.

"We aren't going to our rooms," I snapped. I didn't know where the sudden confidence came from, but I liked it. "We'd appreciate it if you'd show us to the library, though. We have some studying to do," I said, stepping into her space.

Amalie stepped back. "I don't have the time. I'll send Nissa to help you out," she said before scurrying away.

I shook my head, turning back to Koen and Lianna. "What a bitch," I said.

Lianna shook with barely concealed laughter. "What's gotten into you?" she asked. "I've never seen you like this with anyone."

"I don't know. Something about her pisses me off. It's like I lose all anxiety factory settings."

Nissa bounded up beside us. "I heard you want to check out the library. I can take you there, but I have to hurry. I want to grab a shower before my date with Nico."

We gathered our things and followed her to the library.

Chapter Twenty-Three

Nothing Like a Little Ass Kicking

Riona

The rest of the month passed similarly for us; we'd go to our classes and end the day in the library. We felt like we were miles behind and wondered if this was true for everyone.

At the end of the month, Aithan taught us our first combat move, dodging an oncoming attack. He'd spent an hour running at breakneck speed at us while we tried to get out of his way. Most of the time, it was a disaster, and one of us went flying. Usually me and Lianna. Koen held his ground and let Aithan bowl into him at full speed. Lia and I cringed every time, but Koen seemed unfazed.

I hit the ground once again. And the impact reverberated through my body. I sprawled out on the floor, pain radiated through me, and my chest heaved as I gasped. Sorcha's voice sliced through the air, adding to my disorientation. "What the hell is going on over here?"

I clambered to my feet, wincing at the pain that shot through my body from the movement. Sorcha's eyes passed over me before she turned to Aithan. "What're you doing? You're supposed to be training them to maneuver out of your way, not knocking them down repeatedly. If you can't do the job you're expected to do, then get out, and I'll find someone who will."

Aithan let out a low, barely audible growl. Even I could tell it was a challenge. Sorcha's meadow-green eyes frosted over, every muscle tensing. They locked in a heated stare-down, and I almost admired Aithan's stupidity because he wouldn't win the battle.

He lasted a grand total of forty-five seconds before he caved and mumbled, "I showed them. It's not my fault they're slow."

Sorcha looked at us. "Did he show you any maneuvers to move out of his way, or did he just tell you to move?"

"He told us to get out of his way," Lia answered, earning a glare from Aithan.

Sorcha looked back at Aithan, one eyebrow raised. Then she stood between Koen, Lia, and me. "Watch and learn," she said to us. Then she looked at Aithan and said, "Attack."

Aithan flew at her, his feet moving so swiftly it almost looked like they didn't touch the floor. He landed where Sorcha had been only a moment before, except now she was a couple of steps to the left. I hadn't even seen her move.

"Again," she said.

Aithan returned to his original position. This time, he launched himself at her and landed in front of her. This time, she took a simple step back. She was still within his attack range, and he lashed at her, swinging his fists wildly, trying to make any connection. Sorcha blocked his attack easily. She dropped to a crouch and swiped her leg under him, knocking him flat on his back.

"Again," she said.

She knocked him on his ass several more times, and each time she did, the three of us smiled a little wider. We watched her every move, which she slowed down for us after the initial attack so we could better understand what she was doing. After she was done kicking his ass, she turned to us. "Try again," she said, looking at Koen and Lianna but clearly avoiding my gaze. With that, she walked back to her class.

Xenryn watched the exchange and stared at Aithan with a frown before returning to her own charges. Aithan turned to us, fury burning in his eyes after the humiliation he'd suffered at the hands of his superior.

I went first and ran through the maneuvers I'd seen Sorcha perform. Aithan ran at me, and every move Sorcha had just shown us flew from my mind. I did the only thing I could think to do and jumped straight into the air.

I hovered there for a moment.

Aithan skidded to a stop below me. "What the hell?" he said. The room went quiet and every set of eyes turned to me. I lost my concentration and plummeted back to the ground. Gasps filled the air as pain slammed through me as I rolled my ankle.

Lia rushed to me. My ankle already black and blue and swelling.

What the fuck was that?

Aithan strode over. "Perhaps you should make sure you have control over your magic before you try to use it in class," he sneered. "Take her to the infirmary," he said.

Once again, Koen scooped me up in his arms and carried me from the gym. Peals of laughter and some concerned murmurs followed us, but I blocked them out as the pain in my ankle sent shockwaves through my body. Sorcha's face was etched with worry when the gym doors closed behind us.

"Ignore them," Lia said from beside my head.

I barely registered what she said. The agony was unbearable, and I clamped my teeth down on my lip to prevent myself from screaming. I was pretty sure that my ankle was broken.

"Back so soon?" Ophelia asked as we arrived at the doorway to the infirmary.

"Training accident," Lia explained as Koen set me on the bed. "I think her ankle might be broken."

Warm hands touched my ankle, poking and prodding before Ophelia said, "It would appear you're correct." Then, without warning, she grasped my ankle with firm hands and yanked. I screamed as the bone reset.

I awoke a short time later. I looked down at my leg, expecting to see a cast, but there was nothing. The ankle was no longer swollen or black and blue. It looked normal.

"Oh, good. You're awake," Ophelia said, crossing the room toward me.

"What happened?" I asked. "My ankle was broken."

"It was. I fixed it," Ophelia said. "Fae healing," she said by way of explanation when I looked confused. "Fae healing and a bit of magic go a long way. There's little healers can't fix, if given the proper time. A broken ankle is easy."

"What about crutches or anything? Do I need to stay off it?"

She laid her hand on my ankle, poking and prodding it for a moment before answering. "Nope. You're one hundred percent good."

"Then why did I have to rest after fainting a few days ago?" I asked.

"That was different. It was difficult to tell what made you faint, and it was tinged with magic. It's more difficult when magic is involved. Not impossible, but difficult both for the healer and the patient and in rare cases more damage can be done by trying to untangle the magic. I rarely like to mess with magical injuries unless I have to, because the injury is life-threatening. In your case, it wasn't a necessity, so I let you heal naturally."

"But I was using magic when I fell," I argued. Even if I couldn't believe I'd used magic for the first time.

"You were using magic *before* you fell. No magic was involved *when* you fell, so no magic was present in your blood at the time of injury," Ophelia explained patiently.

"I see," I said, though I didn't see at all. I was more annoyed than anything that I'd lost an entire day. But at least I got to spend the day in bed with Lianna.

Chapter Twenty-Four

UNDECLARED

Riona

A week after I broke my ankle, Lianna, Koen, and I entered our physiology class to find Cyrus with two males I'd never seen before.

"Hey, Cyrus." Koen greeted the instructor with a familiarity I still cringed at.

I struggled to call our physiology instructor by his name, even though that's what he requested—and what pretty much all the instructors requested. Being so friendly was utterly exhausting for me. I didn't understand how he and Lianna could be friendly with anyone in such a short time.

"What's going on? Who are they?" Koen said, gesturing toward the two males.

"We'll get to that in a minute," Cyrus said. "Please take your seats."

We sat, looking between Cyrus and the males. Once we were seated, Cyrus picked up three mulberry envelopes and laid one of them on each of our desks. "These are your blood test results. You may open them."

Koen and Lianna eagerly tore into their envelopes, but I held mine. Trepidation crept in as I stared down at the little envelope with my name in a fancy gold scrawl.

"Yes!" Koen exclaimed from beside me. "Combat intrinsic."

"I'm healer intrinsic!" Lianna exclaimed from the other side of me. "I knew it!"

They both looked at me.

"What did you get?" Lianna asked.

My mouth was bone dry. "I don't know," I said, frowning at the envelope in my shaking hands.

"Hurry up and open it!" Lianna exclaimed.

I flipped the envelope, opened it, and dragged the letter out.

Undeclared was written across the top of the page in bold letters.

"Undeclared? What does that mean?" Lianna asked, looking over my shoulder.

"It means she's special," Cyrus said, gesturing the males forward. "Riona, this is Kallik," he said, gesturing to the taller of the two males. His skin was a rich brown, his black hair was cropped close to his scalp, and he carried an impressive-looking sword on his hip. The other male, the exact opposite of his partner, shorter with warm beige skin and long blonde hair, came forward, and Cyrus called him Oryn. "They're members of Queen Nasryn's Queen Guard, and they've come to get you."

What the fuck?

"Riona Vandeleur, Queen Nasryn has requested your presence at the palace. We're here to escort you," Kallik said, coming to stand closer to my desk.

"What? Now? Why?" Lianna fired off the questions, but they ignored her.

When I didn't move, Kallik and Oryn flanked either side of me. Each took an arm and smoothly lifted me from my chair. Adrenaline coursed through my veins as I was manhandled. The males were nothing but gentle, if not a little demanding. But I was right back to when Elik turned his fists on me, and I'd had no control.

My body kicked into fight mode. I yanked my arms, trying to pull them out of the men's grasp, but they tightened their grips, not understanding the fear engulfing me.

I whimpered. The fight left my body as quickly as it had come.

"Stop! You're scaring her! Take your hands off her!" Lia exclaimed, jumping out of her chair.

"Move, girl, this doesn't concern you," Oryn said, nudging Lia out of the way. He must've underestimated the strength behind the nudge because Lia crashed to the ground between the desks.

Blinding white-hot rage consumed me. Wind blasted into the room. Strength coursed through my veins. I broke out of the men's grasp, which had been unbreakable vises moments before, and stood between Lianna and the males.

"Don't fucking touch her again!" My voice was low and deadly. I glowered at the two males, and Koen stepped around me and helped Lia to her feet.

Oryn held his hands up. "It was an accident." His voice shook a little on the word *accident*, and for some deep-seated reason, that pissed me off more. Elik always insisted it was an accident, and I was having none of those excuses for harming my girlfriend.

The wind picked up and turned frigid as I considered the males. Lia's teeth chattered, and her shivering broke my concentration. I dropped my gaze from the males, and the wind stopped. Kallik, Oryn, Cyrus, and Koen stared at me with apprehension, but Lia had awe in her gaze.

I turned back to the queen's goons. "If you ever touch her again, I swear to the goddess, you'll regret it."

Both males bowed their heads. Kallik said, "We need to go. Will you come willingly?"

I paused. "I will." I wanted answers. Otherwise, I never would've agreed to this. "See how easy that was? No one had to get hurt."

I followed the males out of the classroom, throwing a concerned look over my shoulder to check on Lianna. She was upright and moving, so I took that as a good sign.

Every faerie we passed stopped and gawked as I was led through the school and out the front door, where a swirling portal in the courtyard transported us straight into Queen Nasryn's throne room.

"Riona, how lovely to see you again," Queen Nasryn said, her voice saccharine sweet. She sat on her throne, dressed in black jeans and a black V-neck sweater.

Per custom, I bowed and remained quiet, waiting for her to tell me what the hell I was doing here.

"I called you here because we have something important to discuss," she said, rising and walking down the steps toward me.

With a wave, a table and two chairs appeared. "Sit, we've much to discuss," she said, gesturing toward the chair as she took a seat in hers. I sat in mine after a slight hesitation and a stern look from Queen Nasryn.

"I've called you here to discuss your intrinsic ability. Typically, this would be discussed at Vakmore, however your case is special."

"How?" I leaned back in my chair and crossed my arms.

"Generally, after receiving your results, you would be enrolled in your pre-intrinsic classes, which are introductory classes about your ability. Your blood test showed special properties. Those properties have been prophesied about for years as a key to breaking The Mortal Curse." She paused, letting me take the information in before continuing. "It explains why your ascension differed from other faeries before you. Your colors with the gold and purple hues, instead of the traditional purple with golden hues, occurred because you're a direct descendant of a deity."

A burst of laughter escaped me. The queen's lips pressed into a thin line.

"You're serious?" I asked. "I'm literally the least suitable person for this."

The queen glared at me, and I blanched. For a moment, I swear I saw sparks in her eyes. "Of course I'm serious. I'm not in the habit of making jokes about such serious things. It's your destiny. It's been prophesied for centuries, and you will do it."

"Prophesied? By whom?" I asked.

"Seers. Some of whom you've come into direct contact with and grew up around."

I sifted through my human memories until it landed on a face and grating voice. "Acanthe," I said.

"Yes, Acanthe. She notified the head matriarch of her coven when she first read your future as an infant. She said your outcome was one of the clearest she'd ever seen, and that you will end The Mortal Curse. The matriarch then notified each faction leader that there was a Magicborn child that could potentially break the curse. We've had our eye on you for a while."

"And did she expound on how I'd do that?" I asked, crossing my arms.

"You'll have to travel through the realms of Ilthyrium and collect keys from each of the factions' monarchs, likely fighting your way in and out, and use them in Erebos, the Underworld, to break the curse. It won't be easy, but you'll do it."

Sweat pooled in my palms. I swiped them on my leggings. This was bullshit. They couldn't make me do it. I ground my teeth, trying to push down the terror that was bubbling in me. I didn't want to go on a crazy quest for something because some old witch prophesied it.

"Of course not. I won't do it." I said, shaking my head vigorously and rubbing my hands back and forth on my leg. "I'm not bonded, and I've no intention of being with a male, let alone having children, and I—I just can't. I can't do this." I stammered, fighting the tears that threatened to come as the panic continued rising."

"Riona, you're not bonded yet. I wouldn't count that possibility out entirely. There's a male in your unit with whom you may bond. Regardless, it's your destiny. It was prophesied."

I rolled my eyes. "Perhaps you misunderstood. I'm gay. I don't ever see myself having children, so I don't care about the curse, the prophecy, or any of it. And I'd like to leave—now."

"You're okay with letting Magicborn children continue to be ripped from their parents? You're okay with them being raised away from their true home and their magic? You're okay with them never returning to the home they were born in?" Queen Nasryn's voice rose an octave with each accusation.

"Maybe they're better off there instead of being raised here and being forced into battle as soon as they can swing a sword. For two, I'm eighteen. Why should I be forced into this when I'm just starting out? It's completely unfair."

Queen Nasryn studied me for several moments before giving a slow nod. "So be it. Riona. You may leave, but it is your destiny to break this curse. Refusing to do so will bring about disastrous consequences."

"Not for me," I said. I turned away. I had to get out of there.

Queen Nasryn looked at the guards who'd hauled me here. "Oryn, Kallik, please return Riona to Vakmore and stay with her. Make sure nothing happens to her. She's our only hope of breaking the curse."

I whirled to face the queen. "I don't need babysitters," I spat.

"Regardless, they'll accompany you," she said, and that was final. She swept out of the room. Oryn and Kallik each took an arm and propelled me through the portal to Vakmore.

It was well after midnight when we returned. Fortunately, only a few students were out and about at that hour. However, those still up and outside their rooms eyed me and the two hulking fae by my side curiously. I cringed as I dashed through the hallways and up the stairs to the room I shared with Lianna. I stopped at my door and turned to my new bodyguards.

"Guys, no way are you coming into my room with me. Go away," I whispered.

The males looked at each other. Oryn said, "I'll check your room first." moving to enter the room.

"No," I protested, blocking the door. "Absolutely not."

Oryn picked me up as if I weighed nothing and moved me aside. He entered without knocking. A shriek sounded inside, and Oryn rushed out, red-faced. He cleared his throat. "It's, uh... all clear," he said sheepishly.

"Perhaps we should speak with Queen Nasryn and Thea about moving you to a single room," Kallik said.

"Nope, no way, absolutely not," I said before pushing past both of them and slamming the door in their faces. I walked into the bedroom to find a seething Lia dripping wet in a towel.

"What the fuck is going on? I was buck naked, and some male walked in without warning."

Emotions flowed through me so quickly that I couldn't keep up. Rage that Oryn had seen Lianna in this state, a hunger as I took in her glistening, soft skin, and finally, humor as the night's events caught up with me.

I raised my hand to cover my laughter. That instinct to fall back on my human method of coping—laugh instead of cry—had my mother's face flooding my thoughts unbidden when I was hit square in the face by a pillow, bringing me back to the present.

"It's not funny, Ri," she said. Her lips twitched, betraying the laughter she was desperately trying to suppress.

"Sorry, Lia. You might want to make sure you're not hanging around naked. You never know who might walk in," I said, trying to make a joke, but the laughter in my voice faded, and tears welled in my eyes.

"Seriously, Ri, who was that? What happened with Queen Nasryn? What does 'undeclared' mean?" She fired the questions off in rapid succession, not allowing me to answer even one of them before jumping to the next.

I stared up at the ceiling, swallowing hard against the lump in the back of my throat, fighting the tears that threatened to fall. I lost, and a tear made its escape down my cheek. "I don't want to talk any of it," I said when she finally stopped long enough for me to get a word in.

Lianna walked over to me and wrapped her arms around me. I melted into her embrace.

"Ri," she whispered, "you know you can tell me anything, right? That I'll always be here for you?"

Tears flowed freely down my cheeks, and sobs wracked my body. Lia held me tightly, offering solace and understanding in her embrace. Lianna whispered soothing words as I sobbed and clung to her like she was my only hope of survival.

When my tears subsided, I was gripping Lianna's bare skin. Her towel had fallen to the ground, and she was shivering, but she hadn't let me go, despite her discomfort.

"Oh, Lia. Shit, I'm sorry," I said, reaching down to grab her towel.

I held the towel out to her. She went to wrap the towel around herself, and I took in her naked body and didn't hesitate. I leaned forward, my hands on her waist, and I pulled her into a kiss.

My pulse quickened when she leaned into me and kissed me back, and I smiled against her lips—slowly and gently.

She pulled back and kissed my cheeks, erasing the remaining tear tracks that lingered. As her kisses burned their way across my skin, a fire ignited within me, and I needed her like I'd never needed her before.

Her lips met mine again as I slid my hands down her body and cupped her thighs, under her ass, and lifted her. She wrapped her legs around me, never once breaking our kiss. I moved to the bed, still kissing her before laying her out beneath me.

I leaned back and gazed down at her, taking in her beautiful naked body. Then I reclaimed her mouth. I took my time kissing her, teasing her. I trailed my hand against her, the lightest touch down her throat, her chest, and when I reached her belly, she arched her hips toward me. I slid my hand down, caressing her inner thigh. She groaned, and I pulled back, gazing at her lying there. Desire pooled in my belly just as much as it did the first time. I slipped out of my clothes without a word.

"Holy fuck." Lianna breathed, letting her eyes languidly peruse my naked body. "You're so beautiful," she said, reaching out to me. She grasped my arm and pulled me down on top of her.

Chapter Twenty-Five

THE BEGINNING
Riona

The acrid scent of smoke and charred flesh surrounded me, burning my nose. I gagged. My eyes burned and watered from the hazy, smoke-filled air. I swiped the tears away, clearing my vision. I gazed all around me at burning bodies, bodies impaled on swords, eyes staring up at me unseeing. I tried to turn, to run, but my body refused to cooperate.

"Watch and learn, child, for you've much to do."

I'd recognize that grating voice anywhere, but still, I looked up at the tall, dark-haired woman beside me, not believing what my ears had already told me.

"Acanthe." I breathed. "What're you doing here? Where are we?"

"Watch and learn," she repeated, gesturing to a figure in the distance.

Then I was within the figure, seeing the world through her eyes, feeling what she felt, and knowing what she knew. She was a fury, the eldest sister of the Erinyes, the three goddesses of vengeance.

Tisiphone stood on the battlefield beside her old friend Thanatos, the goddess of death, wrath building inside her.

"What have they done?" Tisiphone whispered, her eyes wide with horror as she gazed upon the fallen. Her eyes were drawn to the mismatched armor worn by children. "How could they do this?" she asked, her voice cracking with sadness as she kneeled beside a tiny female fae child.

Thanatos stepped beside her, placing a comforting hand on Tisiphone's shoulder. "They've grown greedy."

"They've always been greedy. This"—the goddess spread her arms to the destruction before her— "is so much more than greed."

Tisiphone rose. The carnage inflicted on children and parents was enough to make anyone's blood run cold. Entire families were decimated. The air crackled with the intensity of her swirling vengeance.

She'd thought she'd made peace with allowing the chaos to play out. She'd reasoned that they'd finally end their actions when they were on the verge of extinction. She hadn't expected their solution to be replenishing their troops with children.

Thanatos scanned the smoky, devastated landscape. "What do you intend to do?"

"What I must," Tisiphone said, her voice steely and resolved. "You should leave. I must call my sisters, and Megaera still hasn't forgiven you since the last time she saw you."

Thanatos grinned, pointed teeth gleaming. "Might be worth sticking around. I do so miss her company. If only she weren't so...uptight," Thanatos said, voice coated in laughter.

Tisiphone stared at her old friend. She'd grown used to Thanatos using humor to cope with being surrounded by death, but today, surrounded by dead Magicborn children, she didn't have it in her to crack a smile.

Thanatos sobered. "All right, I'll go." She pulled Tisiphone into a hug before releasing her and disappearing, leaving only a lingering scent of burned sulfur.

Tisiphone stood alone in silence. She took one last look at the battlefield, grief filling every inch of her and released a guttural roar filled with centuries of unadulterated rage and heartache. It was her job. Her and her sister's job as the Erinyes, the furies, to protect the family dynamic and seek vengeance on anyone who harmed it. Too long had they shirked their duties.

"Sisters, come to me," she whispered.

The air crackled with electricity as Tisiphone's sisters, Alecto and Megaera, journeyed topside from Erebos, the Underworld. The world rippled and shimmered as a bolt of lightning split the sky, and her sisters appeared beside her.

Alecto took in the harrowing scene of death and destruction before them. "Sister, what's happened?" she asked, clutching her chest as though she was trying to physically keep the pain at bay.

Tisiphone stepped forward and faced her sisters, the tension in the air palpable. "Something that demands immediate action. We can't allow it to persist."

Lighting crashed in the distance, and thunder rumbled ominously as three more figures materialized beside the sisters.

"We can help," the three said in unison.

Tisiphone turned to the women. "Nice of you to show up, Moirai," she said, addressing the goddesses of fate. "I don't know what more you can do since this is your doing," Tisiphone said, gesturing toward the ten-year-old at her feet.

"It's true," Clotho said. "The threads of the Magicborn children have been cut short as of late, but that's as much your doing as ours, Erinyes. You turned your back on your duties, and we were forced to make up for it."

"By taking the lives of innocent children?" Tisiphone shrieked, the snakes circling her arms and head hissed with agitation.

"When free will comes into play, our control becomes constrained, compelling us to make adjustments to accommodate the choices," Atropos said.

"You said you can help?" Megaera asked, cutting in before Tisiphone could argue further.

"Yes, we can help," the fates said, circling the furies. "Together, the six of us can change the destructive path the Magicborn are heading down."

"How?"

"Simple," Clotho said, a grin spreading across her face. "By casting a curse on all future Magicborn."

I was flung out of Tisiphone's body and back beside Acanthe. "What is this?" I asked.

"The beginning," Acanthe said. She looked down at me, and for the first time, I didn't shrink away from her gaze. I beheld complete and utter sadness on her face.

"What does this have to do with me? I told Queen Nasryn I refused. The Mortal Curse isn't my problem."

"It will be," Acanthe said, then snapped her fingers.

Chapter Twenty-Six

SECRETS EXPOSED
Riona

I bolted upright in bed.

"What? What's wrong?" Lianna cried, startling awake beside me.

The previous night rushed back to me. "Nothing. Sorry I woke you. Weird dream." I laid down and curled up around her, pulling her into my arms. "Everything is fine."

I held Lianna in my arms, reviewing every part of the dream in my head. It's like it had been burned there. I remembered every detail, and it played out like a movie in my head. What was Acanthe playing at? I'd already said no. I couldn't do it. On a good day, I could barely leave my home back on Earth, and things hadn't gotten better since settling in at Vakmore. It wasn't just that I didn't want to do this. I couldn't. Just the thought sent my pulse racing.

Why did everyone think they could make me?

Lianna stretched before cuddling back into me. I glanced over at the clock on the nightstand and groaned.

"We need to get up. It's late. I doubt we'll even have time for breakfast."

"Or we could skip breakfast and do something else..." Lia said, a twinkle in her eye.

"Oh," I grinned. "Let's do that." I captured her lips with mine.

The bells chimed, giving us a fifteen-minute warning before class, and we gave each other one last kiss before we left the room hand in hand.

Oryn and Kallik looked at us, one approvingly, one condescendingly.

"Did you get any sleep?" Kallik grumbled.

My face heated, and I knew pink tinged my cheeks. "None of your business," I said, straightening the hem of my skirt. I didn't even know them, but suddenly, they were privy to every detail of my life. It was a gross invasion of privacy.

I'd need to address this with them and Queen Nasryn. My stomach churned at the idea of confronting the hulking bodyguards and, worse, the formidable queen who was used to getting her way.

Oryn grinned and held out two bagels, one jalapeño bagel smothered in plain cream cheese and the other a French toast bagel smothered in honey cinnamon cream cheese. He turned to Lianna. "My apologies for last night," he said, his face turning an interesting shade of crimson.

"I'll let it slide this time since you brought food," Lianna told Oryn. I grinned and accepted the French toast bagel while Lianna accepted the jalapeño, and we began making our way down to class.

"Are you ever going to tell me who they are?" Lia asked, taking a huge bite of her bagel, leaving a smear of cream cheese on her upper lip.

I was tempted to kiss and lick it away, but I remembered we had an audience, so I settled for wiping it off with my thumb. I sighed and rolled my eyes. "They're my bodyguards, courtesy of Queen Nasryn."

Lia opened her mouth, presumably to ask questions, but I said, "I'll explain later." "We're going to be late for class."

We walked into class and found Koen waiting for us. He looked down at our hands, scowling. I dropped Lia's hand and sat at my desk while Oryn and Kallik hovered behind me like I was about to be attacked.

Who are they? Koen mouthed, tilting his head toward Oryn and Kallik.

Cyrus swept into the room, followed by several other instructors, including Sorcha. My mouth went bone dry. I don't know why I always reacted weirdly when I saw her. It was like time stood still, and everyone ceased to be, leaving us the only two people in the universe.

I didn't have a chance to respond to Koen, though, because the following words out of Cyrus's mouth shook me to my core.

"We will be doing something we've never done before. After Riona's blood work came back yesterday, and we learned she's the only hope the Magicborn community has of being able to keep their children, we are revising how she will be taught. She'll spend most of her time training with Sorcha in advanced magic and combat. She'll continue taking her regular classes. However, she'll also be taking classes on the customs and languages of the other factions of Ilthyrium as well."

I groaned. I was already struggling with Vakrasi. This was bullshit since I'd told Queen Nasryn I wouldn't be saving anything. I opened my mouth to say exactly that when Koen spun to face me.

"You can break The Mortal Curse?" he hollered.

"I told Queen Nasryn I wouldn't be breaking any curses," I said, looking first at Koen, then at Cyrus. Lia's eyes were filled with hurt. She leaned away as if to say, what the hell.

I should've told her last night or this morning. This isn't how I wanted her to find out. I reached out and took her hand. She tried pulling it away, but I held her tighter. *Please, trust me.*

She seemed to get the message because she relaxed, squeezed my hand, and bobbed her head before I let go and turned back to Cyrus.

"I'm not breaking any curses. I'm not taking extra classes. I'm not 'the chosen one' or whatever bullshit you want to call me. Just no," I ground out through gritted teeth.

"I'm afraid it's not Cyrus's call," Queen Nasryn's voice said from the hallway seconds before Thea appeared alongside Queen Nasryn.

"I've taken a particular interest in your training, Riona. It's been rather lax, so I've crafted a new schedule, and you'll follow it according to my order," Queen Nasryn said.

I opened my mouth to protest, but the room filled with suffocating power. My resolve crumbled, and I fought with all my might, but it was useless. I'd barely begun when I was overcome with the willingness to do as she demanded. "Now then, I'm sure we won't have any further issues." She glanced around the room. "Correct?"

I reluctantly agreed. What else was there to do?

I sat back in my chair and crossed my arms as the queen and Thea left, apparently content that they'd managed what they came to do. I'd lost this round, but there'd be others.

"As I was saying," Cyrus continued, "Riona, you'll spend your early mornings with Sorcha in the gym training in magic and sparring, and your afternoons, after your other classes, will be spent with Ismene. She'll be taking over your Vakrasi lessons. She's fluent in every language and custom in Ilthyrium. She's Queen Nasryn's interpreter. But for now, she's at your disposal. Use her wisely. Ismene will arrive today. For now, you'll go with Sorcha."

"What about the rest of my unit?" I asked.

"You'll still undergo the graduation trials together, but for now, you'll be the only one doing additional training. There's no need for them to."

"Doesn't that put us in danger of failing the trials?" Lianna asked.

"You'll be fine. You'll have an advantage since Riona will have been training at a higher level," Cyrus said, putting an end to the conversation. "Riona, collect your things and go with Sorcha. You'll miss physiology today and begin your training with Sorcha. I expect to see you bright and early tomorrow, though."

I didn't budge.

At first, nothing happened, but then my skin started tingling and burning. With each passing moment, the feeling grew more overwhelming until it seemed my entire being was engulfed in fire, and I couldn't take it anymore. I leaped to my feet and snatched my belongings.

"Fine," I grumbled.

I walked to the front of the room, my footsteps echoing in the silence. Sorcha's mouth curved into a wry smile before she strode out of the room.

Lia gave a half-hearted wave before Kallik and Oryn blocked my view, and I was ushered out of the room.

Chapter Twenty-Seven
ALL ABOUT THAT BOND
Lianna

Sorcha led Riona out of the classroom, and I slumped in my seat. Riona provided a buffer between Koen and me and was a welcome distraction from my growing attraction to him. I'd spent the last few weeks avoiding him as much as possible, hoping the attraction would die down, but it seemed like it was only making it more prominent. He was the first male I'd wanted in a long time.

"Guess it's you and me," Koen said, flashing me a grin.

I glanced at him and flushed as an image of him on top of me flashed through my mind.

With difficulty, I turned my attention to Cyrus.

"Now that you each know your intrinsic ability, you'll begin classes in those areas, which will take place in the afternoon. They'll be mixed classes with other units, so prepare for that."

"If they're with other units, won't we be significantly behind?" Koen asked, expressing concern.

"You'll work individually until you're ready to compete against others. You won't engage in sparring until your second year." Cyrus said. "Lianna, since you're a healer, you'll spend much of your time solo. However, you'll be in one large classroom with all the other healers. It's a go-at-your-pace class, so you'll be surrounded by students at various levels and not expected to interact with them too much."

That sounded alright. I worked well independently, even though I loved interactions with others. I was perfectly happy to work alone.

"Now, let's get back to class," Cyrus continued. He flipped the textbook open. "We're working on page three hundred and ninety-four today."

I found the page. My face flushed when I read the title of the chapter: **Faeries and Sexual Intercourse**.

Oh, goddess.

I wished Riona were here. I wanted nothing more than to bury my face in my hands and hide as Cyrus began discussing the ramifications of faeries and their mating habits. I glanced at Koen from the corner of my eye and found him hanging on Cyrus's every word.

I skimmed through the chapter until I landed on a section titled: **Bondmates: What it Means for You**. I started reading, curious how bondmates apply to me as a bisexual, polyamorous individual.

Bondmates: What it Means for You:

New ascendants ascend in pairs to be bonded in their second year, after they pass their graduation trials. If there's only one new ascendant (this is rare), they'll remain unbonded until a Decabonding ceremony takes place (See section on the Decabond) on Mabon. Should they fail their graduation trials, they remain unbonded until then.

In the event of an uneven number of ascendants (extremely rare), the opportunity must be given to allow all unit members to put themselves forward to see if a bond can be forged between any of the members in their second year at Vakmore Academy. If a bond is forged between two of the group, the unbonded will remain that way until a Decabonding ceremony.

Faeries are highly sexual beings. They can have as many partners as they desire. They can't go long without a partner and sex. Faeries may date around, but that's more typical with adult faeries who've lost their bondmate or never had one.

Territoriality Effect:

The territoriality effect occurs once the romantic bond is in place. The traditional bonding ceremony occurs during the Beltane festival at the palace and is presided over by the current monarch. Once the bond snaps into place between the parties, total territoriality also snaps into place. Territoriality is when a bonded becomes territorial over their bonded to where they pose danger to anyone trying to come between them and their bonded.

Multiple Bondings:

Multiple bondings are rare but have happened. In these cases, the bonded face the arduous task of managing the territoriality that comes with the bond. Because of the territoriality effect, most multiple bondings result in the death of one or more of the bonded.

"Ms. Hirovonen, would you care to join us?" Cyrus said, pulling my attention away from the book.

"Sorry," I said, looking up at him.

Cyrus opened his mouth to continue whatever lecture he'd been giving, but I didn't give him the chance.

"Cyrus, are there any faeries bonded to multiple partners today?"

"Not to my knowledge. I believe the last multi-bonded partners were Queen Nasryn, her mate King Elias, and King Elias's other mate Tempest."

"Queen Nasryn was in a multi-bond?" I asked. "Where's the King and his other mate now?"

Cyrus gave me a look.

"Oh," I said. "She killed them?"

"The story is," Cyrus looked back and forth nervously, as though the queen could hear him. "King Elias and Tempest were in a carriage accident on their way back to the palace. Something spooked the horses, and they ran off a cliff and fell to their deaths. It was quite the tragedy for Queen Nasryn."

"I bet," I said snidely. I knew in my bones that she had killed them. "So, Queen Nasryn isn't a fan of multi-bonding?"

"I don't believe she is," Cyrus said, wiping a bead of sweat off his brow. He shot a nervous glance around the room again. "Now, can we please get back to my lesson?"

"Of course," I said. I'd gotten the information I needed. I'd have to share this with Riona.

Chapter Twenty-Eight

SCORCH MARKS AND STRAITJACKETS

Riona

Sorcha led me to a room at the left of the gym that I'd never been in before, not surprisingly since the academy was huge—most of my time had been spent in class, the library, the mess hall, and my room. I looked around, taking in every detail. The walls in the room were dark in some spots and white in others.

I drew closer to look at the unique paint job, except it wasn't paint. I cocked my head. "Scorch marks?" I asked before turning my gaze back to the dark splotches. "What is this place?"

"This is the vortex room," Sorcha said as she followed my gaze. "This is where beginners learn to wield magic. Generally, we'd wait until your fifth month, but since time is short, we're jump-starting your magic abilities.

"You've already displayed some capabilities, and I'm here to push you. It'll be painful, but I don't want to hear any complaints about it. Neither of us is happy to be here, but here we are, so let's leave it at that and get to work," Sorcha said.

She strode to the center of the room, beckoning me to join her. Once I stood across from her, she looked at Kallik and Oryn. "You can go," she said.

"We're to stay with her," Oryn said, crossing his arms and planting his legs as though grounding himself for a fight.

Sorcha took two menacing steps toward Oryn and unleashed a feral growl. Oryn stepped backward. Sorcha grinned.

"Not here," Sorcha growled. "She needs to focus, and you won't help by hovering in the background. Go. Now."

Both males paled, and neither uttered another word, as they tripped over each other to leave the room.

Once the door closed behind them, Sorcha turned to me. Her eyes roved over my body. She lifted my arms to the sides and put them back down. "We'll work on sensing the magic within first. You can't do anything until you understand how your magic flows through your body." She sat cross-legged before me and motioned for me to do the same.

I followed her lead, accidentally knocking our knees together. I flinched, and my shoulders went rigid. "S-sorry." My heart skipped a beat at the accidental contact.

"Why are you afraid?" she asked.

My head snapped up. "How did you—?" I started.

She tapped her head. "I have telepathic abilities. That doesn't answer the question, though. Despite my reputation. I've never harmed a student, and I never would intentionally harm a student for simply bumping into me, so why are you so afraid of me?" Her last words ended in a whisper, and I detected a hint of something... longing, perhaps?

"I don't know," I said. "I guess I'm used to being punished when I do something wrong."

"Why's that?" Sorcha pressed her knees into mine and took my hands in hers.

A shock erupted in my veins, and I stared down at our joined hands for a beat too long. I didn't want to get into the dynamics of my human childhood. How could she possibly understand? I shrugged in answer.

Sorcha cocked her head, and as the silence built, my desire to fill it did, too.

"My adoptive dad was an abusive ass," I said, summing up my childhood in one sentence. The last thing I wanted to do was dredge up memories of him and send myself spiraling into a full-blown panic, but if Sorcha was telepathic, it's not like she didn't know what I was thinking. A warm wave of gratitude swept through me at the patience she'd exercised to allow me to speak when I was ready instead of plucking the thought from my mind and speaking it aloud.

"I'm sorry," Sorcha said. She gazed at me for a long moment. "You carry a lot of anger, but it's buried beneath your fear. Beneath the anger and fear is a fountain of strength. I sense a formidable well of power buried deep within you. It's going to be important that you learn how to control it and quickly because once you release the things holding you back, you'll be unstoppable."

"I don't want any of that. I don't want to be powerful or unstoppable. I want to be left alone with Lianna." My voice dropped to a whisper. "Why can't you guys leave me alone?" I'd only just come into this life. Why was it on me to break the curse? "Why do I have to carry the weight of the sins of our fathers? I want nothing to do with it."

Sorcha sat quietly for several moments, still holding my hands, letting me rant.

"It's *not* fair," she said when I finally stopped long enough to take a breath. "We've been waiting so long for someone to fulfill the prophecy, and I'm sorry it's fallen on your shoulders. But think of the good you'll do."

"What good does it do if nothing's changed? Even now, the ceasefire's a temporary truce. What happens when the curse is broken, and they put children on the battlefield again? What happens when the adults are placed on the battlefield again and pitted against the adult child they don't know is theirs? How's that any better than what happened all those years ago? Nothing has changed." Fire flickered to life in my veins as I spoke.

"Some things have changed," Sorcha said. "There are greater forces at work here than the simplicity of breaking The Mortal Curse. Not all Magicborn wish to return to the ways of before."

"But some do," I insisted, desperately hoping she'd disagree and tell me no one wanted to return to how things were before and the Magicborn had had enough war.

"Some do," Sorcha agreed, crushing every hope I had.

I took a deep breath and blew it out slowly, gathering my thoughts. "The some that do are enough for me to say no. Magicborn children are safer in the human world. At least humans don't want to send them off to war as cannon fodder. I won't allow innocent children to endure trauma and death at my hands."

"Because of your father?"

"What is this, a therapy session? I thought you're here to teach me magic."

"I am," Sorcha said. "Look around," she said, releasing my hands to wave around us.

Already missing the comforting warmth of her hands in mine, I looked to where she was pointing and found us wrapped in an opaque, rippling bubble.

"Congratulations on your first shield bubble. Defensive magic is deeply ingrained within us and is often tapped into through trauma. It's most accessible when you feel protective. When one has deep-seated trauma like you do, you can access defensive magic without even trying if you feel the need to be protective. In your case, it seems to be tied to protecting children. Likely because of the lack of protection when you were a child."

"I did that?" I asked in awe, watching as the bubble dissipated.

"You did. Now that we've gotten the question of whether you can do it out of the way, we can delve into how, so we don't have to sit down and discuss feelings every time. After all, this isn't therapy, as you so eloquently stated." Sorcha deadpanned.

I smiled. I couldn't help it. I'd done magic. And I hadn't hurt myself this time. "Show me how to control it," I demanded.

"We'll start working on that tomorrow. We don't want to risk you burning out before we've even begun."

"Burning out?"

"Yes. Think of it like building physical endurance. Usually, you'd learn in a classroom and slowly build your endurance over your first year. We don't have time, so we have to build your endurance quickly and ensure we do it safely because if we do it too quickly, we risk you burning out and losing your ability to do magic at all."

"That happens?"

"Rarely, but yes, it has happened. There was one who came before you. We thought she'd be the one to break the curse. But her training was rushed, and she couldn't build her endurance quickly enough to combat the strenuous schedule."

"What happened to her?" I asked. A bottomless pit of dread built in my stomach, and I wasn't sure I wanted to know.

Sorcha's silence was answer enough.

"You're not making me want to do this more," I said, pulling away from Sorcha and rising to my feet. "So you're telling me there's a chance I might burn out and never be able to use magic for the rest of my immortal life? Would I be immortal if I burned through my magic?

"You would be immortal, yes…" Sorcha hesitated.

I braced myself for whatever would come next.

"Immortals who can't do magic don't always live for long, though."

"Why?" I asked, thinking it was because they struggled to earn a living since Magicborn relied on their magic for work.

"It's not that," Sorcha said, clearly reading my mind. "Vakrass isn't like Earth. Every citizen is cared for, no matter their status. Those who have more receive less, and those who have less receive more. A series of checks and balances exists to ensure everyone lives with as much dignity as possible. The reason those who burn out don't live for long is because they can't cope. After feeling magic sing in their blood and power course through them, not being able to feel even a smidge of it causes many to go mad or sink into depression so deep they can't crawl back out. The suicide rate among immortals who've burned out is 98 percent."

"What about the other 2 percent? What happens to them?" Dread settled in my stomach. I felt I knew the answer but needed to hear it. I needed my suspicions confirmed.

Sorcha hesitated again. "They're insane. So insane that they spend all day every day in a padded cell because they're a danger to themselves and they're a danger to everyone around them. They don't have contact with a single person. Their meals are delivered through a tiny slot in the door. Their rooms are windowless." The longer Sorcha spoke, the quieter her voice became until she only whispered the last words.

"How are they dangerous if they don't have magic and everyone around them does?" I asked.

"They don't have magic, but they're still fae. I know you've felt the viciousness lying inside you. We all have it. Imagine what you would do if you couldn't access magic. All that remained within you was that viciousness and the need to release it. What would you be capable of?"

"Anything," I whispered, not giving myself the chance to think it through. Because there *was* a monster within me, and I'd spent so much time pushing it down that I hadn't considered any options involving letting it out. But if I were insane, I could see myself gladly relinquishing control.

I stared at Sorcha, waiting for her to say anything to make this sound less horrible, but she didn't say a word.

"I'm not doing this. I'm returning to my regular classes and will learn magic how I'm supposed to. I'm not going to be one of the 98 percent, and I sure as hell won't be one of the 2 percent." I'd never thought I'd fight so hard to live, but the future she was laying out was bleak. I'd be miserable. I'd make those around me miserable. I couldn't do that to Lianna. I leaped to my feet. "I'm done here," I said, turning to leave.

My body froze, and my skin blistered and welted as fire burned through me from the inside out. I opened my mouth in a soundless scream as Queen Nasryn's power engulfed me.

Sorcha met my eyes, and I could see the sorrow in hers. "I'm sorry, Riona, but you're not leaving. Queen Nasryn won't let you."

Despite the overwhelming agony enveloping me, I refused to succumb. Instead, I fought back. I wanted to believe my will was more powerful than Queen Nasryn's.

"You're not strong enough to take her on," Sorcha whispered. "But you will be, if you train. You will be, if you let me teach you all I know."

Her words crashed through me, and I met her gaze. My mind spun in the way it always did whenever I looked Sorcha in the eye, but this time, it balanced out more quickly, and as it dissipated fully, I saw her for the first time.

Her eyes held a desire for something. I wasn't sure for what, but it was enough for the fight to dissolve from my body. Something told me she was on my side—at least a little bit.

"Fine," I said, and the pain ceased. "I'll train, but I won't break the curse."

Sorcha shrugged like she knew differently and agreed with me to let me think whatever I wanted to think to get through.

"What's next?" I asked.

"We're going back to the gym. Since you've already used magic today and you can't decipher how much you used and how much you have left, we'll go spar." She stood and held a hand out to me.

"Fine," I said. "Lead the way."

Chapter Twenty-Nine

BALANCING ACT
Riona

Classes were in full swing when Sorcha and I reentered the gym for sparring, but that didn't stop all eyes from turning to us as we walked in. This was going to be hell. Several students, including Aithan and Xenryn, glared at me.

Great. Not only did I have to endure training, but I also had to deal with my peers' jealousy. I tried to shake off the overwhelming jealousy and rage directed at me as I followed Sorcha's directions to change into athletic clothes, but it lingered and grew. I left the dressing room and followed Sorcha to the opposite side of the room and through a door into a much smaller room that was set up for sparring. Soft, padded mats lined both the floor and the walls. Not that I'd ever been in one before, but it looked like a padded room in a psych ward.

"All I need is a straitjacket," I quipped, immediately wanting to smack myself. After the conversation with Sorcha, which involved me potentially ending up in a real straitjacket, the joke missed its mark.

Sorcha didn't respond. She didn't even look at me or act like she'd heard me.

I sighed. Sorcha's ever-changing personality was wearing on me.

"Today, we're going to work on your ability to balance," she said. She flicked a switch that blended into the wall so well I'd missed it. The mats on the floor parted. A balance beam rose through the floor, and the pads closed again. The beam rose about an inch above the mats.

I'd never had the best balance as a human, and I struggled with it even now. My mom joked that my inner ear must be faulty because I constantly tripped over my feet or invisible barriers on clear paths.

"Come on. Take off your socks and shoes and step up on the beam," Sorcha urged.

I slipped out of my sneakers and trudged toward the beam. I feigned confidence and stepped onto the beam with one foot. My arms windmilled, but it was useless. I lost my balance before I could get my other foot on the beam. Somehow, my feet ended up entangled, and I was going down face first.

Then Sorcha was there. She caught me before I hit the ground. My legs finally got their shit together and found the floor.

"Looks like this'll be harder than I thought," Sorcha said, still holding on to me. "Though I shouldn't be surprised. I've been catching you since I met you."

I blushed, recalling crashing into Sorcha on Ascension Day. And falling down the steps during the ceremony and Sorcha catching me again. "What can I say? I have a habit of falling for pretty females." I clamped a hand over my mouth, horrified. *Oh, my goddess. I can't believe I said that. What the fuck is wrong with me?*

"But you did," Sorcha said, "so thanks for the compliment. The only thing that appears to be wrong with you is your balance is shit. Perhaps we can focus on the task, and you should consider working on that nasty case of negative self-talk you have going on during your free time. After all, nobody likes a Negative Nancy."

My face heated at the realization that she heard that. Mind reading felt like an abuse of power. The thought of my thoughts being wide open to the world around me was frustrating.

"Once you learn to control your magic, you'll be able to shield your mind. Everyone is entitled to their privacy, and when new students come into the school, they are shielded by Thea so their minds aren't accessible to anyone except the person shielding them. That person doubles the shields around themselves to block out the thoughts of the students until they can do so on their own. It requires special training. However, you seem to be a special case because your thoughts keep coming through loud and clear, despite the wards and shields around your mind and mine. We're going to have to work on that, but in the meantime, we will both have to suffer," Sorcha ground out, rubbing her temples as though she had a headache, which she must, if she could hear every thought running through my head. "I'll do my best not to intrude."

Damn, that must be exhausting. How do I stop thinking? Oh, my goddess, I'm probably so annoying right now. Oh, goddess Riona, stop thinking.

"Riona, focus on the balance beam," Sorcha said, pulling me out of my spiral. "Preferably before my head explodes," she added under her breath.

"Right. Balance beam. Got it," I said, hopping up onto the beam too fast, then falling off and nearly twisting my ankle. "Ouch! Shit!"

"Perhaps slower," Sorcha said wryly, gesturing for me to try again.

We spent the rest of the afternoon working on that balance beam until I could walk the whole thing forward and backward without falling. As I was completing my twentieth trek across the beam, an elegant Black female entered the room, breaking my concentration and nearly causing me to topple. However, I found my center like Sorcha had shown me and completed my walk before turning to address the female from the beam.

"I'm Ismene. You're Riona?" the new female asked, eyeing me warily.

I looked to Sorcha, who inclined her head, and I stepped off the beam. "Yes, I'm Riona. You're here to teach me everything there is to know about Ilthyrium, right?" I said.

Ismene was stunning. Her skin was a deep ebony that seemed to capture and reflect light in a way I'd never encountered before. This striking contrast made her light gray eyes pop like two shimmering stars against the night sky. Their captivating depth drew me in and held me longer than I intended. Her canary yellow dress, a color I'd previously thought no one could pull off, set her dark skin aglow.

"Sure am," she said, clearly tired of me staring. "If you're done here, we can head to the library and get started," she said.

I glanced at Sorcha again, and she nodded once, releasing me to Ismene.

"Sure," I said. "Let me change. I'll meet you there."

Ismene set a stack of books on the table when I sat down.

"These are your new reading materials. Read the first five chapters of each by midweek," Ismene said.

I looked at the stack of books before me. "Midweek? As in tomorrow?" I asked. There had to be at least ten, and they were all several inches thick. This would take the entire night.

"Yes, tomorrow," Ismene said sharply. "We're on borrowed time, and I have the impossible task of preparing you to survive Ilthyrium in a few short months."

"But what about graduation and spending time with my unit? How are we supposed to go through the graduation trials if I'm spending all of my time training, in class, or reading enormous old books?"

"I'm sure Queen Nasryn and Thea will discuss that with you when you get closer to graduation. I don't know beyond that. I go where I'm told and do what I'm directed to do," Ismene said, leaning on the table.

I glared at Ismene. "Are you serious? This is my life you all are messing with, and you don't know?"

"Look, you're not happy about this arrangement. I get that. I don't have the power to do anything about it, so let's focus on what I can help you with, which is surviving Ilthyrium. Starting now, every conversation we have will be in Vakrasi, and I won't respond to anything else. Once you've mastered Vakrasi, we will move on to the other languages of Ilthyrium."

I scowled. "I suck at Vakrasi," I said in English. "So, I wouldn't hold your breath on getting to any of the other languages."

Ismene ignored me. She opened a book and stared at it pointedly.

I sighed, pulling a book off the top of the stack. If she wanted to do the silent treatment, I could do the same. The title of the book was *The History of Vakrass* by Ora Farrow. Luckily, it was the same text we were already reading in history, so I'd already completed most of the required reading for that text.

I pulled the next book off the stack, *The Rules and Regulations of Vakrass* by Ora Farrow.

Blech, next.

I grabbed the third book, *Maps of Vakrass* by Ora Farrow. I set that aside and reached for the next tome, which was much larger than all the others I'd already picked up. *The Rise and Fall of Ilthyrium: Everything You Need to Know About The Mortal Curse* by Unknown.

I groaned. So far, every book on this list looked horrible. I picked up the final book from the stack, *The Languages of Ilthyrium* by Ora Farrow, Xoassie the Victorious, Zhaleh, and Trena. I cracked it open and was met with pages filled with unreadable (at least to me) text. I set that book aside, returned to the first book, and pretended to read it.

Ismene looked up and spoke in Vakrasi.

"Huh?" I said. "I have no idea what you said. You can speak in Vakrasi all you want, but at this point, I don't know what you're saying or how to respond.

"You know I'm telepathic, right?" Ismene repeated, this time humoring me by speaking English.

I grimaced. "Let me guess, you can hear my thoughts despite the shield," I said.

"Well, yes, but Queen Nasryn also said I should use my abilities to access your mind to help speed up your training."

My mouth dropped open. I knew Sorcha and Ismene could read my mind, but I hadn't realized the extent. It seemed like such a gross invasion of personal space, not to mention highly unethical. "What the fuck!" I said finally. "Why? How are there no laws about that? Shouldn't my consent matter?"

Ismene raised an eyebrow, brushing a stray hair out of her face. "There are laws about it, of course, but Queen Nasryn can veto them. You've already proven that you're not on board, so she vetoed your consent and overruled you as your monarch."

"That's not okay." I sputtered.

Ismene shrugged. "This isn't a democracy. And what the monarch says, goes."

"And you're okay with that? What if it were being done to you?"

"Whether or not I'm okay with it, I'm here to serve my queen, and if that was what was demanded of me, I'd do it without complaint."

"That's—that's ridiculous."

"That's Vakrass. If you were reading that book rather than pretending to, you'd learn that." Ismene looked at the timepiece on the counter behind her. "That's all we've time for today. I'll meet you here tomorrow at the same time. Read the first three chapters of *The Rules and Regulations of Vakrass* by then." Ismene rose and collected her materials.

I kept my face serene. But internally, rage billowed, and I pushed it down. It wasn't Ismene's fault. But at the same time, it was. How could she participate in something so debased and not be morally compromised?

Ismene looked at me. "Because sometimes the world isn't fair, and we don't always have a choice." Ismene turned on her heel and walked out of the library.

Well, shit, I thought, gathering my books. I should learn to filter what goes through my mind.

That evening, as the sun dipped below the horizon and cast a warm glow around our dorm room, Lianna turned to me. "Do you want to explore the school with me and Koen?" Her voice bubbled with enthusiasm.

A wave of guilt washed over me as I glanced at the mountain of assignments on my desk. "I can't. I need to focus on schoolwork." It was only my first full day of mandated extra classes, and the pressure felt like an anchor.

Lianna stepped closer, her expression softening. "I can stay with you," she offered, her brow furrowed with concern.

"No. Go have fun," I insisted, attempting to sound unbothered. I could see the restlessness in her eyes.

"Are you sure? I don't mind keeping you company or helping you," she replied, uncertainty creeping into her voice.

"I'm sure," I reassured her with a smile. "You'll just distract me, anyway. Besides, you deserve to enjoy yourself."

A grin broke across her face, and her spirits lifted. "Thanks, Ri! You're the best." She rose on her tiptoes and brushed her lips against mine.

Then I was alone in our dimly lit dorm room, sitting at my cluttered desk, surrounded by ancient texts filled with tales of Vakrass's wars and traditions. The weight of history loomed over me as I tried to immerse myself in the complex narratives, but a part of me longed for the laughter and camaraderie that Lianna and Koen were enjoying outside.

Chapter Thirty

THE HEART WANTS WHAT THE HEART WANTS

Lianna

I walked into the dining room alone and scanned the crowded space. I wasn't nervous, but I hated going there alone. I missed Riona. Her early mornings with Sorcha were cramping our style, both in and out of the bedroom. She was so tired every night that the moment she completed all her homework, she fell into bed and fell asleep almost immediately, leaving me alone. I'd be lying if I said I wasn't getting lonely after a month of this.

"Lianna!" Koen's boisterous voice filled the space.

I flinched when all eyes turned on me. I'd always loved being the center of attention, but I was finding I didn't like it as much when Riona wasn't around. I wondered if I only liked to be the center of attention because she hated it, and I wanted her to be comfortable. Maybe it was this new life that I struggled to integrate myself into.

Koen bounded up to me. "Morning. Want to eat with me?" he asked.

I sighed with relief. I wasn't alone. Even though Koen got on my nerves sometimes, it was nice to have someone to take the edge off. The downside was that the more time I spent with him, the more I wanted him.

"Sure," I said, a little too enthusiastically. "We can since Riona's off training with Sorcha," I continued when I saw his eyes light up. I was trying to keep my distance, but it was getting harder to do that when we spent all our time together with no buffer.

"Lianna," he started when we sat.

I braced myself. "What's up?"

"I was wondering if you wanted to hang out tonight. We could go for a walk or hang out in my room and do something?"

I studied him. We'd been hanging out a lot over the last several weeks, but Koen's nervousness implied this would be a different kind of hanging out. I could say no. But I was fooling myself. Of course, I wouldn't say no. I was falling hard for him. Maybe I needed to stop fighting it and see what would happen.

I smiled shyly at him. "I'd love to. Riona doesn't return until late, so that would be nice."

Koen grinned. "It's a date," he said.

I stood outside Koen's door and drew a deep breath. I felt like doing this was going to change everything. Like stepping through this door would start something I couldn't take back. It was dumb. I shouldn't do anything, at least not without talking to Riona, but I was afraid of how she'd react. Past partners hadn't been understanding, and I was afraid I might lose her if I told her I had feelings for Koen. She'd been understanding in the past, but those instances had been flings. Somehow, I knew if I started something with Koen, it would be more than a fling.

I stepped back, planning to return to my room, when the door swung open. "Lianna, come on in," Koen said, moving out of the way.

For once, take care of you, my brain screamed at me. *You always take care of Riona. Tonight, do something for yourself instead of sitting around being bored.*

I stepped inside and Koen shut the door behind me.

Koen's room was smaller than ours, but that made sense because he had a room to himself while Riona and I shared one. His space was surprisingly clean and not like he'd done a quick clean before I came over by shoving all his crap under his bed like my adopted brothers would have. His kitchenette and living room were spotless, and everything had a home. His adoptive mother must've taught him well.

"Would you like something to drink? I have water or wine."

"I'd love some wine," I said.

"Have a seat," he said, gesturing to the couch as he walked into the kitchenette and collected two wineglasses.

The rich, fruity scent of the red wine permeated the air when Koen popped the cork and filled the glasses. He brought them over and handed me one before sitting down on the other side of the couch, maintaining a respectful distance between us.

Awkward silence filled the room for several minutes while we sipped our wine.

"So..." Koen cleared his throat. "How are you doing with Riona having all this extra training? You two are together, right?"

"Yeah, we've been together for years," I said, planning to leave it at that. But I surprised myself when I added, "It's been hard. I'm so used to having her around all the time. I hate that she's always busy doing other stuff, and I'm always alone."

Koen was quiet for a moment.

"I'm not Riona, but I am part of your unit. You can always hang out with me. I've been incredibly lonely since coming here too. I grew up in a big, noisy household with tons of siblings. Here, I've spent most of my time alone, and it sucks." Koen admitted.

It was my turn to be silent. I hadn't even thought of how isolated Koen must feel stuck in a unit with Riona and me. He only had us, and we were so involved in each other, not realizing Koen was spending all his time alone. As lonely as I'd been the last couple of weeks, I couldn't begin to fathom how lonely Koen had likely been since arriving here.

"Do you hate it here?" I asked.

"Yes and no," Koen said, crossing a leg over the other. He averted his gaze and looked at the wall. "I enjoy the classes. I thought it would be different that first day when we stepped into the dining room, and I saw all the fae there. I thought I'd make friends easily, and it wouldn't matter that my unit was two gay females who wanted nothing to do with me. But then we found out there was no fraternization, and more so that nobody wanted to mingle outside of their unit. It made it harder."

"I'm not gay," I blurted, addressing the least important part of Koen's monologue. "I'm sorry that Riona and I've abandoned you. It wasn't intentional. We're used to it being the two of us."

"You're not gay?" Koen said, his voice tinged with hope.

"Nope. Bisexual and polyamorous," I said, throwing that last bit in for some unknown reason.

"Oh. Is Riona bisexual and polyamorous also?" Koen said.

I chuckled at the hope in his face as I imagined what he was likely thinking. "No. Riona is strictly lesbian and not at all poly. But she lets me be me, which is amazing. She's a good person."

"She doesn't seem to like me," Koen said.

I was surprised he'd picked up on Riona's aversion to him. She'd always been friendly toward him, though she maintained her distance, and I'd caught her give an eye roll or two in his direction when he wasn't looking. Still, I couldn't remember any particular moments where Riona was outright unfriendly.

The longer we talked, the easier it became, and I learned all about Koen's siblings and his home and how much he missed it. My attraction grew, as did my respect for him. Deep down, he was sensitive and slightly anxious, which he covered with his cockiness. I could respect that he was willing to admit that rather than continue to try to cover it up.

As the night deepened, I moved closer to Koen as we shared our favorite memories before we became fae and our struggles with our new lives. I could like him. I could see myself having a relationship with him. The thought surprised me, though it shouldn't have. We'd been skirting around each other and our attraction for weeks.

"Lianna," Koen said, interrupting my thoughts. "It's getting late, so I'm assuming Riona will worry if you don't return to your room, but I wanted to ask you something before you go."

I checked the time. Riona would be back soon, if she wasn't already. I stood to gather my things. "What is it?" I asked.

Koen's face went red as he tried to find the words. "I-I was wondering, if you'd give me a chance, too? I know you're with Riona, and that's cool, but I like you—a lot. And I'd like to see if there's anything between us."

I stood there for a moment, torn between the idea of starting a relationship with him and knowing how all of my other relationships with men had gone.

"I'd like that," I said. "I need to let Riona know though."

"I figured." Koen walked me to the door and opened it for me. "Can we have breakfast together tomorrow?"

"Yeah," I said, contemplating whether I should hug him or not. Then, I impulsively reached out and wrapped my arms around him.

He responded by wrapping himself around me, and his arms felt like the other half of home. I inhaled his scent of pine, cedarwood, and faint arousal. I jerked away, knowing if I could smell his, he could smell mine. Not to mention, his arms felt a little bit too good wrapped around me, and if I stayed a moment longer, I might do something to embarrass myself, like throw myself at him and beg him to take me.

"Good night, Koen," I said, hurrying out his door and into mine.

I dropped my things in the doorway of the dorm room and proceeded to the bedroom, where I intended to tell Riona everything, but she was already fast asleep on the bed. I let her sleep, and I settled for a hot shower.

I'd tell her in the morning.

Chapter Thirty-One

MAGIC TRAINING, AND SPARRING, OH MY!

Riona

I fell into a daily rhythm of waking before dawn each morning and running through the paces with Sorcha. When she decided she'd sufficiently kicked my ass for the day magically, she switched to kicking my ass physically. After, I rendezvoused with Koen and Lianna to begin a jam-packed day of regular classes. I was so utterly bone-tired that my eyes felt like lead weights. Ismene remained unsympathetic, and her expression hardened whenever I complained about my exhaustion.

The mental challenges Ismene hurled at me were as demanding as the physical ones. She spent the time lecturing me on the rules, regulations, and languages of Ilthyrium, ensuring I was prepared to travel the realms, fight if necessary, and break The Mortal Curse. I fell into a coma-like sleep each night until I woke up the following day and did it all over again. I functioned on autopilot for weeks, my stamina growing with each passing day.

By the end of the month, I finally had the energy to focus and retain information as I worked with Ismene. After training with Sorcha and my other classes, I showered and joined Ismene in the library.

"How was training?" she asked in Vakrasi.

"Sorcha kicked my ass, per usual," I said in English, proud that I'd understood her.

"Vakrasi!" Ismene demanded.

I repeated myself in Vakrasi, and Ismene smiled, seemingly content with my pronunciation.

After weeks of studying four hours every night with Ismene, Vakrasi was flowing off my tongue correctly about 75 percent of the time. More than once, Lia woke me in the middle of the night and asked what I was saying because it was all in Vakrasi. I still had a long way to go, but I was surpassing Queen Nasryn's initial goals much faster than anyone anticipated. However, magic and sparring skills remained elusive.

Chapter Thirty-Two

SO MANY THINGS TO TELL HER

Lianna

With each passing day, I grew closer to Koen as Riona spent all her time training to break The Mortal Curse. I wasn't angry with her, but I missed her so much. Koen was doing everything to fill the void that had opened because of Riona's training. We spent each afternoon together, after our pre-intrinsic classes, and we reconvened in his room to study together. The more time we spent together, the more I saw the real Koen. The confidence that had attracted me to him in the beginning was still there, but the cockiness he'd used to cover up his insecurity had passed.

After a month of this, pre-intrinsic classes were canceled one day, so we retired to his room early to study, but things quickly took a turn. I entered his room and found it filled with lit candles and the scent of jasmine. Soft music played in the background.

Koen cleared his throat. "I know you and Riona are together, but we're also together. Lianna, I care about you deeply, and I thought maybe we could take this relationship to the next level."

I took in the room, appreciating the care and thought he'd put into it but also feeling a twinge of frustration. I still hadn't had the chance to talk to Riona about any of this, and the weight of it hung around me like a shroud. Koen's hands landed on my shoulders, their firm yet gentle touch expertly unraveled the knots and induced a sense of tranquility.

"Koen, I—I want to be with you, but I haven't been with anyone other than Riona in so long. Especially a male. I'm out of practice, and it feels a little off without Riona knowing." I wasn't sure why I felt the need to tell Riona first. In the past, when I'd been with others, I'd always told her after the fact, and it'd been okay, but those instances had felt different.

"I understand, but you've been trying to tell Riona for a month," Koen argued, his voice soft and seductive. "But, if you aren't ready and you want to wait, Lia, that's okay too," Koen added after I still hesitated.

My heart melted and I leaned into him. What he was talking about would change everything. But him giving me the choice and backing off to let me decide whether I was ready for this change solidified in my mind that I wanted this. Wanted him.

The warmth from his chest against my back spread through my body. His heart raced. Or was that *my* heart? I couldn't be sure anymore. He slid his hands from my shoulders down to my waist and wrapped them around me. He dropped his lips to my neck, brushing them against the sensitive skin there.

His breath grazed my ear, and a wave of anticipation washed over me. The soft press of his lips on my neck shoved all arguments to the back of my mind. His hands glided up and down the sides of my body. My heart skipped a beat and then doubled its pace. An electrifying heat surged through me, leaving me momentarily breathless. I stopped thinking and leaned into it. Everything about it felt right.

I turned, rose on my tiptoes, and wrapped my arms around his neck. I pulled his face to meet mine, losing myself in his embrace.

He didn't hesitate. He picked me up, and I wrapped my legs around his waist. Koen walked us through the dorm into his bedroom and laid me gently on the bed. And everything changed.

Our sweaty bodies lay intertwined, the sheets clinging to our skin as if they, too, were part of our embrace. The air was thick and warm, infused with the heady scent of desire and the subtle musk of our intimacy. I could hear nothing but the rhythm of our breathing, each inhale and exhale creating a soft, syncopated melody that echoed in the quiet room. The faint sound of a clock ticking somewhere in the distance was drowned out by blood pounding in my ears. Everywhere our bodies touched was electric, igniting sparks of warmth across my skin.

I lay there, coming down from the high of an amazing orgasm and reveling in the new closeness I felt to Koen. As I returned to my senses, I glanced over at the clock beside Koen's bed and bolted upright. "I have to get back. Riona's going to be back soon, and I don't want her to find out about this" — I gestured between him and me— "this way."

"Are you going to tell her about us?" Koen asked, leaning back, his arms under his head.

"I'm going to tell her when the time is right, Koen. I'm not going to drop it on her. I don't want to hurt her, but I do want to live my life, and that includes being with you, so I'll tell her soon." I crawled out of bed and grabbed my clothes. His scent was all over me. I needed to shower before Riona got back. I didn't want her nose to tell her before I did. I said goodbye to Koen before returning to the room I shared with Riona.

As I entered the room next door, a wave of relief washed over me when I saw it was empty. Stripping down, I entered the bathroom and stepped into the shower. The powerful jets of water eliminated any lingering scent from the intimate moments I'd shared with Koen. When I finished, I collected the clothes I'd worn to Koen's, careful to hold them away from my body. I was beginning to feel like I was hiding my relationship with Koen, but I was too deep to back out now.

This is wrong. The thought shoved its way into my mind as I hurried to the laundry room and tossed my clothing into the washing machine. *Riona deserves so much better than this.*

I added a generous amount of soap, filling the washing machine with a fresh, clean scent. The washing machines in Ilthyrium were much like the ones on Earth, except they ran on magic instead of electricity.

You have to tell her. Tonight. No matter what.

I glanced in the mirror above the washing machine. "I'm going to tell her," I declared to my reflection. My voice shook with anticipation and anxiety. I'd decided. No matter what mood Riona's in, I was going to tell her what's going on with Koen and me. She deserved to know, and it was unfair of me to keep it from her.

I made my way back to the dorm room, ready to wait until Riona returned to pounce on her with the information, but when I returned from the laundry room, Riona's bag was on the floor inside the door.

"Ri?" I called softly so as not to scare her, but when I walked through our bedroom door, I found her sprawled across the bed, still in her clothes and shoes, fast asleep.

I slumped against the wall, feeling defeated as all of my plans of telling Riona what was on my mind vanished. I wouldn't disturb her sleep. She struggled to sleep, tossing and turning all night. And whenever she didn't get enough rest, her anxiety levels skyrocketed the following day.

With a heavy sigh, I returned to the living room and plucked a romance novel from the shelf. I curled up on the couch and pulled a large blanket over me, enveloped in its cozy warmth, but the book remained closed at my side. The fear of confessing to Riona consumed me. It almost felt like it was too late to do it without it dissolving into a fight.

This is wrong. You never should've slept with him without talking to Riona first. You knew it was different with him.

I clapped my hands over my ears as if that would help, but it only made it worse. "It's already done. I can't undo it," I said the words aloud, trying to calm the storm in my mind, but I'd messed up, and I knew it. Goddess, please let Ri forgive me.

Chapter Thirty-Three

MISUNDERSTANDINGS
Riona

After gathering my dinner tray, I met Koen and Lianna at our designated table. They sat beside each other on one side of the table rather than on opposite sides like they usually did, and they were deep in conversation.

"What's going on?" I asked, setting my tray across from them, and Lia looked up guiltily.

"Nothing," she said, becoming fascinated by the food on her tray. She scooted away from Koen, and I frowned.

The delicious scent of my roast and potatoes had my stomach growling, and I was starving, so I pushed the confusion out of my mind and dove into my dinner.

Exhaustion swept over me as I took the last bite. I glanced up at Lia, staring down at her plate, pushing her food around, and my heart picked up its pace as a rush of desire flooded me. Goddess, how long has it been since I'd last held her in my arms?

"I'm tired. Lia?" I said and waited until she looked up at me. "Want to head back to our room? Maybe we can hang out for a bit." I said, raising an eyebrow, indicating what I meant by 'hanging out.'

Lia shook her head. "No thanks, Koen and I are going to take a walk," she said, almost coolly.

"Oh, okay. Want me to come?" I asked, even though I could barely stay upright.

"No!" Lia said quickly—too quickly—and my mind started putting two and two together, and I didn't want to believe it. I'd known there were others before we came to Vakrass, and I'd known there would be more, here. But I didn't think it would be so soon that she wouldn't tell me, or that it would be Koen, of all people.

"I see," I said somewhat frostily.

Lia looked down. "You need your rest," she said, providing the world's flimsiest excuse.

"I don't need that much rest," I said. "I'm sure we could find a way to wake me up a bit. Plus, I'm not nearly as tired as I've been," I said, gritting my teeth. But the two of them continued avoiding my eyes.

When they said nothing, I stepped back. "Fine, I'll see you tonight."

"Don't wait up," Lia said. "Like I said, we're going for a walk and might hang out," she said when I glanced at her.

"Right, 'hang out.'" My voice dripped with sarcasm. I was pissed. Here I was, forced to participate in this ridiculous training, and suddenly, my girlfriend would rather spend time with Koen than with me. *If that's how they want to play, we'll play.*

I could be a downright petty bitch when the situation called for it, and boy, did this situation call for it. I was okay with her seeing other people, if she was honest. But fuck secrecy. I walked around the table to stand beside Lia. "Don't stay out too late, love," I said, dipping down to brush my lips against hers.

Lianna hesitated, and I bit her bottom lip in the way I knew she loved and could never resist, and she kissed me back hungrily. Then I pulled away, leaving her breathless. "Night," I said, leaving quickly.

I didn't make it halfway up the steps before Lia grabbed my hand and pulled me to her.

"You can't kiss me like that and then walk away," she said. Her voice was low and husky, filled with lust and need.

"What else was I supposed to do? You were practically mounting Koen in the fucking dining room, Lia. It hasn't even been that long since you and I last had sex. What the fuck's going on?" I asked. I wasn't even sure I wanted the answer because it was clear something was going on. "Did you cheat on me?" I asked. I knew the words weren't exactly right because we'd agreed she could sleep with other people.

"I can't cheat on you. We aren't exclusive," she said defensively.

I stared at her as she tried to dance around the issue.

"You know what I meant. We agreed. No sleepovers with other people, and you promised you'd tell me if you wanted to see someone else," I said.

"Yeah, well, things change when one partner is unavailable all the time," Lianna yelled, throwing her hands up.

I stepped back, surprised at her vehemence. Rage welled within me. "I don't have a choice!" I shouted. "You could've at least had the courtesy to tell me you were changing the rules!"

"When? You're never around."

"What kind of excuse is that? Who even are you? Because I have no idea!" I shouted, crossing my arms.

Lianna stepped back as if I'd slapped her. "What do you mean, you don't know who I am? We grew up together. You know exactly who I am. I'm your best friend and your girlfriend."

She sounded defeated, but I didn't care. I wanted to sort this out.

"Clearly, I don't know you as well as I thought, because I thought we could be honest with each other. My being busy isn't an excuse for lying. So, what gives? Why wouldn't you be honest with me? That doesn't seem like something that should be difficult for someone who claims I'm their 'best friend and girlfriend.'"

Lianna's shoulders dropped. "Look, you know I'm not monogamous. I like Koen, and I enjoy—" She broke off, blushing. "I enjoy what he brings to the table," she said, avoiding my eyes. "But you're available tonight, so how about instead of arguing and talking about Koen, we take this to our room and do something else..."

I waited for her to acknowledge the rest.

"What?" she asked.

"Why not tell me, Lia? We promised honesty when we started this. I think that stands more now."

Lianna stood there for a moment. "I—" She started and then hesitated. "I mean... you aren't the first person I've dated. Nobody else has ever been cool about it. They'd say they were, and then everything would blow up when I told them I was considering seeing someone else. I didn't want to lose you."

I stayed silent, shifting from one foot to the other.

"Because..." Lia paused for several moments, and I waited. "I was afraid you wouldn't love me anymore," she said, the words coming out in a whisper.

I narrowed my eyes. It couldn't only be the fear of my rejection, something deeper was at play. What kind of person would change the rules of the relationship without notifying the other party and think that wouldn't cause their partner to leave them?

"Look, I've never been monogamous, and when I've had girlfriends in the past, they had an issue with me being bisexual. They especially had an issue when I wasn't monogamous and would sleep with men while I was with them. So, I was used to keeping my other partners a secret. I know that was wrong. I should've told you."

"So you judged me according to your past girlfriends?"

"Come on, Ri, you're one of the most rigid people I know. You hate when the rules change. You hate change."

"That doesn't make it okay to lie to me, Lia. I might not like you sleeping with other people, but I'd never try to control you, and I'd never lie to you."

Lia flinched. "I didn't lie."

"Omitting the truth is the same as lying. Sneaking around behind someone's back is the same as lying," I said. "It's cheating."

Lia peered at me and tears welled up in her eyes. "I'm sorry, Ri. I didn't mean for it to happen this way. I swear. I was afraid I'd lose you now that we have a real shot of being together without thinking one day we'd have to say goodbye."

Her fear washed over me like it was my own. Her anxiety of losing me was as intense as my fear of losing her. It was overwhelming and threatened to consume the whole of me. My rage melted. The hurt and betrayal stung and remained, but I understood fear better than most and how it made you do cowardly shit.

I took her chin in my hands. "Don't lie to me again," I said. "I want to know. I hold no judgment for you, and I don't want to end this."

Lia's shoulders slumped, and she leaned into me. "Thank you, Ri. I'm sorry I didn't tell you. You mean so much to me. And I tried to tell you sooner, and there never seemed to be time to discuss."

I looked at her and saw the remorse in her eyes. I'd always been able to read her well, but the distance between us had been hindering that. But looking at her now, I saw it. She gnawed at her lip, anxiety and doubt clouding her features. "I can guarantee you'll lose me a hell of a lot faster by not being honest. Be straight with me, Lia. That's all I ask. No matter how busy or exhausted we are," I murmured, reaching out to pull her into my arms. I hugged her.

"Okay," Lianna said, smiling. "Now, can we please stop talking about Koen? Let's go to our room. I want to do things to you that can't be done in this hallway."

I leaned into her, kissing her deeply, thankful that no one had witnessed our argument. "I think that sounds like a great idea," I said when I broke off the kiss. *Guess I win this round.*

"Good, because it's been way too effing long since I've had you inside me," she said, grabbing my hand and pulling me up the stairs behind her.

Later that night I lay in bed mulling over this turn of events. It made sense that Lianna and Koen would hook up, and I don't know why I didn't think of it before. There wasn't anyone else that she could safely sleep with at the school because everyone was already bonded, so it made sense that she would consider the only male in our group.

Strangely, I wasn't jealous. I was angry that she'd kept it from me, but I would never want to be with Koen. Bondings happened within groups that ascended together, and we were all platonically bonded, so it made sense.

Shit, bonding.

When Lia and I ascended together, I'd assumed we'd bond, but now she was in an intimate relationship with both of us. What did that mean for our bondings? It was far more likely that she'd be bonded to Koen since they were opposite sexes, and they could further the races together.

Shit, shit, shit. Lianna snuggled into me, deep asleep and unaware of my inner turmoil.

I wrapped my arms around her, and she settled into my arms. I tucked away my worries about bonding and focused on Lia's steady breathing and the way she felt cuddled against me.

Chapter Thirty-Four

TERRITORIAL
Riona

Lianna and I walked down to breakfast together the next morning, Oryn and Kallik trailing behind me like always. I paid little attention to what I scooped on my plate, gearing up for my first face-to-face with Koen after Lianna's big reveal last night. When I sat down at our little table across from Koen, I averted my eyes so I wouldn't catch his gaze.

Koen eyed my tray, then arched an eyebrow at me. "Interesting choice," he said.

I looked down at my tray. I'd scooped oatmeal and put it all over my eggs. I said nothing.

I'd agreed to try, but at this moment, I wanted nothing more than to reach across the table and strangle the fuck out of him. The image of him and Lia tangled up together twisted my gut, and I shoved my tray away. "I'm not hungry. I'm going to head to training. I have to talk to Sorcha about something." I didn't wait for a response. I left my tray on the table and rushed out of the room.

I didn't need to speak with Sorcha. I needed to be alone. I glanced over my shoulder at my ever-present hulking shadows and huffed.

I needed to work off some of this excess energy, and the gym seemed the best place to do that.

When I stepped into the gym, it was empty. I was thrilled. There was almost always someone working out. So, I hurried to the locker room, changed into some gym clothes, and headed back out to the floor where I began stretching. I tried to clear my mind of the images of Koen and Lia threatening to take over, but it was no use.

I started jogging. I hated running, mostly because I was clumsy, and as a human, I'd often tripped over my own feet. It wasn't something I had to worry about as a faerie because I'd finally acclimated to my fae body. My movements were almost always graceful now.

Gracefulness was definitely a supernatural trait. But my ears were different, my face, my body. Little of the old Riona, the human One Twenty-Seven, remained. Even my human memories had faded so much that I had to fight to recall certain memories while others were gone completely. I knew I was missing memories because when I thought about my time as a human, there were areas that were crystal clear, areas that were fuzzy or blurry, and areas that were blank spots. Those were frustrating, but what was more frustrating were the crystal-clear memories. The memories of my family.

I missed my mom. And Rosalyn and Dahlia Lane. Damn it, I even missed Acanthe being around—but only a little. Maybe I missed the familiarity they provided. Tears welled in my eyes, and I struggled to keep them at bay. I wouldn't cry. It would throw off my running, and I desperately needed this.

Someone fell into step beside me, and I looked up to see the tall, red-haired female running beside me. I nearly stumbled, but I righted myself. I sighed, but lucky for me, I was a little winded, so it sounded like I was panting.

"What're you doing?" I demanded. Why couldn't I have a single moment of peace?

"I could ask the same of you," Sorcha retorted. "I've never seen you come down here to run before training or any other time," she probed. "What gives?"

I shrugged, indifference washing over me. The last thing I wanted to do was get into my relationship woes with Sorcha. "I had some energy to burn off and some thoughts to deal with."

"And what? My workouts are too tame? You're going to run yourself ragged before we even get to our session if you keep up this pace. What's going on?" she asked again. "Maybe I can help."

I looked her up and down, and my face heated. She looked good. Her lithe body took each stride effortlessly. I'd never let myself admire her. I was with Lia and that had been it. But I'd be lying if I hadn't checked her out once or twice during our sessions.

"Riona?" she prodded.

I shrugged and slowed my pace a little. She couldn't help. "Like I said, I had some extra energy to burn off this morning, so I thought I'd run."

The sound of our feet hitting the gym floor filled the silence. "Makes sense to me," Sorcha said after we'd done a full lap. She seemed to have dropped the interrogation, realizing I wouldn't talk about it. "Physical workouts are one of my favorite ways to get rid of excess energy."

The way she said *one* had me glancing at her, wondering if I was misreading how she said it, but she'd said it in a way that was full of innuendo, which was weird because so far, I'd thought she hated me, and merely tolerated me.

Sorcha stopped, and I stopped beside her. "Let's head outside and get to work."

I didn't respond. Rather, I followed her out the side door into the chilly winter air and sucked in a deep breath, held it for a few moments, and released it.

"Let's do this," I said.

Sorcha put me through the paces that day while I replayed her words. I had to be imagining it, right? I mean, she was my teacher and way older than me. But as I caught her stealing glances at me as I worked through my stances, my thoughts trailed off in a different direction.

The idea of being in a relationship with more than one person had never crossed my mind, but it was intriguing. Considering non-monogamy or polygamy seemed overwhelming and unfamiliar to me, even with Lianna being poly. It had always come so naturally to her, but it hadn't even been a blip on the radar for me. However, I couldn't deny that the idea held a certain allure when it came to a certain crimson-haired female warrior.

"Riona, care to join me instead of whatever world you're engrossed in?" Sorcha's voice cut through my thoughts.

"Sorry," I said like I hadn't been caught daydreaming. At least I'd mastered how to shield my thoughts, most of the time. My face heated. I hoped none of those thoughts slipped through.

I spent the rest of the class attempting to focus on what Sorcha wanted me to do, but I was distracted by Sorcha's hair, lips, and body as she flung herself through the air.

A half hour before the first bell rang, Sorcha must have realized her efforts were futile because she released me to go to class. I was relieved to escape early. I was horny as hell, so I decided the first thing that had to happen before I went to class was an ice-cold shower to get my mind out of the gutter and into Ilthyrium. I raced to the dorm room and found myself blissfully alone. I didn't have time to wonder where Lia might be, and truthfully, with the racy thoughts of Sorcha in my head, I didn't mind. I turned the water on, shed my clothes, and stepped into the stinging cold spray, all thoughts of sultry redhead teachers dissipating—for the moment anyway.

After getting my ass thoroughly kicked by Sorcha all morning and listening to lecture after lecture, I was happy to meet Ismene in the library. The only thing pushing me through the day was the plans Lia and I'd made for tonight. I'd be damned if I was going to let Koen hog all of her attention.

"Hello, Riona," Ismene said in Vakrasi as soon as she speedwalked through the door. "Sorry, I'm late. Queen Nasryn had some things she wanted us to work on today, and she was providing me with the material, but I lost track of time, so here we are."

I groaned at the mention of Queen Nasryn's name. "Alright, what horrors does she have for me today?" I asked in Vakrasi.

"First, it's pronounced this way," Ismene said, repeating my words back to me with their correct pronunciation and making me repeat it until I had it right. "Secondly, since you're making excellent progress, the queen decided it's time to focus on breaking the curse. So today, we'll go over what it will take to end The Mortal Curse."

"I'm not breaking the fucking curse," I said, panic filling me at the mere thought of it.

Ismene sighed, "So you've said. We both know Queen Nasryn thinks otherwise. She has ordered that you're trained and educated for it, regardless. So, can we go through this, please?"

Ismene looked as exhausted as I felt, and I could understand why. I hadn't been the most cooperative student, and I was too tired and distracted to give it a whole lot of argument, so I shrugged and said, "Yep."

"Great, I'll start with what I know," Ismene said. "Then we will have to research the rest. We don't know where the curse was created—"

I do, I thought, remembering the dream I'd had weeks ago. Ismene gave me a puzzled look.

"What do you mean, you know? What dream?" she asked.

I froze as if that would make my mind shut up. It never worked, but I never stopped trying. "Uh, nothing," I said. I didn't want them to know about it, but the cat was out of the bag. I needed to get a grip on my thoughts.

Ismene stared at me, waiting. I sighed and relayed my dream about the goddesses of fate and fury converging to create a curse to change the course of the Magicborn.

"How interesting," she said. "Well, it may have been a dream, although it sounds prophetic, so we won't dismiss it entirely or rely on that information as fact, but I'll certainly look into it.

"Now, here's what we know is fact. Six magical items must be gathered to unlock the portal to the realm you must travel."

"So, the magical items are keys?" I asked.

"Yes. The first we already have, bone dust from a faerie queen or king. The second is the wings of a dead pixie queen. They'll be kept close to the current pixie queen herself."

I groan at the thought of dealing with our mischievous cousins.

"I agree, but it must be done. So, that's the second key. The third key's the vocal cords of a mermaid queen."

I groaned again.

"Are you going to keep groaning, or can I get through this?" Ismene snapped.

"Sorry," I replied. "Please continue."

"The fourth is a werewolf fang, also from an ancient queen and highly protected."

"Are any of the keys not protected? I mean, if they aren't, that sounds like piss poor management," I said, throwing my hands up, exasperated.

Ismene smiled for the first time that day. "Fair point. We'll assume all the keys are well protected."

"Great, so what's after the werewolf fang?"

"Dragon scale and vampire blood," Ismene said, ticking them off her fingers individually.

"Excellent," I said, with a wry smile and an eye roll. "When exactly am I supposed to begin collecting these items?"

"The sooner, the better. But you'll need to make more progress with Sorcha before you can do anything. Traveling to these realms will kill you if you don't have any training first."

"Fantastic, and why does this have to be me?"

"Only someone with the blood, your blood, can collect the items and pass into the Underworld with them. And they must be collected and earned by the person trying to enter Erebos, where we believe the Cursemaker resides. Your blood is the seventh key."

"Perfect," I said. "So, you're not even sure where the Cursemaker is?"

"I'm afraid not, but we're working on it, and I'm confident we'll know by the time you begin collecting the keys. Plus, with the dream you shared, maybe we'll be able to crack this sooner rather than later.

Ismene continued going over things for a little longer, but I tuned her out and practiced shielding my mind instead. I'm sure she knew, but maybe she needed a break that day too because she kept droning on until she finally released me.

I raced to find Lia, who was with Koen at dinner, but, at least, tonight, she was sitting on the opposite side of the table from him and was waiting for me.

I slid into the seat beside her without a tray of food.

"Are you done?" I asked. The need to have her in my arms was all-consuming.

She took one look at me, seeing the fire I was sure burned in my eyes, and said, "Absolutely."

We barely made it back to our room before I undressed her and claimed her as my own again.

Chapter Thirty-Five

INSATIABLE
Riona

My days passed in a blur of fighting and fucking. My mornings were spent with Sorcha, sparring with magic or in physical fights, learning the combat techniques I needed to break the curse. My afternoons were spent with Ismene as she drilled all the seemingly useless facts of Vakrass into my brain. "You never know what might be useful," Ismene said every time I grumbled about our lessons. I'd picked up on Vakrasi and was now fluent, so we'd moved on to Oxli—the mermaid language—which pleased Queen Nasryn. And I spent my nights buried in Lia, trying to fulfill the insatiable lust that ripped through my core every evening. I could never get enough of her, and I was never left feeling satisfied. We only stopped when the sun rose, and I had to meet Sorcha again.

After a month of no forward progress in combat or magic, Sorcha decided if I had so much energy to expend at night, (someone had informed Sorcha about my late-night extracurricular activities with Lia each night. Damn, Oryn and Kallik.) then we could start training at night as well to ensure we were getting as much done as possible, and maybe she'd start seeing some growth.

Seriously? They already occupied my days, and now they're taking away the only time I have with Lianna. It was bullshit.

Despite my heavy protests, Sorcha wasted no time and went straight to Queen Nasryn, who promptly issued an order for me to comply with my instructor's demands. So, I trained morning and night and attended all my regular classes in between, leaving me with only morning meal times to catch a glimpse of Koen and Lia.

A month passed with no alone time with Lia. Ismene kept me late in the library every night, well past dinner in the mess hall, and instead, opted to have dinner delivered to us. When I'd return to my bed, exhausted from my late-night sessions with Sorcha, sometimes I'd find Lia already nestled in our bed, but other nights, she'd be nowhere to be found. Yet, she was always in bed when I woke up the next morning.

Until the morning I woke to find she hadn't returned to our room, and I was furious.

I shouldn't blame her. She'd been open with me from the beginning that she'd date others, and I'd been okay with that when I thought I'd be the one she'd be coming home to every night. But I was far from okay with her staying all night with someone else since she promised she wouldn't do sleepovers. I climbed out of bed, padded down the hallway to Koen's room, and knocked on the door.

Koen answered the door shirtless and in his boxers, and I cursed. "Is she here?" I asked, heart thundering and blood pounding in my ears.

Koen scoffed. "Yeah, she's here. We're busy,"

Unadulterated rage consumed me until all I saw was red. I knew Koen had wanted her for himself since we first met, and now I knew he'd been playing the long game. He was trying to take her from me.

"I'd like to see her," I said, refusing to back down.

"Like I said, she's indisposed at the moment. I'll let her know you stopped by." He moved to close the door in my face, and I shoved my foot in it, stopping him from closing it.

He was strong, but I was pissed, and my strength when I was enraged outmatched most. I threw my body against the door, and it crashed into him. He staggered back.

"What the fuck," he said, coming at me. I ducked around him and dashed into his bedroom, where Lia was lying naked and asleep in his bed.

"Lia, wake up," I said. My anger pulsated through the room, an ugly, treacherous living thing. Lia's eyes flew open and widened when she saw me. She grabbed the blanket, pulling it over her naked chest.

"What're you doing here?" she asked.

"You promised you wouldn't do sleepovers." I was seething and cut straight to the point as my fury spun into a wild thing, untangling itself from my control. The candles in the room flickered to life and sputtered out again. The bed beneath her trembled, and I reached for her, but she shrank away from me, her blue eyes wide.

I stepped back several steps as if I'd been slapped. "You're afraid of me?" I asked incredulously.

The bed stopped trembling. I took another step back and held up my hands. "I'm sorry. I don't want you sleeping in other people's beds. I don't care if you have other partners, but we had an understanding. We have rules," I said, the betrayal and hurt coloring my voice.

Lia stood, pulling the sheet off the bed with her.

"I'm sorry," she whispered. She moved to wrap her arms around me, but Koen's scent was all over her, and I backed away, refusing to allow her to touch me when she was covered in him, afraid of what the monster within me might do if she touched me now.

"Come back to our room and get cleaned up," I said, resigned. "We have class soon." I didn't bother waiting to see if she followed. Instead, I left with a sharp ache in my chest like a knife was twisting in my heart when Koen walked into his bedroom and closed the door behind him. I went to meet Sorcha. I didn't trust myself to return to the room anymore. I didn't want to see if she'd stay with Koen longer or return.

I stomped to the training field, where Sorcha had moved our training now that it was getting nicer out. I trampled every flower I saw, trying to emerge despite the spring snow until I reached Sorcha in the middle of the field.

"Bad day?" she asked.

I glared at her.

"Okay then," she said, setting aside her ever-present sword and daggers. "Why don't we work on tackles and pins today?"

I didn't bother responding. I glared at her, waiting for her to make the first move.

I didn't have to wait long. I'm pretty sure knocking me on my ass gave her some sick pleasure. Any other day, I might find that sexy, but I was in no mood.

She lunged at me. I tried sidestepping to use her momentum against her as she'd taught me, but she was so fast. At the last minute, she turned and casually flipped me over her shoulder and pinned me to the ground.

"Again," she said, staring down at me.

I worked to draw air into my lungs. "Yeah," I gasped. "Give me a second."

She reached down, grabbed my arm, and hauled me up. "You won't have a second to regain your breath on the battlefield. Breathe through the pain and never stop moving or you'll die."

Before I could fully regain my footing, she knocked me on my ass again. This time, I was quicker to regain my footing until Sorcha swiped a leg under mine and knocked me to the ground again.

My nostrils flared, and I stayed on the ground. I was fucking done.

"Get up," Sorcha commanded.

"No," I said. I sat up and brought my knees up to my chest, then wrapped my arms around them. I laid my head on my knees, letting my hair fall around me like a shroud to hide the tears leaking from my eyes. It was all too much. I couldn't bottle it up anymore.

Sobs wracked my body. Tears of frustration and rage. Tears of loneliness and exhaustion. Tears of constant unfulfillment and fear.

I felt, rather than saw, Sorcha sit on the ground beside me. She sat there with her arm against my arm, knee against my knee. She said nothing as I struggled through my emotions.

I don't know how long we sat there, but when the tears subsided, I was presented with a different problem. My excessive crying had resulted in a massive amount of snot.

Well, crap. You've done it now. Sorcha's going to see you covered in your own snot. Ew. You're never going to live this one down.

I kept my head bowed, debating my options when Sorcha came to my rescue.

Sorcha stuffed something in my hand. "Meet me here tomorrow, first thing in the morning," she said brusquely, grouchy Sorcha reappearing. As her footsteps faded away, I was left to deal with my tear-stained face.

When I looked to see what she'd given me, I was surprised to find an antique handkerchief with the initials AM stitched into the delicate material. The cloth was meticulously cared for, and I could tell it was an important keepsake. After wiping my face clean, I folded it and put it in my pocket to be laundered and returned.

I sat for a long while until the sun set and the moon rose and the night grew chilly. But I didn't care. I gazed up at the twinkling stars, contemplating everything.

I hadn't asked for this. I resented it, and in resenting my task, I resented Koen and Lianna for the time they got to spend together while I was stuck training. I resented them for their freedom to live life on their terms and together.

"I'm so tired of being alone," I said aloud. The sound of my voice echoed through the stillness of the night, unanswered by even the faintest cricket's chirp.

Chapter Thirty-Six

GO EASY ON ME
Riona

Sorcha didn't mention my breakdown when I returned her handkerchief the following morning at training. She just put it in her pocket. We stared at each other for several minutes before I broke the silence.

"So, wise teacher, what masterful plans do you have for me today? Will you be knocking me on my ass some more?"

"Nope," she said, continuing to observe me.

"Then what?" I asked, my impatience getting the best of me.

She assessed me for another minute before she said, "We've pushed you harder than we typically push new students, partly due to our frustration. We were forced into this as much as you were. The other part is the time constraint."

"What's your point, Sorcha?" I asked.

"My point is, today I'm going to go easier on you," Sorcha said with a smirk.

"Easier?"

"Well, easier in that I won't waste our time by knocking you on your ass over and over. We'll do something more meditative and work on your balance more. Have you ever done yoga?"

"Yeah, but I've always sucked at it."

"Well, you're fae now, so let's give it a go," Sorcha said, gesturing for me to stand before her.

I took my place in front of her.

"I'll walk you through each position, and we'll start training with these exercises each day, so do your best to memorize them."

"Okay," I said, trying to match her positions. Sorcha moved me through each pose, and I breathed a little easier as some stress melted from my shoulders. I was glad balance training had paid off as my fae body managed the position easily. For the first time in weeks, I started to relax.

"This doesn't look like sparring." Koen's condescending tone sliced through the air around us, disrupting all the peace I'd found within myself.

My muscles tensed. My arms windmilled as I lost my balance and tumbled to the ground.

"Ouch! Damn!" I said, sprawling out on the grass. I'd mastered catching myself on the balance beam weeks ago, but with a few words, Koen undid all that training in seconds.

"Do you need something, Koen?" Sorcha asked, but her voice had a hard, threatening edge.

"Came to check on the progress," he said, shoving his hands into his pockets. "Looks like there isn't any." With that, he scowled at me and then turned back to the school, grabbing Lianna's hand and tugging her with him. "I'm going to get back to keeping Lianna company," he tossed over his shoulder. "She sure is a wildcat, and it looks like I'll have plenty of time to keep her to myself."

It was a dig. I knew it was a dig meant to get a rise out of me, and I took the bait. I leaped off the ground, bellowing a challenge.

There was a gleam in his eye as he turned back to me.

Stars danced in my vision when his fist connected with my face. He swatted me away as though I were nothing more than a pesky insect, which only enraged me further. My hands and skin burned with trapped magic, begging me for release. Instructor Christina's words rang through my head. *Without balance, your magic is trapped.*

So, my magic stayed trapped as Koen advanced toward me. What a mistake I'd made taking him on. Lia had told me that Koen excelled in sparring. I scrambled to get my feet under me while stumbling backward away from him.

Damn, he hit me harder than I thought. I was off balance, trying to regain my equilibrium, then Sorcha appeared between us, her twin daggers drawn.

"What the fuck are you doing?" Koen asked, and even in my disorientated state, I was surprised by his arrogance when he spoke to Sorcha. She could end him with a flick of her wrist, but he didn't back down.

"You may not attack my student." Her voice was low, dangerous, and downright terrifying, and to my surprise, there was a note of protectiveness.

"She attacked me first," he complained, inching away, and a flicker of fear shuttered in his eyes. He still feared, Sorcha. He was trying to hide it, but I could see that his arrogance was a bluff.

"No, she didn't," Sorcha enunciated. "You provoked her. Therefore, you attacked first. Now, go."

When he didn't budge, she released a low feral growl, and the hairs on the back of my neck rose at the challenge.

Koen turned tail and ran back to the school without looking back, leaving Lianna behind.

Lianna's eyes flicked between Koen's fading form and Sorcha and me. Sorcha attempted to help me up by extending her hand, but I slapped it away.

"I don't need you to fight my battles," I growled, the sound escaping through clenched teeth as I rose.

Sorcha cocked an eyebrow and stated, "Technically, you do until you have the knowledge, strength, and training to protect yourself. It's my job to keep you safe... even from those living here or your own unit, if I have to," she said, glancing at Lianna.

"Super," I said. I brushed the snow and mud off my clothing, thankful that for my sparring sessions with Sorcha, I could wear something other than my all white uniform. I turned around to regroup.

Lianna glared at Sorcha. "Was that necessary?"

I spun at the malice in her tone.

"Was what necessary?" Sorcha asked coldly. "Was it necessary that I defend your—she looked to me—"whatever Riona is to you from that asshole because you refused to? Yes, it was necessary."

"You didn't have to be so harsh," Lianna said, surprising me. Challenging Sorcha took guts, but what surprised me more was that Lianna defended Koen, despite what he'd said to me.

"You're taking his side? Even after what he said?" I said incredulously.

Lianna had the grace to look contrite.

"What the hell, Lia?" I said.

"It's just that—" She stopped, looking at Sorcha. "We can talk about it later."

My gaze shifted to Sorcha, who was suddenly engrossed in cleaning her nails with a dagger. "Oh, by all means, don't stop on my account," she said. "After all, I have absolutely nothing better to do than hang out while you guys have your little lover's quarrel or whatever this is."

I sighed and turned back to Lianna. "We'll finish this later. Tonight. In our room," I said.

Lianna sighed. "Don't worry about it. I'm over it." She turned on her heel, walking away without another word.

I turned back to Sorcha. "Sorry about that."

"Don't worry about it. Let's get back to training."

"Aye, aye, captain."

That night, I returned to my room, and Lia was nowhere to be seen. I stripped down to my tank top and boxers, crawled into bed, and cried.

Chapter Thirty-Seven

JACK-IN-THE-PULPIT MIGHT BE THE CULPRIT

Lianna

Startled awake, I scrambled out of bed and hurried to the bathroom, my sheets threatening to trip me up in my haste. I barely made it to the toilet before the contents of my stomach were forcefully expelled. I did my best to be quiet while my stomach turned inside out for the fifth morning in a row. When it finally stopped, my legs wobbled beneath me, and I sank onto the cool bathroom floor. Exhaustion took over.

From the moment I'd woken up every morning, I was plagued by sickness that lingered the entire day. I'd been successful in concealing it from Riona and Koen thus far, but the situation was worsening rather than improving.

It had to be some weird bug. I felt like shit. I had a horrible headache that had been on and off all week. I was exhausted all the time, so much so that it nearly rivaled Riona's exhaustion after she finished training with Sorcha, taking her classes, and then spending her evenings with Ismene. I rested my head against the cool wall in the bathroom until I found the energy to drag myself up. I splashed cold water on my face before I rinsed my mouth out.

In the mirror, I glimpsed my tired eyes and disheveled hair. My eyes were bloodshot, and I was pale—paler than usual. I looked worse than I felt. It's getting worse. I need to go to the infirmary. I tiptoed out of the dorm room, careful not to disturb Riona, waved at Oryn, who was standing watch, and headed toward the infirmary, my queasy stomach protesting with every step.

Please let me get to the infirmary without puking.

I breathed a sigh of relief when I made it.

"Good morning, Ms. Hirovonen," Ophelia said. "What can I do for you?"

"I'm not feeling well. I think I might have a stomach bug. I can't keep anything down. I've had a headache on and off all week, and I'm exhausted."

"Well, let's get you checked out," Ophelia said, ushering me into a room.

I sat on the edge of the bed and lay back.

Do you allow me access? Ophelia's voice sounded in my mind, and I remembered the class we'd taken on mind speak.

Yes, I grant you access, I replied, allowing the healer to assess my body telepathically.

Ophelia raised her hands above my body, closed her eyes, and fell into a deep trance. She was silent for several minutes until her eyes popped open.

"What is it?" I asked.

"You don't have a stomach bug," she said, a grin crossing her face.

"Then, what is it?" I asked. Dread filled me as I waited. I already had a feeling, but it couldn't be.

"You're pregnant," she said.

No. That was all I could think. *No, no, no. This isn't right. Riona is going to freak out. Fuck, fuck, fuck!*

"Wasn't planned?" Ophelia asked.

"No. It wasn't planned."

"There are ways to both avoid pregnancy and enhance your chances. Did you take anything to avoid pregnancy?"

"No—I didn't think. I thought pregnancy was rare in fae. I didn't think it would happen so quickly."

"While it is rare, it's obviously not impossible. One should always plan for the inevitability of what happens when you have sex. Do you know if the male did anything to enhance the chances of pregnancy?" Adding a dose of jack-in-the-pulpit would be more than enough to give him a chance to plant a seed, no matter where you are in your cycle.

"I-I don't know," I said, tears filling my eyes. I wasn't ready for a baby. I hadn't even made it halfway through my first year of school. I hadn't passed my graduation trials. Oh goddess, I was going to be hugely pregnant by the time trials come along. *What am I going to do? I'm going to be a burden to my unit. What if we fail because of this?*

"Lianna, calm down. I can feel your tension from here. We'll figure this out. I need to notify Thea, but you'll be the one to tell your partner."

"Partners," I whispered. "I have to tell my partners. One will be ecstatic, and the other is going to be heartbroken. Fuck!"

"Well." Ophelia cleared her throat. "I'm sure Riona will come around eventually," she said kindly.

"I hope so," I said through my tears.

"Now, let's see if we can't do something about managing those symptoms. You said headaches, nausea, vomiting, and exhaustion. I have a few things we can try for each of those." Ophelia walked over to the cupboards that lined the wall in the room.

"First," she said, pulling out a small pink bag, and setting it on the counter. "Peony ensures a healthy pregnancy, but be careful to follow the dosage instructions I'm going to give you because it can be toxic if not followed correctly."

She reached into the cupboard again and grabbed two more small bags. One was light brown, and the other was light green. She held up the brown bag. "Ginger tea is best for nausea. However, for morning sickness," she said, holding up the little green bag. "Add a little catnip. It should help with the nausea and vomiting." I arched an eyebrow, surprised at the use of catnip, but it's a plant, and I'd try anything to find some relief from the near-constant nausea.

"For the headaches," she said, pulling another green bag from the cupboard, though this one was darker than the catnip bag. "Try this yerba buena tea. It should help with the headaches, but if any of these don't help, come back, and we can reassess. Now, regarding fatigue, I'm going to recommend two options. First, valerian root tablets for sleep," she said, pulling a dark pink bag from the cupboard. "And pine needle tea for energy. Take the valerian root before bed and add the pine needle to the ginger and catnip tea."

My head spun with all the instructions, and I started bobbing my head to everything she said, wondering how on earth I'd remember everything.

"Don't worry," she said, turning back to me. "I'll write it all down, along with the dosages, for each and brewing instructions. It'll be straightforward once it's all written out. The important thing is if any of them don't work for you, then return immediately. If you have any weird or increased symptoms, return immediately."

"Okay," I said. "I can do that." I felt numb. It was like I was floating around the room, and life wasn't real.

Ophelia seemed to know it too. "Why don't I brew you a cup of ginger and catnip tea to help with the nausea now? You can drink it before heading to class."

"I need to return to my room before Riona leaves for training. I don't want to worry her."

Ophelia glanced at the clock on the wall, and I did too. It was well past the time Riona would have left for training. I sighed. She'd know something was up.

"Ginger tea would be great," I said as my stomach pitched wildly. I covered my mouth with my hand, searching the room wildly for something to catch what was inevitably coming. Ophelia shoved a basin into my hands as I started retching. All that came up was bile. When the retching stopped, I wiped my mouth with the cloth Ophelia handed me, then took a swig of water from the cup Ophelia held out to me before spitting it into the basin of sick. "Yuck."

Ophelia took the basin, handing me a clean one before setting about making the tea. I lay back on the bed and fought the rising nausea. Goddess, morning sickness sucked.

"Ophelia, how long does morning sickness last for fae?"

Ophelia hesitated. "Morning sickness rarely subsides until the child is born. So, you can expect to be sick the entire time."

I groaned.

"But, on the plus side," Ophelia continued, helping me sit up and handing me a hot mug of tea, "fae pregnancies are much shorter than human pregnancies. They only last seven months, so you'll give birth shortly after Samhain."

I groaned again. Samhain seemed so far out.

"There are other options. If you wish, there's always the option to terminate the pregnancy..."

"No," I whispered, my voice barely audible but filled with determination. "I'm sorry. I respect any female who makes that choice, but that's not a viable choice for me," I said vehemently.

"Alright, in that case, stick with the teas and follow the instructions. If anything feels abnormal, report to the infirmary immediately. Otherwise, go about your life as best you can. Like I said, I'll notify Thea, but telling your partners is on you."

Chapter Thirty-Eight

SOMETHING TO LOSE
Riona

A week after Koen attacked me and Sorcha so valiantly came to my rescue, I returned to mine and Lia's room, half expecting it to be empty, but it wasn't. Lia was red-eyed, sitting on our rumpled bed surrounded by used tissues, staring at the floor.

"Lia, I'm glad you're here—" I started, but when she looked up at me, her eyes were filled with tears.

"Ri," she choked out, her voice filled with anguish as tears fell from her eyes.

I rushed to her side and settled beside her, pulling her into my arms. "What? What is it?" My mind immediately jumped through worst-case scenarios—someone died, someone was seriously hurt—

"I-I'm pregnant," she said, gulping as huge wracking sobs overtook her body.

I jerked back. That scenario had been nowhere on my list, but it took the top spot of worst-case scenarios. "What do you mean you're *pregnant*? How?"

She looked at me like I was a complete and utter moron.

"I understand *how*. But we haven't even finished our first year. We haven't declared or bonded, and now you're pregnant—with Koen's baby?" I paused. "It is Koen's, right?"

"Of course, it's Koen's. Who else's would it be?" Lia said through her tears.

I shrugged, running a hand through my unruly curls. "I don't know. I was making sure. What does this mean for us?"

Lia gaped at me in disbelief. "You're worried about you right now? Or our relationship? I'm fucking pregnant, and I'm going to lose this baby because of the fucking Mortal Curse, and you're worried about—what—us? How selfish are you?" Lia spat at me.

It was my turn to stare at her in disbelief. "That's not what I meant. But maybe if you didn't feel the need to sleep around, you wouldn't be pregnant right now," I barked. Regret washed over me instantly, and my face heated with shame.

"Fuck," I muttered. "I didn't mean that."

The look of pain etched across her face had me reaching for her with an apology on the tip of my tongue, but she jerked away. "Don't fucking touch me," she said viciously.

"Lia."

She held a hand up, cutting me off before I could apologize. Rage burned in her eyes. I knew she'd have sex with other people, so how was I accusing her of cheating on me?

"Sorry, I didn't mean what I said," I said, trying to diffuse the situation, knowing it was too late. I couldn't take it back, and I wasn't entirely sure I wanted to—not fully. I meant some of it, but I absolutely could've approached it differently.

"I think it's clear that you said what you'd been thinking and feeling for a while. At least now it's out in the open.

"Does he know?" I asked, ignoring her words. The cat was out of the bag, so to speak, and there was no coming back from it, so I plunged ahead.

"Not yet. I thought it was only fair that I talk to you about it first since you and I are—well, I guess I don't know what we are anymore. I'm guessing you don't want to be with me anymore."

I didn't answer her. I didn't know what to say. Of course, I still wanted her, but her having Koen's baby changed everything.

Except it wouldn't.

Once the baby was born, it would descend into a human and live in the human realm. None of us would know what happened to it after that. Everything would go back to normal. I breathed a sigh of relief. We only have to make it through the pregnancy, and I'd have her back.

"What am I gonna do, Ri?" she whimpered.

"It's going to be okay," I said, sitting beside her again on the rumpled bed, flicking some of the used tissues onto the floor. I pulled her into my arms and rocked her gently. "It's going to be okay. We will figure this out. How did you find out you're pregnant? Are you sure it's not a mistake?"

"I went to the infirmary because I haven't been feeling well. Ophelia worked her magic, and voila, baby. So, it's not a mistake."

"Okay, well, you'll have the baby, and things will return to normal after you have it. We'll continue like this never happened," I said.

Lianna recoiled and leaped up off the bed. "You think I'll pretend this never happened? You think I'll give birth to a child and forget about it? Are you kidding?" Lianna shouted.

The door burst open, and Oryn and Kallik spilled into the room, weapons drawn. In a split second, they assessed the situation in my room. Lianna standing over me, screaming at me as I cringed on the bed. Oryn grabbed Lianna and jerked her away from me, and I bolted up off the bed.

"Stop!" My voice was filled with power, and it ripped through the room. Both guards froze. "Oryn, release her, right now," I commanded.

To my surprise, he dropped Lianna immediately, and I pulled her behind me.

"Get out," I growled.

The air wrapped us in a suffocating embrace as tension crackled like electricity. It seemed to vibrate with my unspoken rage. Oryn stood frozen, his breath hitching as he gazed at me, obviously torn between his mandate to protect me and the violence swirling in the air aimed at him. Shadows shifted around us, deepening the sense of foreboding. Every heartbeat echoed loudly as I stared down my guard, daring him to make a move.

"Get out," I ground out when he didn't move. My voice was low and deadly, and a shiver ran down my spine as the wind in our room picked up.

Kallik grabbed Oryn, and they sheathed their weapons and backed out of the room without a word, keeping a wary eye on me the entire way out of the room.

"Are you okay?" I asked, turning and catching Lia's arm to examine it. She yanked it out of my grasp before I could assess any damage.

"Leave me alone," she said. She grabbed her hoodie and slipped her shoes on.

"Where are you going?"

"To stay with Koen. I—I need to be with someone who doesn't care only about themself."

I flinched and began pacing, frantic to make her understand, to make myself understand. "That's not fair, Lia. You know that isn't fair or true. What do you want from me?"

"I want you to tell me it'll be okay. I want you to care about how this is going to affect me. I've always wanted a baby, Ri. You know that, and now I'm pregnant, and The Mortal Curse is going to take everything from me. This is the worst possible scenario for me. You know I'd planned to never get pregnant, and now I am, and there's nothing I can do. Why—how can you not see that?"

"I—I figured since The Mortal Curse was going to take the child from you, we could—I don't know," I said, my voice cracking with frustration.

"Well, I'll leave you to ponder that, but I can't be here," Lia said as she pulled the door open. Oryn and Kallik stared down at her, blocking her way out. They both looked at me.

"Let her pass," I said. I'd never hold her anywhere against her will, and seeing Kallik and Oryn block her way brought me back to when Elik used to keep my mother locked up in the house. "Now!" I demanded when they didn't move fast enough. They moved aside.

Lia stalked from the room without a backward glance. Oryn and Kallik closed the door, leaving me to ponder what she'd said. Was I *really* so selfish? Tears welled in my eyes, and one slowly slipped down my cheek as I wrapped my arms around myself, trying to keep from shattering.

What happens if she has her baby and loses it, and you didn't do everything you could for her? That mysterious voice whispered in my mind.

She'll never forgive me. The answer slammed into my head with heartbreaking clarity. Losing Lia would devastate me. I didn't know how I'd survive in this world without the only friend I had. The one person I loved more than anything in this new world. The one tie I had to my home on Earth. I couldn't lose her.

I sank onto the edge of my bed, lay down, and pulled the covers up over my head. I clutched my knees to my chest as my sobs echoed off the walls.

I didn't want to lose her.

I wanted to keep her in my life, and Lia wanted to keep her baby. Nobody in the world could help her, except for me.

And now you have something to lose. Something to risk your life for. That mysterious voice rang through my mind again, and damn it, it was right.

I bolted upright, my tears ceasing. *I* can help her.

Well, damn, I was going to break The Mortal Curse or die trying.

Chapter Thirty-Nine
RAGING HORMONES
Lianna

Tears coursed down my cheeks as I raced away from the room I shared with Riona. I cursed the hormones running through my rapidly changing body. I'd never been a crier, but it was all I seemed to do these days.

Who the hell did she think she was? I stormed through the school with no destination in mind. I'd planned to go to Koen's room, but he hadn't answered when I knocked, and I was sure as hell not returning to my room, so I opted to stomp through the castle.

The heels of my boots clacked against the marble floors, and the sound fueled my rage. There was something about the sound that enunciated the feelings rolling through my body. Tonight, the sound resembled a woman on a mission for vengeance.

Would it have killed Riona to be a little understanding about the situation?

I sighed, turning a corner. Once I was out of sight of our dorm, I slumped against the wall. I groaned, scrubbing my face with my hands. I should've realized how difficult it would be for her to hear I was carrying Koen's baby. I should've handled the whole situation differently.

I swiped the tears away, only for several more to fall.

"Come on, Lia, get yourself together," I scolded myself. I stood up straight, swiping at the tears again and swallowing back more. I needed to apologize to Riona. She hadn't deserved how I'd treated her. I wiped my face one last time and stepped around the corner to return to my dorm.

"Ms. Hirovonen, there you are." Thea's voice reverberated off the walls as she walked down the hall toward me.

"Hello, Thea. Can I help you with something? I was returning to my dorm." I hoped I didn't look like as much of a mess as I felt. But I'm sure I did.

"Your presence is demanded at the palace," Thea said, taking my arm and leading me away from my dorm's hallway.

"I need to speak with Riona." I protested, trying to pull my arm out of her grasp.

Her grip was ironclad, though, and it tightened around my arm. "There's no time for that. We must hurry. It took me a fair amount of time to track you down. The Queen isn't known for her patience." She dragged me through the school. Our hurried footsteps echoed through the empty hallways until we reached the courtyard, where Koen was waiting at the entrance of an arched portal.

"What's this? What's going on?" I asked.

The portal opened, and Thea ushered us to the other side without a word.

Queen Nasryn was waiting for us when we stepped out of the portal. Her eyes lit up at our arrival. "Lianna, Koen," she said as she hurried toward us with an enormous grin on her face. "I'm pleased you're here."

"Why, exactly, are we here?" I asked, irritated by our abrupt departure from Vakmore.

Queen Nasryn's piercing gaze dropped to mine, and I stepped back. Malice was in her eyes, and then it was gone, replaced by a smile. "Of course, I'm happy to explain that. However, it's late, so Charis will show you to your room." She snapped her fingers, and the female who'd taken us to the market all those months before came forward and inclined her head toward us. Her hair was a vibrant shade of purple. When she lifted her head, she grinned at me.

"Hello, Charis," I said, smiling back at the female.

Before Charis could respond, Queen Nasryn cut in, "Charis, show Koen and Lianna to their room." Then she turned to us. "Meet me tomorrow morning for breakfast, and we'll discuss why you're here."

"But—" I trailed off as Queen Nasryn swept out of the room with all of her attendants.

I turned to Charis. "What're we doing here?" I demanded. "Riona doesn't know, and she'll freak out if I don't return!" My voice was rising, and I didn't care. I didn't want Riona to panic because she couldn't find me. "When are we going back? What's going on?" I looked at Koen, waiting for him to chime in, but he seemed unbothered by this turn of events.

Charis looked between Koen and me. "Queen Nasryn will meet with you in the morning. I'm not sure what's going on. All I know is I'm supposed to take you to your room, so if you'll follow me…" Charis led the way out of the throne room and down the hall, where our room was. This was the first time we stayed at the palace after the Ascension. "Here you are," Charis said, opening the door. "Here's your room."

Koen strode through the door, and I waited for Charis to take me to my own room. But she didn't. She remained there stoic.

"Aren't you going to take me to *my* room?" I asked after a long, awkward silence.

"I'm sorry. I thought you knew. You and Koen will share a room. I assume this isn't an issue. As I understand it, you're together."

I flushed. I wasn't sure if it was from embarrassment or anger. Most likely, it was a combination. "I'd like my own room, please," I mumbled.

"I'm sorry," she said, her voice filled with regret. She gestured toward the open door where Koen was silhouetted by the last vestiges of sunlight. "This is the only room I'm allowed to give you."

I sighed. I didn't want to room with Koen, especially after fighting with Riona and knowing how Riona felt about me spending the night with anyone other than her. "Fine," I said, not wanting to cause Charis any trouble. "I'll stay here for tonight and deal with it tomorrow morning. Thank you, Charis." I stepped inside, and Charis pulled the door closed behind me.

I glanced back at the door, then around the room.

It'd be fine. I'd sleep on the couch, and Koen could have the bedroom. Problem solved. I glanced at Koen to tell him my plan and found his eyes burning with lust.

"We're alone, babe. For once, Riona is nowhere near us and won't interrupt anything."

"She rarely interrupts anything anyway," I snapped. I was exhausted by the constant animosity between them. If I were being honest with myself, Koen's animosity grated on my nerves a great deal more than Riona's. I couldn't deny I cared for both of them, but I was less concerned about Koen's feelings. Maybe that made me a crappy partner, but I'd been connected to Riona since we were kids. It would take time to build that type of intimacy with Koen.

"Even so, we're alone... in our own room... We may as well take advantage of it. Come on, babe, let's have some fun."

"I'm tired, Koen. Not tonight. I'm going to sleep on the couch."

Koen looked frustrated, maybe even slightly angry, but then he checked himself. "Okay. If you're not up for it, that's fine. I'll take the couch. You can have the bed."

I relaxed. This was the side of Koen that had me falling for him. He often came across as an asshole, but he was all about consent. "Thanks," I said, crossing to him and wrapping my arms around his tall frame.

He responded instantly by wrapping his arms around me and respectfully maintaining space between us.

"Koen," I said, pulling back and looking at him. "There's something I need to tell you before we go to bed. And it's likely why we were pulled away."

"You're pregnant," Koen stated as if it were the most obvious thing in the world.

I took several steps back. "How did you know?" I asked hesitantly. I hadn't told him. I'd told no one, except Riona, and the only other people who knew were the healers in the infirmary.

Koen assessed me for several moments. "Did you think you could hide it from me? I'm the father. Of course, I was notified."

"That was my responsibility. Whoever told you had no right."

"And when, exactly, were you planning to tell me? You've known for a week. Does Riona know?"

I crossed my arms across my chest. "I was going to tell you when I was ready."

"Did you tell Riona?" Koen stepped toward me, and I stepped away from him. I wasn't afraid of him, but I wanted my space to deal with this turn of events.

"Yes, today," I whispered.

"So you told Riona before you told me, the actual father?" Koen's voice raised an octave.

"Yes. I owed it to her."

"But you didn't owe it to me?" Koen asked, but he wasn't accusing me. He sounded heartbroken.

I took a small step toward him, closing some of the distance between us. "Koen, I messed up with Riona by not telling her about us the first time. She's my partner..."

Koen opened his mouth to interrupt, and I held my hand up and continued.

"Just as you're my partner. But she and I have a history. We have rules and boundaries, and I broke those with her already. I don't intend to hurt her like that ever again, if I can help it. So, yes, I told her first. I also told her first because I knew you'd rub it in her face. She deserved to hear it from me. So, I'm not placing blame at your feet, but that's part of the reason. Because you take pleasure in rubbing our relationship in her face. She doesn't deserve it."

Koen had the grace to at least look contrite. "I'm sorry. It bugs me that you two are together and have that history. I want you to be only mine."

I looked up into his stormy gray eyes. "I'll never be *only* yours, Koen. I'm hers too. If you can't figure out how to handle and deal with it, you and I will never work out. I'll choose her because she lets me be me."

I swept into the bedroom without giving Koen the chance to respond. I couldn't take it anymore. The constant arguing between Koen and Riona was exhausting, and I was worn out from having to defend them to the other.

My feelings for Koen were growing, but they were still new. However, I loved Riona. I'd always loved her, and I needed to do a better job of showing her how much she meant to me before I lost her. Balancing my love for Riona, my feelings for Koen, and their jealousy of each other might just tear me apart.

The following morning, Charis led Koen and me to Queen Nasryn's private dining room. Entering the room, the scent of freshly brewed coffee and warm pastries turned my stomach.

After we were served heaping platters of piping hot food, Queen Nasryn greeted us with a cheerful, "Good morning. I'm sure you're wondering why I've called you here."

Koen and I exchanged a glance. Neither of us slept well the night before, and neither of us was in the mood to play guessing games with the Queen.

"As you may already know, the upcoming weekend marks the celebration of Beltane. During this festival, Vakmore Academy second-year students can participate in the bonding ceremony, joining with their potential bondmate."

"What does that have to do with us?" I asked, my voice echoing through the room.

"It's come to my attention that you're pregnant, Lianna, so it makes sense to forge the bond between you and Koen now. Since you're pregnant, you're likely mates because it is challenging for non-mates to get pregnant together. This means you and Koen will go through the bonding ceremony at the end of this week."

I glanced at Koen. Pure elation spread across his face.

"No," I said, still looking at Koen.

His grin dropped, and I felt a fraction of satisfaction. I hardly knew him, and now I was expected to tie my life to him through a bond?

Queen Nasryn ignored me and continued, "You'll remain at the palace and be instructed on the intricacies of the Beltane festival and the bonding ceremony. Typically, you would attend these classes during your second year, but since we're moving up the timeline, you'll get a crash course and undergo the ceremony, whether you want to or not. I command it." A shiver ran down my spine and lingered like a dark shadow.

Her voice, smooth yet piercing, wrapped around me like a tightening grip, leaving no room for resistance. The weight of her gaze was heavy and compelling, as if her essence was woven into the air around us. Each word pulsed through me, compelling my muscles to obey against my will. My heart raced, caught in the relentless tide of her words—this wasn't persuasion. It was magic, a force I couldn't hope to resist.

I won't do it. My stubborn thoughts triggered an immediate response from the Queen's power, which sent a jolt of pain through my body. Agony engulfed me as my skin blistered, and I cried out.

Queen Nasryn's piercing glare met mine. "I suggest you don't fight it. I've made my decision, and you *will* obey,"

I was helpless against the crushing strength of her power, and I crumpled.

"Your will be done." The words dragged themselves from me against my will, and Koen echoed them.

"I'd like Riona to go through the ceremony with us," I said.

"That won't be necessary," Queen Nasryn said.

"Why not? She's also my partner, and if I have to go through the ceremony with Koen, I'd also like to go through the ceremony with Riona. It's my right." I pushed, recalling the passage I'd read on mating bonds.

Queen Nasryn wrinkled her nose in disgust. "If you believe you and Riona will be bonded, you can attempt the ceremony with her next year, at the appropriate time. I'm only allowing this due to the special circumstances of your pregnancy with Koen's child." Queen Nasryn stood. "Now, I have much to attend to before this weekend." She left the dining room, leaving Koen and me to finish breakfast.

I glanced at Koen, whose face was lit up with a wide grin as if he'd hit the jackpot. "Did you do this?" I asked.

"How would I've done this? This was all Queen Nasryn, but I can't say I'm not thrilled. We get to go through the bonding ceremony a whole year early."

I said nothing. I wanted to tell Riona, and I wanted her here. I didn't want to go through the ceremony without her. I didn't want to be bound to only Koen in this way. She deserved her chance too. I shoved my plate and rose. "I'm not hungry," I declared and left the room, finding Charis waiting outside the doors.

"I need to speak to Riona," I told her as she led me back to the room I shared with Koen.

"I'll ask the queen if that could be allowed, but for now, I'll leave you in your quarters until Koen is ready and then you'll begin preparations for the bonding ceremony."

Charis left me at the door, her footsteps echoing through the hallway as she set out again to collect Koen. I entered the room, found a piece of paper, and sat down to draft a letter to Riona.

Chapter Forty

IT'S ABOUT TIME
Riona

I walked out to the training yard the following day with a different attitude. Lia hadn't returned to our room, and I was dying to tell her about my plan, but she wasn't there when I rushed to breakfast to find her. I checked Koen's room, and neither seemed to be there. I couldn't find her anywhere, and when the time came, I had no choice but to make my way to the training yard for class with Sorcha.

Sorcha began putting me through my paces, but after repeating the same instruction for the third time and me acknowledging what she was asking me to do and doing the opposite, she finally snapped. "Where are you today? I know you don't want to do this, but you usually at least follow directions. Stop wasting my time." She walked to the fence, grabbed her water bottle, and took a swig.

"Have you seen Lia?" I blurted. I couldn't help it. My mind was filled with all the possibilities—most of them horrible. I kept picturing her lying dead in a ditch or hurt or something equally horrific. My mind always went to the worst case possible, even when I was little, before Elik tried to kill me and my mother. My mom used to call me her morbid little pumpkin. Of course, she stopped calling me that when the worst case almost happened, and we nearly died. I think she understood it more after that.

"I haven't, but I know she's not here."

"Well, where is she? Is she okay?"

"She's fine. Queen Nasryn summoned her and Koen to the capital early for the Beltane festival. You're going to meet them there next week. Now, let's focus, shall we?"

"You know?" I asked.

"Know what? That Lia's pregnant? Yeah, I know. I was informed almost immediately."

"Can I do this in time? Before the baby's born, can I break the curse?"

Sorcha walked up beside me and set a hand on my shoulder. When I looked at her, she said, "That's up to you, Riona. I believe you can, but if you don't believe in yourself, you won't. It won't be easy."

"Most things worth doing aren't easy," I said. "What do I have to do?"

Sorcha must've seen the change in my eyes. She grinned. "It's about time."

Chapter Forty-One

BELTANE BONDS
Riona

After what felt like the longest six days of my life, I arrived at the palace among the throngs of fae, clambering to get into the throne room where Queen Nasryn sat on her throne. The smell of incense and flowers hung heavy in the room, and the flickering candles cast an ethereal glow over everything. After ten minutes of being jostled about, Queen Nasryn stood and the crowd stilled.

The queen's voice echoed through the throne room, filling the air with a sense of awe and wonder. "Welcome," Queen Nasryn announced.

The crowd murmured, their voices a vibrant hum. Goose bumps danced along my arm, a visceral physical reaction to the magic in the atmosphere. Each breath was heavy with a sense of wonder that made my heart race.

"Gather close, for tonight we celebrate a truly momentous occasion on this sacred Beltane! This night, steeped in tradition and magic, signals a time for deepening bonds and nurturing the flames of love. Beltane is not only a time for revelry. It is a celebration of the heart where we honor those who've found their true mates.

"Tonight, under the starlit sky, we're privileged to witness the enchanting bonding ceremonies that unite souls in profound and everlasting connections. Traditionally, only those who've completed their first year at Vakrass Academy and proven their mettle in the trials are honored in this way. But this year is different!

"We have a delightful surprise that will fill your hearts with joy and excitement! Join me in celebrating Lianna and Koen, remarkable souls who've recently ascended and have proven their love as Lianna is pregnant.

The crowd was utterly silent for a moment before a ripple of sorrowful murmurs ran through it. Everyone attending knew what this meant for them. Heartbreak thanks to The Mortal Curse.

"Tonight, they'll join the ranks of our second-year students as we unite them in the sacred Beltane bond!" Queen Nasryn continued, ignoring the murmurs.

What? No! That can't be right. My stomach clenched, and my mouth went dry.

"May this Beltane ignite not only fires in our hearths but also within our hearts. Here's to love, to bonding, and to a night filled with magic and joy! Let the festivities begin!"

I stared up at Queen Nasryn. My mind became increasingly befuddled because with each word Queen Nasryn spoke, the air shimmered with magic, and the sway of power and acceptance of what was to come spilled over me.

Trepidation turned to excitement.

Don't give in. The magic flowing through the air was taking over my feelings. *You aren't happy about this. Don't let the magic fool you.*

The thoughts were meant to ground me, but as I was swept with the crowd outside to the courtyard, it was impossible not to give in to the euphoria in the air.

The scent of blooming flowers filled the air, and the crowd's excitement was like music to my ears. The moon cast a soft, silvery glow over everything, and the cool night air caressed my skin lovingly. As we reached the raised platform, my heart thundered, and I fought through the haze of the heady magic, nearly breaking through Queen Nasryn's thrall. I shifted from one foot to the other and back again before locking my knees to remain still. My mind slowly cleared, and I considered what Koen and Lia's bonding meant.

Another burst of power emanated from the queen, and for once, I reached for my anxiety like it was a lifeline. Opening myself to the panic would give me something else to focus on and help me push against the might of Queen Nasryn's power.

Would Lianna bonding with Koen make her leave me behind? Would she still want me if I told her I'd break the curse for her? It's nearly impossible to break or interfere with a bond. I gulped a breath, then another, fighting the rising tide of nausea at the image of Koen and Lianna bonded and me left behind.

Bonding? How can Lianna even consider testing their bond when I'm still around? Has she given up on me so entirely after our first big fight? Each thought raced through my head as the crowd surged toward the raised platform, everyone clamoring to get a good view. I allowed myself to be carried by it, only to find myself stuck in the middle of the writhing mass when the crowd finally settled.

The claustrophobia settled in, and a vise wrapped around my heart, squeezing. I searched for an escape route, but bodies crushed in around me from every side.

No! No! No!

I tried to drag in a breath, but my chest refused to expand and allow the much-needed oxygen into my lungs. My stomach flipped wildly, and I thought I might be sick on everyone around me. My sharp nails dug into my skin, drawing blood. The pain grounded me.

I inhaled deeply through my nose and blew it out through my mouth, working to regain control as the panic attack threatened to engulf me.

I wanted to ground myself with my anxiety against Queen Nasryn's power, not let it take over me in a crowd of strangers. I focused on my breathing and the pain in my palms as I drew my blood. I hated crowds—worse, I hated being stuck in the middle of them with no escape.

It's okay, you're okay. I chanted this mantra to myself over and over, even as the crowd grew more energetic, pressing against me as Koen and Lia took their places on either side of Queen Nasryn and the others who intended to go through the ritual. Only two other couples were on the stage, and I vaguely recalled seeing them around Vakmore between classes. However, the memory slipped away as the panic continued.

"It's okay, you're okay," I repeated, this time aloud.

Queen Nasryn's voice interrupted my mantra. "Tonight, Lianna Hirovonen and Koen Trevarthen, Vesper Ravenscroft and Sotiria Ashbourne, Calyx Dvorak and Astraea Havilland seek their bondmate, and as tradition demands, we will see if they're to be a bonded pair."

Everything faded away the second I saw Lia on that stage. She was dressed in a flowy, shimmering gown that cascaded around her like a gentle waterfall. The fabric, a soft blue, so light it flirted with silver, caught the moonlight with every movement. The delicate layers of the gown danced against her skin, enhancing her ethereal grace. Her striking, deep blue eyes sparkled like sapphires against the gown's hues. She was a perfect image of elegance and grace, as if she'd stepped out of a dream.

Koen stood beside her, and he couldn't take his eyes off her. Seething jealousy bubbled inside me, and I pushed it down before I did something stupid, like leaping on stage and tackling Koen to the ground.

"Lianna, Koen, step into the rings, please." Queen Nasryn's command yanked me from my thoughts.

Lianna hesitated, glancing out into the crowd as though searching for something or someone before she stepped forward into the glowing ring in the center of the stage, and Koen followed. The gold rings rose, encircled them, and swirled. Seconds passed before Koen's band soared toward Lianna, encasing her and linking them.

My heart ached while I waited to see if Lianna's band would encircle Koen. Lianna's band slowly unwound and snaked out. It hung suspended for what felt like eternity before a blinding flash filled the courtyard, and her ring split in two. The crowd gasped as the twin bands hovered before they struck out. One tentacle encircled Koen.

The other wrapped around me.

Murmurs flooded the courtyard as everyone witnessed our triad bonding, and all eyes turned to me. But I didn't pay them any mind. Lianna and I locked eyes.

Ri? Lianna mouthed. Her entire face lit up when she saw the brilliant gold band glowing and pulsating around us, binding us together.

"Well, this is certainly an interesting development," Queen Nasryn said, her tone filled with derision and disgust. She continued looking between Lianna, Koen, and me. "You may remember that these three ascended together, which was rare, but it appears Lianna has completed a bonding with Koen. However, she's also trying to bond with Riona Vandeleur."

"Test their bond!" a voice cried from within the crowd.

Murmurs of agreement erupted, and I was pushed toward the stage as the crowd chanted, "Test their bond!"

"Yes, of course," Queen Nasryn stammered, looking as though she'd rather do anything but test our bond. "We must test them together and perform the ritual."

"But she's bonded to me! I'm her bondmate!" Koen interjected, squaring his broad shoulders like he was gearing up for a fight. I knew he'd wanted that since we'd met, and for a moment, he thought he'd won.

Queen Nasryn raised her hands, gesturing for Koen to calm down. "Yes, you certainly are," Queen Nasryn said, her tone placating. "However, it appears that Lianna may have two bondmates. And the law states all potential bonds must be tested."

"That's preposterous. I won't entertain this," Koen seethed.

The chanting nearly drowned him out entirely. Their focus was on me as I inched through the crowd that was parting for me. I wanted to rush to Lianna and tell her what an idiot I was, but I sure didn't want to do it when everyone's attention was focused on me.

"Ah, yes, Riona, join us on stage," Queen Nasryn said, like I wasn't already making my way there. "Koen, congratulations on a successful bonding. Now, please step out of the circle."

I climbed the steps as Koen said, "You can't be serious. She's a female. They can't be bonded." Koen turned to the Queen. "You said if we bonded, she wouldn't—" Koen's words choked off. He clawed at his throat.

Queen Nasryn's expression was ice, and the air in the courtyard chilled considerably. "Perhaps you misunderstood me, Koen Trevarthen. Remove yourself from the circle, or I'll remove you forcibly."

Dark, suffocating power emanated from Queen Nasryn. I struggled to draw a breath, but Koen appeared to feel something different. He fell to his knees, still clawing at his throat. His eyes filled with terror as the queen fixed him with a menacing glare. Then, as suddenly as it started, her magic relented, and the pain in my chest eased. Queen Nasryn released us, but the tang of her magic hung thickly in the air. Koen stayed on his knees for a moment before he rose, bowed his head in submission, and then quietly stepped out of the ring. Once he was clear of it, Queen Nasryn lifted her power entirely.

Koen neared me and sneered, "Watch yourself. She's mine. You lost her."

I said nothing. But a wave of icy dread washed over me. I couldn't have lost her. I know she was mad, but please don't let me have lost her.

"Riona, dear, come step into the ring," Queen Nasryn said. Her saccharine, sweet tone grated.

I made my way up the steps, eyes on Lianna when my foot caught on the lip of the top step. A calloused hand caught me before I fell, and I looked up into Sorcha's green eyes.

"Thanks," I said after regaining my balance.

Her lips were drawn in thin line as she took in the gold band encircling me. "Good luck," she whispered. Her voice was thick with emotion, but her face gave away nothing.

I couldn't tell what she was feeling; she was feeling something strongly. Strangely, in that moment, when everything I wanted was within arm's reach, it bothered me that I couldn't read Sorcha's mind like she could read mine. I wanted—no, I needed—to know what she was thinking.

"Riona, dear," Queen Nasryn's voice jarred me out of my stupor.

I shook my head. I glanced at Sorcha one last time, wondering why what she was thinking or feeling suddenly mattered so much when everything I ever wanted was within my grasp. I pushed all thoughts of her from my mind and stepped into the inner circle with Lianna's band still linking me to her.

My bonding ring rose from the ground and swept around me. Without hesitation, it wrapped itself around Lianna. Our bonding bands glowed brightly. Far brighter than Koen and Lianna's had.

The sweet scent and magic of our bond coated the air around us.

Lianna beamed, and I grinned back. She was all I'd ever wanted; our bond was a testament to that. The magic around us grew heady as we gazed into each other's eyes. Then, I caught movement out of my periphery.

I glanced back at Sorcha, who'd gone bone white and was hurrying away toward the stairs. She disappeared into the crowd, so I started to turn my attention back to my bondmate, but as I did, I glimpsed Queen Nasryn. Her brow was furrowed as her eyes followed Sorcha's retreating form. Lianna squeezed my hand, drawing my attention away from the queen.

I stared into Lia's ocean-blue eyes and offered a tentative smile. "Lianna, I'm sorry I was an ass," I whispered.

Tears slid down her cheeks. I stepped forward, took her face in my hands, and wiped her tears away.

"I missed you so much," she whispered, not that it mattered. I'm sure everyone heard it thanks to their sensitive hearing. The courtyard's silence added to it.

"I missed you too. This was the longest week of my life," I said, leaning down to kiss her, but before my lips met hers, I was hoisted into the air and thrown.

I flew through the air and crashed into a marble pillar that held up the domed ceiling. An audible crack filled the courtyard. Agony engulfed me as the ribs on my right side shattered. I fell to the ground, cracking my head against the marble floor. Starbursts filled my vision before it went blurry. I screamed and immediately regretted it because pain sliced through me when my lungs expanded against my broken ribs. My head throbbed, my vision darkened, and the last thing I saw before everything went black was Koen advancing toward me, eyes filled with violence and a blur of crimson racing toward me.

Chapter Forty-Two

HEALING
Riona

I lie on my plastic floating raft, dipping my toes in freezing Lake Superior. Laughter sounds from the beach, and I lift my gaze to take in the scene. Black Beach has always been one of my favorite places to relax and float, and today's no exception. It's my mother's birthday. The first after Elik was forced out. The covens rallied around my mom to throw her a huge bash to celebrate her thirtieth. Rosalyn putters around the picnic tables, ensuring all the food is perfect, and the coven children, human and Magicborn alike, run around playing tag on the beach. It's a perfect day. I close my eyes. The sun's warmth chases away the coldness of the water coating my legs—

"She's healing more quickly than normal. Likely because of her blood," a smooth male voice said, interrupting my bliss. My eyes flew open; the warm sun, the frigid lake, and the laughter of my family were gone, replaced with stark white walls and a hospital bed.

The pain in my head was unlike anything I'd ever felt. It was as if a searing hot poker was being forced through my eyes. I gasped when agony engulfed me as my lungs expanded against my broken ribs. I closed my eyes against the brightness and pain, the conversation continued around me. They seemed unaware that I was awake.

"Excellent, thank you, Garen. Will she be okay to transfer back to Vakmore?" Queen Nasryn said.

"Yes, Your Majesty. And what're your plans for the male? They should be kept separate, don't you think?"

"I haven't figured out the logistics of their living arrangements yet. For now, he'll return to Vakmore as well. Oryn and Kallik will continue to guard Riona. I don't see a way around that. Koen must be allowed to continue his education, despite this unfortunate turn of events." The queen heaved a tremendous sigh. "Multiple bondings are such a disgrace, and they're difficult to manage, but at least this one works to my advantage, so I'll let it play out."

What the hell did that mean? I kept absolutely still, hoping the queen would expound on that comment, but she didn't.

"I'll address the concerns with Thea and see what arrangements she can make to keep Riona safe. Our survival depends on her, but I won't hinder the male's opportunity to graduate with his unit because of a little tension over a multi-bond." Queen Nasryn's tone was filled with disdain and annoyance as if the attack and the threat to my life were a big inconvenience.

"Then it's best she returns to Vakmore, though she shouldn't be alone. She'll need someone to stay with her."

A commotion sounded at the door, and my heart skipped a beat when I heard Lianna.

"Let me pass. I need to see her! I need to see her now!" she demanded.

I risked the pain and cracked an eye open. Lianna's furious expression greeted me as she stood outside my door in front of the guards with her hands on her hips as they barred her way into the room. I drew in a breath at the sight of the fierce girl I loved and was rewarded with a sharp, stinging pain in my chest. I couldn't hold back the groan.

The room fell into silence.

Then Queen Nasryn spoke to me in a near whisper. "Riona, you've suffered severe injuries to your head and ribs, which will heal in time. We are planning for you to return home to Vakmore. Oryn and Kallik will accompany you and offer protection." She paused for a moment before adding in a comforting tone that I could hear the falseness in. "I'm afraid Koen must return to Vakmore as well. However, he won't be allowed near you until his bond stops causing him such distress."

"Okay," was all I could muster.

How freaking long would his bond cause him distress? And how safe would I be if he were so out of control?

"The physician says you'll need someone to take care of you, so we will arrange for a caretaker to accompany—"

"I'll take care of her," Lianna interrupted.

"You'll have class and your bondmate when you return home to Vakmore. How do you also intend on taking care of her?" Queen Nasryn said.

"My bondmate is lying in this bed, injured, and I'll care for her as long as she needs," Lianna insisted. Her voice rose an octave. "So, you'll need to figure out the ramifications, but that's what's happening."

I gripped my head as the pressure in my skull grew. "Too loud—please," I said. Nausea surged through me, intensifying to sync with the relentless throbbing in my skull, each pulse echoed like a drumbeat, amplifying the sense of discomfort that enveloped me. "Too loud," I moaned again.

"I'm sorry, Riona. We'll continue this discussion elsewhere. We'll get you back to Vakmore as soon as we can," Queen Nasryn whispered. "Garen will give you something to help with the pain and to help you sleep."

Garen waved his hands over my body, using his healing magic. Warmth spread throughout my body, easing the pain in my skull and ribs from a crescendo to a dull roar.

"I'll be back soon, my love," Lianna said, kissing my forehead.

I listened as the footsteps receded, and I could've sworn I heard the queen tell Lianna her place was at Koen's side. I fought the medicated fog clouding my mind long enough to hear Lianna utter a low growl at the queen before the dark claimed me again.

Over the next several days, Lianna nursed me back to health slowly and caught me up on the events that had transpired, like how Queen Nasryn had plucked her and Koen from school and demanded they go through the bondmate ceremony since Lianna was pregnant. Lianna told me that Queen Nasryn had given her no choice and wouldn't allow her to contact me. I was furious upon hearing this but could do nothing from the bed I was confined to. Then she told me how Sorcha swooped down like an avenging angel and kicked Koen's ass after he attacked me. He still bore the bruises, and the queen reprimanded Sorcha for the amount of damage she'd done. I was surprised to hear about Sorcha coming to my rescue so aggressively, and I made a mental note to thank her later.

All meals were delivered to us, and I was given time off training to recover. Lianna's tutors provided her with work because she refused to leave my side for anything that took longer than a shower, and I wondered how Koen felt about being separated from his new mate while she nursed me back to health. It didn't sound like Lianna was giving him the time of day, though. I guessed he wasn't taking it well, but he couldn't do anything about it because he wasn't allowed within fifty feet of our room. They'd even moved him to temporary quarters on another floor.

A week after Beltane, I woke one morning, and the pain in my head was gone. I took intention breaths, testing my ribs. My lungs expanded without pain. I grinned, rolled over, and found Lianna sleeping peacefully beside me. There were several pillows between us, a barrier. Likely to keep her from hurting me. I lay there, taking in her beauty. She'd been pretty as a human, but she was breathtaking as a fae. Strands of her pale blonde hair fell across her face while a smattering of light brown freckles bridged her nose.

I shifted the soft pillows that lay between us and inched closer to her. I brushed a strand of her silky hair away from her face, revealing the delicate features beneath. Her eyelids fluttered open, and I was entranced by the depth of her piercing blue eyes.

"Morning," I whispered.

"Riona? Are you okay?" she asked, immediately sitting up.

"I'm fine. I feel better," I said, pulling her back down beside me.

"Seriously? No more pain?"

"None," I said, my voice husky.

Lianna gazed at me, assessing if I was telling the truth. When she was satisfied that I seemed better, she said, "Good morning, beautiful."

Her melodic voice sent shivers down my spine. For years, I had wished for this, and now, finally, she was mine. I didn't have to worry about Ascension separating us or anything else because we were bonded. Nothing stood in the way of us being together anymore, except the silly notion the queen had about me ending the curse. Lianna was finally mine.

Not all yours, though.

The voice crashed into my mind uninvited, and visions of Koen looming over me, enraged, killed my moment of happiness. I pushed the voice out of my mind, reinforcing my mental shields. I picked my cuticles, a habit I'd given up years ago, as I tried to figure out who it was. When I couldn't, I pushed the thought aside and distracted myself instead of letting my anxiety take over.

"Let's go get breakfast," I said a little too brightly to cover up the anxiety coursing through my body.

Lianna frowned and reached for me, but I crawled out of bed before she could catch my hand and pull me to her. "What's the matter?"

"Nothing," I said too quickly, my voice was an octave too high. I grabbed a shirt and pants off the floor and slipped into them, glancing around our messy, cluttered room. I added "clean dorm" to my never-ending mental to-do list. I was the neat freak, and after a week of me being out of commission, our dorm room showed it.

"Obviously something is up. Please don't do that. I know you well enough to know when something's off."

"It's—this is almost perfect. Almost everything we ever wanted... Except..."

"Except Koen," she inserted.

"Yeah, except for that, and the curse."

"Just because I'm bonded to him doesn't change my feelings for you. I can care for both of you," she said defensively.

"I know that, but you're having *his* baby. Feelings between you are bound to increase. He can give you something I can't. Something I can never give you. You two will share something that'll change your lives so much that I worry I'll become obsolete to you," I admitted.

Lianna climbed out of bed and wrapped me in her arms. "Riona, you give me things he can never give me, too. You'll never be obsolete to me. Besides, as you said, the baby will descend into a human after it's born, and I'll never see it again." Her breath caught in her throat as she uttered the words, and I remembered I hadn't told her yet that I'd decided to end the curse for her.

I opened my mouth to tell her, but she held up a hand.

"Please let me finish," she said, and I closed my mouth, biting back the words.

She adjusted her sheer camisole, momentarily distracting me, but her following words pulled me right back. "I love you. I loved you long before we became a thing. I loved you when we were kids. I'll never love him the way I love you."

I looked at her, knowing it wasn't that simple.

"Say something, Ri," she begged, grabbing my hand and squeezing it.

"I don't know what to say. You think that now. Maybe you think you won't, but I think we both know it's not true, especially since I'll be breaking the curse for you, and you'll be able to keep your child. Your and Koen's child," I said, finally spilling my secret.

"What? When did you decide that? Don't I get a say about you traipsing off worldwide to do this? I didn't ask this of you."

"Except you did. I'm the only one who can break the curse. You want this baby more than anything. Perhaps more than you want me or Koen, and we both know you'll be destroyed if you can't keep it. So, no, you don't get a say because I can't live without you!" I leaped to my feet and made my way to the bathroom.

"Let's get breakfast," I said over my shoulder, ending the conversation before closing the door.

Chapter Forty-Three

HOLDING BACK
Riona

Breakfast was waiting for me on the table when I exited the bathroom a short time later.

"I thought we were going to *get* breakfast," I said, looking at Lia.

"Koen might be down there," Lia said. "And I thought we should finish our conversation." Lianna patted the seat beside her.

"Pretty sure we finished that conversation, and it's not up for debate." I sat at the table with my tray and took a bite of the scrambled eggs and moaned. Faerie food was so fucking delicious.

"So, what exactly is the plan? Is he going to try to kill me again or—"

"Well, Kallik and Oryn are here to ensure that doesn't happen. Everyone's gone out of their way to make sure you two don't even see each other. Plus, Thea temporarily relocated Koen, so his room's on a different floor, but he'll be returning to his room now that you're better.

"But I don't know. You know how the bond can be. If he seeks you out..." She didn't finish her sentence. There was no need.

"Got it," I said, gritting my teeth against the bond in me that was equally outraged by the idea of my bondmate being bonded with someone else. For once, I understood Koen. For once, we agreed.

I wanted to destroy him. The thought startled me. I'd never been violent, but as a fae, a viciousness was welling within me I hadn't previously known was possible.

"How do you not feel it? How is it not tearing you apart?" I asked between clenched teeth as I wrestled the monster within, that had a single goal: find Koen and destroy him.

"The theory everyone's working with right now is that the absence of territoriality of the bond on my end is because of the unique aspect of my bond with both of you, since neither of you is bonded to anyone else. If either of you were to get close or bond with someone else, the territorial aspect would likely snap into place for me." She sat for a moment, staring at the wall before she looked at me. Unshed tears shone in her eyes. "Fuck, Ri, he wanted to kill you," she said.

"The feeling's mutual," I said through gritted teeth. "I don't know how we're going to get through the first-year graduation trials. I'd rather kill him myself than work beside him."

"Well, we're going to have to figure it out."

A knock on the door startled us, and I cowered at the thought of it being Koen.

"It's not him," Lianna said reassuringly. "It's probably Ophelia. She's been coming to check on you every day around this time."

Sure enough, when Lia opened the door, Ophelia stood between the hulking figures of Oryn and Kallik.

I rolled my eyes at them. The only danger I was in was because of Lianna. "So, what exactly are Queen Nasryn's plans to ensure my safety so I can live long enough to break The Mortal Curse?"

"Queen Nasryn's plan is relying on Oryn and Kallik to protect you and having you avoid Koen as much as possible. My plan's talking you out of it."

I stared at her, and she realized what she'd said was ludicrous.

"It sounds ridiculous. I don't know what else there is to do, and until I can talk you out of it, I don't see any other options."

I groaned.

"She has a point, Riona. There aren't many options. The school will do what they can, but it comes down to whether you and Koen are willing to come to a truce for Lianna's sake. She's going to need both of your support, and you won't be able to offer support if you are trying to kill each other. The choice is your and Koen's," Ophelia said, stepping in. "Now, I'd like to perform my examination so I can get back to the infirmary."

After Ophelia poked and prodded my head and ribs a bit, she gave me a clean bill of health and said I could return to training and classes as long as I didn't overdo it and as long as I avoided Koen.

"Damn, fae healing is nothing to sneeze at," I said after Ophelia left.

"Right?" Lia looked me up and down and finally, looked me in the eye. I could see a question brewing in her ocean-blue eyes.

"What is it?" I asked.

"Are you really feeling better?"

"I am. Why?"

"I...uh—" she started and stopped. She licked her lips, then she closed the distance between us with two quick steps. With a firm, but delicate, grip on my face, she pulled me closer and our mouths collided in a passionate, all-consuming kiss.

She withdrew for a quick breath, searching my eyes for something: permission, forgiveness maybe, I wasn't sure.

"I've wanted to do that for so long. Ever since I walked out the door after our fight, but Queen Nasryn whisked us off so quickly that I wasn't able to come back to the room. Goddess, I've missed you," she said. "I'm sorry for what I said. I don't think you're selfish. I was scared, and I didn't know how I was going to handle losing my baby. I've wanted one ever since I was little, and never thought I'd be able to have a baby and keep it. So, when I realized I might have a shot at keeping my baby because you're all chosen one over there, I lost my mind a little bit, but now I realize I was out of line to assume that you should do that and I—"

I put my fingers over her lips. "I missed you too."

Someone rapped on the door, bringing us back to reality.

"Classes will begin shortly," Oryn said through the door.

"We're coming," I called, but I claimed Lianna's lips once more, instead of making our way to the door. "Later," I promised when I broke off the kiss and saw the desire in her eyes. I nearly lost myself in their brilliant blue depths, but another knock on the door had me clearing my throat and pulling away.

Lianna reached out and grabbed my hand, pulling me back to her. She slipped my hand down the front of her sheer lace panties, and my fingers gently grazed her. I was tempted. I was so tempted to take her then and there, right against the wall, on the couch, on the kitchen table. Anywhere—everywhere. But a more insistent knock on the door broke the spell. "Yes, we're coming," I called.

"Well, we're not if you stop what you're doing," Lianna quipped, grinding against my hand a little. I pulled my hand out of her panties.

She moaned. "Fuck. Maybe we should skip class...." She slipped into a skirt and threw a navy blazer over her camisole.

"I doubt they'll let us skip when we've already missed so much. Plus, I'm feeling better. Let's get it over with. We'll continue later," I promised, slipping on my shoes.

As it turned out, I ended up skipping physiology that morning anyway. Queen Nasryn demanded that since I'd missed my morning sparring session with Sorcha, I make it up during physiology. When I reached the training yard, Sorcha observed me quietly.

I stepped into the ring and set my water bottle on the fence. "I heard you saved me from Koen," I said, uncomfortable under her scrutiny. "Thank you,"

I didn't expect an answer. So, I was surprised when she came closer and brushed a stray curl from my face. "You're welcome. Are you alright?" she asked softly.

"I am."

Sorcha put me through the paces, but I could tell she was going easy on me.

"Stop holding back," I grunted as I parried one of her half-hearted punches.

"It's your first day back after major injuries. Queen Nasryn would kill me if you were injured again, especially by me," Sorcha said, deflecting the next punch I threw.

I retreated and signaled for a time-out. "Holding back won't help me break this fucking curse, so do your job and teach me or get the fuck out, or I'll find someone who will." I huffed. "I'm running on a tight schedule."

Sorcha stepped back, and I dropped my arms.

"Fine. I'm clearly wasting my time out here today." I turned to stalk away when I was flipped through the air. I landed flat on my back. Sorcha's knee pressed into my chest, cutting off any air that hadn't been knocked out of me already.

I tapped her leg twice to let her know I was tapping out, and she moved off me. I coughed. "That's more like it," I wheezed. "Teach me how to do that."

"Why don't I let you catch your breath?"

I panted. "Yeah—that would be good," I said, "but I thought I wouldn't have time to catch my breath on the battlefield," I retorted.

"It's a good thing we aren't on the battlefield," Sorcha said, eyes darkening as she looked me up and down as I lay splayed out.

The look ignited desire in my core like I'd never felt before. Lianna had never looked at me the way Sorcha was staring at me, and breathing became difficult for an entirely different reason.

"Sorcha—"

The look was gone, and her face was wiped clean of any emotion.

What the *fuck* was that?

When I could breathe again, we practiced that move over and over until I perfected it, ignoring the moment we'd shared. I couldn't catch Sorcha by surprise, but I could execute the move perfectly, and when she brought others out to have me practice on them, I took down several upperclassmen.

Aithan was pissed when I could put him flat on his back. He'd been the top fighter for his entire Vakmore Academy career. "This is bullshit," Aithan complained. "I've been asking for private lessons for years. I've been the top fighter, and now this—"

Sorcha threw him a look that would terrify the queen herself. "I didn't have a choice. I never provide individual training sessions for anyone. Queen Nasryn ordered it, and I'm following my queen's orders." Sorcha said, glaring at him. "But even if I offered private lessons, I wouldn't have taken you on as a student because you're cocky and arrogant. I don't waste my time on cocky and arrogant males," Sorcha spat.

I wondered about the malice in her words. Her eyes flicked to me. I dropped my gaze to the ground and was immediately plowed into by an upperclassman who I was supposed to be fighting.

Sorcha stalked over and hauled me to my feet. She looked at the crowd around us. "What's the first rule of combat?" she asked.

"Never get distracted," the students around me parroted. Something that had obviously been drilled into them.

She looked back at me. "Maybe if you spent less time eavesdropping and more time paying attention to your surroundings, you would know that, and you wouldn't have gotten knocked on your ass."

My eyes shot up to meet her gaze. "Is it eavesdropping if you say it loud enough for everyone to hear?" I snapped, embarrassed to be called out and for getting knocked on my ass.

She stared at me until I averted my eyes, and then she stepped back and looked at the upperclassmen. "Head to the gym. I'll be there shortly for class." Looking back, she said, "Go meet with Ismene for your afternoon classes. I'm done with your attitude."

I didn't say a word as I limped out of the training yard. That last hit had done me in, and now that I'd stopped focusing on beating everyone, I paused, taking several shallow breaths against the pain building in my ribs. I rolled my neck, trying to relieve some of the tension building there too.

A hot shower might ease my aching muscles, but there wasn't time. I hurried to the library with Oryn and Kallik in tow, reaching my seat as the bell rang. I sat across from Ismene, who was teaching me the names and unique properties of the plants I might encounter and use during my trek across Ilthyrium.

"Valerian," Ismene said in Vakrasi.

"Valeriana officinalis. Properties include purification, protection, and opening doors between realms," I responded in Vakrasi.

"Good. Medicinal properties?"

"Helps with sleep, anxiety, and stress," I said, filing that information away for myself as something to try for my seemingly never-ending anxiety.

"Magical properties," Ismene demanded.

"A grounding plant that promotes calm minds and harmony. It can help facilitate tough conversations by keeping you calm if you're carrying it."

"Good. Native area?"

"Commonly found in Vakrass, Menefos, and Airestia," I responded, listing off the faerie, Lycan, and pixie realms. "Less commonly found in Erastrith because of lack of sunlight and not found in Oxlis or Nivothia because of the unsuitable weather in those regions," I said before she could ask me why.

"Excellent. I'm glad to see your head injury didn't have a lasting effect."

"Nope, no issues. Hit me with another," I quipped.

Ismene wasted no time, though she used the plant's formal name this time. "Arisaema triphyllum."

"Jack-in-the-pulpit. Typically used as either a contraceptive in women, but has the opposite effect for men as it enhances fertility. It's poisonous in its raw form." I briefly wondered why Lia hadn't been using it to avoid pregnancy, and I made a mental note to ask her.

"Correct," Ismene said. "Where is it likely to be found in Ilthyrium?"

"Same as Valerian for the same reasons," I said.

"Good." For the next several hours, she listed different plants, and I got every one correct, so she released me with several more to memorize and homework to label where in Ilthyrium I might run into each plant. "Tomorrow, we'll put everything you've learned together to assess where you are and what you still need to learn," Ismene said.

"Can't wait," I said, hoisting my bag over my shoulder.

Chapter Forty-Four
OCEANIC VIEWS
Riona

"You're late," Sorcha barked as I ran onto the field the following day. I'd overslept after staying up too late with Lianna.

"Sorry," I said breathlessly, "I—"

"I don't want your excuses. I don't have time. Get in the ring."

I ducked my head, trudged into the center of the ring, and stretched, wondering what had her in such a piss-poor mood. When I reached the middle, I stopped and turned to face her.

"We need to work on unlocking your magic further. You've used magic once or twice, but it was instinctual and without control. I'm sure you noticed you injured yourself when you used magic defensively. So, it's time to learn to channel your magic to use it intentionally without injuring yourself or anyone else."

"Um, okay... how do you propose we do that?"

"Like this," she said as she hurled a fireball at me with no warning.

The flaming ball hit me square in the chest and knocked me to the ground. My breath left my lungs in a whoosh.

"What the hell!" I leaped to my feet only to be hit with another fireball in the arm, then again in the leg.

"Come on. Get your shield up," she taunted. "Do magic. No one's going to save you."

She kept lobbing fireballs and taunting me like it would be incentive enough to elicit my magic to surface.

It wasn't.

Make me deal with emotional trauma, and I could craft a perfect shield bubble, but with physical danger? Forget it. Yet, the taunts put me back into my childhood memories of Elik berating my mother and me.

I only lasted five minutes before I curled up in a ball on the ground.

"Please, please stop," I begged.

Sorcha relented with a growl. "You'll never be able to protect her if you don't unlock your magic."

I sat up, trying not to jostle the burns on my neck, hands, and face. My training tunic had protected the rest of me, but the unprotected areas took the brunt of my injuries. I stood slowly, afraid that if I moved too quickly, I'd tear open my ruined skin. I looked down at my burned skin and turned to leave without a word. Rage bubbled within me.

Fuck this.

She wasn't teaching me shit. It was vengeance. I wouldn't stick around for it.

I was about to leave the clearing to see Ophelia in the infirmary when Sorcha touched my shoulder. "I'm sorry," she whispered. "Come here."

No fucking way.

The last thing I wanted to do was get anywhere near her. I turned to glare at her and noticed her face was pale, paler than I'd ever seen it. She was taking in the full damage of what she'd done to me.

"I'm sorry," she said again. "Please let me fix it."

I hesitated for a moment, then I did as she directed. She placed a hand over the burn on my wrist. Warmth flooded my skin, not a painful warmth like the burns, but a comforting, healing sensation as Sorcha wielded her magic and healed me.

"Can you...remove your shirt?" she whispered. She leaned her head close to mine, almost intimately, and my face flushed.

I pulled the soft fabric of my shirt over my head and winced as it grazed the tender burns on my neck. In my black sports bra, I felt exposed under her intense, probing gaze. An instinctive urge to cover myself rose within me.

She reached out, skimming the raw skin of my neck while her other hand found its way to my stomach. Her fingers grazed my ribcage below my left breast, sending a shiver through me as she pulled me closer. Her eyes closed, and a serene smile crossed her face as she channeled her healing magic into my body. A gasp escaped my lips when the edge of her finger brushed against the sensitive underside of my breast, a mix of surprise and warmth cascading through me.

Her eyes flew open. "Sorry," she said, and I could've sworn she sounded a little breathless as she moved to the burn on my cheek. She placed a hand over it, and as that healing warmth flowed through my body again, I caught her eye.

I had the urge to lean in and kiss her. I licked my lips nervously and angled my head toward hers. She did the same. Someone cleared their throat nearby, and I leaped away from Sorcha, turning and ducking my head sheepishly. I started to mumble an excuse to whoever had cleared their throat, but when I lifted my head, I came face to face with Lianna and Koen.

"Well, isn't this cozy?" Koen sneered.

Lianna's face contorted with rage. Her blue eyes flashed when she directed her glare at Sorcha. "Get away from her," she snapped. Her face twisted into a grimace. I could smell her fury in the air around us. Thunder rumbled in the distance.

"Excuse me?" Sorcha retorted, eyeing Lianna warily, as if Lianna were a petulant child Sorcha was tired of dealing with.

Lianna snarled, "Stop touching my bondmate and leave!" She paced like an agitated cat, ready to strike at any moment. I was surprised. Lianna seemed jealous, even territorial.

I opened my mouth to respond, and calm Lianna down, or to convince her nothing had happened, but Sorcha didn't give me a chance.

"No," she said, her voice eerily calm. Sorcha appeared relaxed, but I'd trained with her enough to recognize the steely concentration and determination emanating from her. She looked unguarded, but the subtle shifts in her body showed she was prepared to protect herself if the need arose.

"She's mine," Lianna said, stopping in front of Sorcha. She crossed her arms, and I swore it looked like she was trying to hold herself back. Lianna glowered at Sorcha before she growled. "I've seen the way you look at her. You can't have her. She's mine. Get the hell away from my bondmate!"

Sorcha took a dagger from her weapon's belt and began cleaning her nails, appearing unbothered. "If you have a problem, take it up with the queen. For now, though, Riona and I have training, so I'm going to have to ask *you* to leave," she said.

"We aren't leaving." Lianna planted her feet as though she thought Sorcha would physically remove her.

"Fine, stay," Sorcha said. Then she took my hand. "Hold on tight, and don't let go," she said, looking at me. "Trust me." Then we were rolling and tumbling, weightless through space, and then the world pressed in around me. Air was squeezed from my lungs, my ears popped, and an excruciatingly intense pressure built at the base of my skull. And just as quickly, solid ground was under us again and the pressure was gone.

The world wobbled, and I staggered, almost falling. Sorcha's strong arms caught me as my stomach roiled and I dry heaved. Nothing came up, and I was thankful I'd missed breakfast that morning because vomiting in front of the female you'd been seconds away from kissing didn't seem like the best impression to make.

Sorcha lowered me to the ground, and hot sand met my clammy skin in a warm welcome.

"Stay still for a moment. The nausea will pass," Sorcha said, lying down beside me.

"What the hell was that?" I asked. "And what was Lianna talking about? How do you look at me?"

"Spaceshifting," Sorcha explained, ignoring my other question.

I waited, but when she offered nothing further, I said, "Uh, okay... what's *spaceshifting*?"

"It's a teleportation ability that some Magicborn possess. I happen to be one of them." She heaved a sigh when I stared at her expectantly, waiting for some explanation as to why she'd spaceshifted us to wherever the hell we were. "I wasn't in the mood to argue with Lianna or train in front of them, so I brought us here," she said. "I hope that's okay," she added.

"Where's here exactly?" I asked, taking in my surroundings. At first, I'd thought we were in another field, but as my equilibrium returned, I caught the briny scent of salt water and heard waves crashing behind me. I whipped around and came face to face with a gorgeous white, sandy beach and the welcome sight of a crystal-blue ocean. I gaped at the sight before me.

I recalled the maps I'd studied with Ismene during our sessions. "Vakmore Academy is at least a hundred miles from the ocean," I said.

"Yeah, we're several hundred miles away," she conceded.

"There wasn't somewhere closer?"

"I missed the ocean," she said, wistfully staring at the waves. Then she looked at me. "Sorry, I should've grabbed your shirt," she said, addressing my lack of a shirt.

I sprawled out on the warm sand, enjoying the warmth as I breathed in the salty ocean air. I looked over and heat blossomed on my cheeks when I caught her staring at my body, and I fought the urge to cover myself. When she saw that I'd caught her staring, she quickly averted her eyes.

"I've never been to the ocean before," I said, looking up at the cerulean sky. "I used to beg my mom to take me, but she couldn't since I was Magicborn. I lived next to one of the biggest freshwater lakes in the US, though. I spent a lot of time there. The water's freezing year-round, so most of the time, it wasn't ideal for swimming. Did you know that Lake Superior is so cold that if someone drowns, the body doesn't float?"

Sorcha looked at me like I'd lost my mind. Maybe I had. Spouting morbid facts about a home that was no longer mine seemed certifiable. But lying on the beach, the sun shining down on me, and the sound of waves nearby triggered memories I'd thought were gone.

"Do human memories ever come back? I thought that with time, they'd go away, but lately, some of mine have been cropping up."

"Like what?"

"Well, when I got hurt, I dreamt about my mother's thirtieth birthday on the beach. I was lying on a floating raft in the lake. And, just now, I remembered not being able to go to the ocean as a kid and spending time on the lake. Stuff like that." I sat back up and looked at her.

"Well, they say all memories fade eventually. But I have one or two human memories too. They're elusive, and if I try to chase them down, they disappear, but sometimes triggers will bring them to the surface, and when they come, I let them without trying to hold on to them. Sometimes, I think it's better to do that than lose them entirely.

"Other fae I've talked to remember nothing of their human lives. They've told me they used to chase their memories, thinking the more time they spent thinking about them, the easier it would be to remember them. But I don't know if we have any control over it."

I nodded, staring out at the water.

I rose. "What're we working on today?"

"Pinning," Sorcha said without a smile.

"You just want me under you." I quipped. My eyes widened at my unfiltered boldness.

"Perhaps," Sorcha replied calmly. "But today, you'll do the pinning. If you can pin me, I'll be under *you*." She smirked.

She wants me under her? I had no comeback for that. My face heated. "Okay," I squeaked. I cleared my throat and tried again. It came out more forcefully and louder than I intended, so I closed my mouth and gave up before I made a bigger fool of myself.

Chapter Forty-Five

CORE MEMORIES
Riona

Sorcha maneuvered me into position and showed me various ways to take down an adversary and pin them. Regardless, I failed repeatedly, too distracted by the thoughts invading my mind.

Sorcha on the ground under me.

Me on the ground under her.

Her hands on my body when she healed me.

During one pass, I was wholly distracted by the thought of what her lips would feel like against my skin, and I missed her as she flew past, stopping short of the ocean's edge.

"Riona!" Sorcha scolded, "Focus." Her nostrils flared, and I wondered if she could scent my arousal. My cheeks burned at that.

"That's enough for today," she said abruptly, moving several paces away.

"I'm sorry," I said.

"It's fine," she said. Then surprised me by pulling her shirt over her head, revealing her toned, muscular stomach, which was marred by scars. She turned around, and I saw a vicious, puckered scar that started at the waistband of her pants and traveled up her spine to the base of her neck, only to be partially hidden by her sports bra.

"How did that happen?" I asked.

"Fell in love with the wrong woman," she replied, turning to face me again. She winked, but I saw the pain and fury in her eyes.

"How does that happen by falling in love?" I asked.

Sorcha sat beside me. "Are you sure you want to hear this story? It's not a pretty one, and there's no happily ever after."

"Sure," I said, hoping my face looked encouraging.

"Anysia and I weren't bondmates. She was bonded to a male named Anxo, but that didn't stop me from pursuing her. She had only to look at me once, and I knew I wanted her for myself. I thought she belonged with me, even if it meant sneaking around and hiding it from Anxo. Or at least we'd thought we were hiding it…" She stared at the water, but I could tell that wasn't what she was seeing.

"Turns out the bastard knew all along," she said after a long moment. "He played the long game by letting us do our thing. I fell in love with her in a way I hadn't thought possible. I dreamed of running away with her. I was so sure she was my bondmate too." Sorcha had a faraway look in her eye, like she was somewhere else.

"One day," she finally said, "when we were scheduled to meet like always, she didn't show up. I went home thinking she mustn't have been able to get out—that happened sometimes—but then it happened another day and then a third day. It wasn't like her to not at least send word that she couldn't make it, so I decided to hell with it and went to her home." Sorcha's voice trembled, and she cleared her throat before beginning again.

"Anxo answered the door, and he had a terrifying, wicked gleam in his eyes. I can still see it now." Sorcha shivered. "'I've been waiting for you,' he said to me."

"Without warning, someone grabbed me from behind, and a sack was thrust over my head, plunging me into darkness and panic. Someone yanked me forward, and I was disoriented as I was dragged down a seemingly endless flight of stairs. Absolute terror gripped me. I was untrained, helpless. There was nothing I could do to fight back."

Sorcha swallowed and took a deep breath before continuing. "When they took the bag off, I stood in what can only be described as a torture chamber."

"I was shackled to the cold floor, but my heart stopped when I saw Anysia, bound to a stone table. She was lying there, stripped naked and undeniably pregnant. I'd noticed her body changing, the subtle signs of life growing within her, but I'd failed to grasp the profound reality of it. I was devastated—I realized I wasn't as attentive as I should have been. I was too wrapped up in the chase and the sneaking around. I couldn't help but feel the weight of my negligence.

"I won't go into detail about everything he did to her on that table in front of me, but he had no regard for her or her dignity." Disgust, tinged with remorse, filled her face, followed by overwhelming sadness.

"I was powerless. She begged me for help at first, but eventually, I think she realized there was nothing I could do, and when she retreated into herself. I knew I'd lost her."

"Lost her?" I asked, unsure of what she meant.

Sorcha jumped. She turned to me like she was coming out of a trance. She'd immersed herself so deeply in her memory that she was reliving it, and I'd startled her.

"Sometimes, when a person experiences severe trauma, the mind has ways of protecting itself. Anysia succumbed to the torture, and her mind broke. She became a shell of who she was before. Anxo put her into special care and forbade me entrance. I couldn't even sneak in to see her. So, I understand loneliness. I understand wanting something you can't have fully because someone else has it. I wish I could say it gets better or easier, but in my experience, it doesn't."

"What happened to the child?" I asked.

"Anysia gave birth to a girl. A girl named Haelyn. Anxo had a final parting gift for me. Anxo went to Queen Nasryn and asked that my punishment for interfering with a bond be that I be the one tasked with taking the child to the portal to deliver her to the witches. Queen Nasryn agreed—the reason is a story for another time. So, I brought Anysia's child to the witches. I kept track of her, even though we weren't supposed to. It was easy because Haelyn was born with a large birthmark that covered half of her face. She transitioned nearly fifty years ago. She's a dragon and the spitting image of her mother. I'd do *anything* to protect her," Sorcha said.

"Have you seen Haelyn? As an adult?"

Sorcha hesitated for several long moments before admitting, "I have. Though I'd appreciate it if you'd keep that to yourself."

"Of course," I said.

"What happened to Anysia?" I asked tentatively. "Is she still in the hospital?"

Sorcha stayed quiet for a long time. "No. She's dead. The story I was told was that while I was delivering Haelyn to Earth, Anysia threw herself out of the tower window. But I know that's not what happened. I know he killed her. He didn't want to be bonded to her anymore, and the only way to rid himself of the bond was for her to die."

Silence palpated between us. I contemplated everything Sorcha had told me, mulling over the fact that this tough-as-nails warrior knew true heartache. I felt her gaze on me, and I turned to face her.

"Find something for yourself," she said. "A hobby, a lover, something you can use as an escape when needed. But save something for you because sharing the person you love has the potential to destroy you faster than anything else," Sorcha said. She opened her mouth to say something else, but stopped.

"What?" I asked.

"Until you break free from the resentment and loneliness, you'll continue to fail in your training. It's tied together. The more balanced your life is, the more control you'll have over your abilities..." Again she looked like she wanted to say more, but didn't.

"What else?" I asked.

"You need to find a release. A satisfying release, by any means possible." Sorcha said. "If you can't find it with Lianna, other options are nearby."

My face flushed. How did she know I hadn't been satisfied? "What? Like you?" I said sarcastically, trying to cover my embarrassment.

"Yes," she said. "I'd be more than happy to provide a satisfying release, and trust me when I say," she said, looking at me, "I can take care of every need you have."

I clenched my thighs as my core heated. An image shoved its way into my mind of being tied down and arching against her as she buried her face between my legs. As quickly as the image came, it disappeared.

I slid my gaze to Sorcha, who was staring out at the ocean, seemingly oblivious to what I'd envisioned, then a sly smile crossed her face. *She'd* sent me that image. I blushed furiously as I thought about her tongue buried in me.

"Oh," I squeaked at the brazen offer to service me. Before I could come up with a more coherent response, she stood, unbuttoned her pants, and pulled them down, revealing black bikini bottoms. My mouth went dry at the sight of her practically naked before me.

"What're you doing?" I sputtered.

"Swimming. I didn't bring us out here just to train and to tell you depressing stories. So, come on, take off your pants and get your ass in the water," she said, grinning in her sports bra and bottoms. Then she raced to the ocean's edge and leaped in. I stripped down to my underwear, thankfully they were black and not the white lacy ones I'd considered throwing on that morning, and joined her.

We spent hours swimming and collecting seashells from the ocean floor. I discovered I could hold my breath much longer than she could. We wrestled and tried to dunk each other, and I relished the feel of her in my hands. Each time my fingers skimmed her skin, I thought about that image of me tied down beneath her as she feasted on me. When we grew tired of swimming, we lay on the sand to dry in the sun.

"Thank you for taking me here," I said, staring into the cloudless sky.

"You're welcome," she whispered, and her voice came from right beside my ear.

I turned. Our faces were inches from each other. I reached over and traced the smattering of freckles on the bridge of her nose and cheeks. My fingers found her lips, and I gently traced them, waiting for her to stop me, but she didn't.

I leaned forward, closed my eyes, and softly brushed my lips against hers. Not even a second passed before she kissed me back. The first kiss was soft and sweet.

The second was not.

Where is she, damn it? They've been gone all day. She needs to come back. Why isn't she back? Thoughts that weren't mine slammed into my mind, and I yanked back from Sorcha's touch. That was Lianna. In my head.

"What is it?" Sorcha asked, looking guarded.

"I'm not sure. I think I heard Lianna's voice in my head."

Sorcha sighed and pulled back from me and stared up at the sky. "It's the bond. You can hear each other's thoughts if the feelings are strong enough. What's she saying?"

I hesitated. I'd kissed Sorcha. I had a bondmate. It felt wrong. It felt like cheating.

Lianna has a paramour. Why can't you have one? I argued with myself. *Because you know about him, but she doesn't know about her.* The answer was crystal clear. If I wanted to continue, I had to tell Lia before anything went further.

I leaped to my feet, "I'm sorry, I can't do this yet."

"Yet?" Sorcha asked, slowly sitting up.

"Without talking to my bondmate. Without letting her know that I'm interested in another. It feels like cheating otherwise."

"What if I don't want you to discuss this with her? I'm your teacher. It might be deemed inappropriate. Plus, I like my privacy," Sorcha said, brushing the sand off her arms and legs.

I looked at her for several moments, weighing the predicament I'd gotten myself into. I wanted Sorcha. I knew I did, but I didn't know if the feelings I thought I had for her were simply lust or if they ran deeper. Or if she had the same feelings. "I can't do anything more without telling Lia. If that's a deal breaker for you, we can pretend this never happened and move on."

Sorcha glanced up at the sky where the sun was setting. "We should head back. It's late," Sorcha said.

"That's not an answer."

Sorcha stood and pulled on her pants and tunic before clipping her thin weapon's belt around her waist. "You made it clear. This was a fun time, and it won't happen again."

"Okay," I said, unsure what else to say. I wanted to try to convince her, but her finality left no room to argue, so I quietly slipped on my pants as confusion settled in. First, Sorcha said yes, but then she said no when I brought up Lianna. I couldn't not tell Lianna, and why shouldn't I tell my bondmate that maybe I had feelings for someone else, and I might want to see where those feelings lead?

Then it clicked.

"Lia isn't Anxo," I said. "She won't hurt me. Not like that."

Sorcha said nothing, and once I was clothed as much as I could be since I was still shirtless, she took my hand without looking at me and spaceshifted us to the front door of the Academy.

"Have a good night," she said, leaving me in the doorway.

It took everything in me not to go after her. To press my lips against hers again, to give in to the desire coursing through my body. She'd tried to hide it, but I'd smelled her arousal. I groaned and went to my room, where Lianna was pacing in our small kitchenette, muttering under her breath. Kallik sat in a chair eyeing her while Oryn was nowhere to be seen. Kallik bowed his head to me and quietly exited.

Chapter Forty-Six

EXPLOSION
Riona

"Where the hell have you been?" Lianna spat before I even made it into the room entirely. "What the hell do you think you were doing? You almost kissed her!"

"So what if I did?" I argued, trudging toward our shared bedroom. I was exhausted, and I wanted to crawl into bed and sleep for as long as possible without dealing with the mess swirling around in my head. I'd kissed Sorcha. She'd kissed me back. She offered sex, then took it back. I wanted to explore polyamory, but I didn't know how to approach it. Yet the spark was lit, and there was no taking it back.

Lia stepped in front of me, halting my trip to the bedroom.

"What do you mean, 'so what if you did?'" Lianna stared at me until I dropped my gaze.

"Did you kiss her?" Lianna asked with her hands on her hips.

"That isn't any of your business," I bristled. I'd planned to tell her, but now that she was treating me hostilely, the last thing I felt like doing was confessing what I'd done and what I wanted.

She won't take it well. I need to wait until she calms down. Old survival tactics wormed their way into my mind. I pushed past Lianna and entered our shared bedroom before she could say another word.

"Of course, it's my business. You're mine," Lianna said, following me into our room.

"Excuse me?" I cocked an eyebrow. "Since when do you own me?" I backed up several paces. "Goddess, you're such a hypocrite, Lianna. You do as you please with whomever you please. You always have. And I've always trailed after you like a puppy, and I keep coming back for more. I'm done with it.

"If I want to see someone else, I'll see someone else. I thought I owed you the courtesy of informing you of that, but I just realized you gave no such courtesy to me when you started shit with Koen. Now, you expect Koen and me to fight against our instincts of our bonds so you can have what you want and leave nothing else for the rest of us? I'm fucking over it. If I want to have an intimate or platonic relationship with someone else. I'm letting you know, I'm going to."

Lianna gaped at me as though I had three heads. "You wouldn't do that."

"Why would it matter if I did, Lia? You can't think you're the only one allowed to jump between partners," I said, pushing past her and crossing the room to the bathroom. Maybe a cool shower would help calm the rage inside me.

"You're selfish, Riona."

Her words immobilized me. Resentment filled every fiber of my being. I turned slowly and glared at her. "*I'm* selfish? I let you have your cake and eat it too. I agreed to go on a quest that has a high possibility of killing me in the hopes of coming out victorious, so *you* can have the child *you* conceived with the partner I'm forced to share you with. The one you didn't bother to tell me about at the beginning. And *I'm* selfish?"

"Yeah. Because you knew who I was. I'm not monogamous. I have a big heart with a lot of love to give. You've always known that. You're trying to change the script, and I don't know if it's to get back at me, but—"

I held up a hand, stopping her tirade. I battled against the feelings within me, trying to calm them. "The world does not revolve around you, Lianna Hirovonen. You don't own me. You have no say over what I do with my body."

Without another word, I swept past her and out the doors. Oryn and Kallik pretended they weren't eavesdropping, so I didn't spare them a word. I took off toward the gym, where I thought Sorcha would be.

I needed to see her.

I needed to figure out what was between us.

Hurried footsteps sounded behind me, and I spun, expecting Lianna to have followed me, but it was Kallik. Oryn waited by my door.

"What, Kallik?" I barked.

"I'll escort you to wherever you're going," Kallik said, his tone leaving no room for argument, but I didn't care.

"How about you leave me alone or find Koen and guard him to ensure I'm safe? I'm sick of you trailing me everywhere. I know it's not your fault, but tonight I need some damn space. So, find a different way to protect me that doesn't involve hovering over me."

Kallik surprised me when he raised his hands and backed off. "I *really* hate saying this to females, but you need to calm down," he said.

His tone was concerned, fearful even, and I didn't understand until he gestured to my arms.

I looked and they were red and blistering at the heat that welled beneath the skin. I didn't take another second to think about it. I knew what was going to happen.

I knew it with every fiber of my soul. I'd felt it building all day, simmering below the surface. Left unchecked, my magic would decimate anything in its path. I turned and raced down the stairs as fast as I could, trying to suppress the fire under my skin. My only thought was to make it to the vortex room because finally, I'd accepted who I was, and with the acceptance came balance, and now my magic was about to explode. My heart skipped a beat, terror engulfing me. If I didn't make it before my magic was unleashed, I'd hurt someone—or everyone.

I burst into the vortex room and found it already occupied. "Get out!" I sobbed. "Please get out now!" Everyone took one look at the blisters on my arms and scattered, slamming the door behind them. My body erupted into flames.

I fought against it, hugging my arms to my chest. Sobs wracked my body. "No, no, no. Please stop."

The flames receded into my body, and I screamed. The excruciating sensation of being burned alive consumed me. "Please stop!" I sobbed.

"Don't stop," a calm female said behind me.

I whipped around and found Sorcha, arms crossed, leaning against the wall near the door, watching me lose control.

"Truly feel every single thing you're feeling right now. Let it fill you up."

"I can't! It hurts!" I wailed, pressing harder against the tide of magic, trying to take over my body.

"It hurts because you're fighting it. Let go," Sorcha said. Then she was in front of me, wrapping her arms around me.

"Let go," she whispered, and the dam broke.

The ache in my chest crescendoed, and my shoulders heaved. Sobs tore from my throat, but I kept fighting it, terrified of what would happen if I let go.

"Let it go. Everything that's holding you back, making you angry, making you doubt yourself, making you *afraid*, let it go. You're so much stronger than you think. You hold the power. Not Queen Nasryn, not me or Ismene, not Koen, and certainly not Lianna. You hold all the cards," Sorcha continued. Her words were my undoing, and everything I'd been holding inside exploded.

I threw my head back and screamed, releasing my bonds of rage, hurt, frustration, and above all else, anxiety.

Everything went silent, and for a moment, calm surrounded us.

Then chaos reigned.

Sorcha hissed an expletive and jumped away from me as my body became engulfed in flames. I was a pillar of fire.

Flames poured from my body, igniting everything around me, and I was lost in the ecstasy of it, riding the waves as the vortex room—a room built to withstand any onslaught of magic—burned to ashes around us. I was vaguely aware of someone calling my name, but I couldn't pull myself out of the pleasure encompassing me as my magic was finally released. And for the first time ever, my chest stopped aching, and the ever-present terror released its grip on me.

Eventually, the pleasure dissipated, but still, I burned.

I was grounded again, staring at the raw carnage I'd wrought. The magic room was *destroyed*. Sorcha's clothing was tattered and burned in some places. She stood as far away as she could get from me while still being in the room. The two-way mirror had shattered, and Lianna, Koen, Thea, and Kallik stared at me with horror and awe. The room was destroyed, but still, I burned. I didn't know how to stop.

"Help her," Lianna said through gritted teeth, looking at Sorcha. I could tell she was pissed she had to involve Sorcha at all, but Sorcha was my magic trainer and the most knowledgeable individual here, other than perhaps Thea, so Lianna had no choice.

Sorcha strolled toward me, flinching slightly when my flames leaped at her. "I can either let it end naturally, forcefully, or help her end it, which might take a while. Forcefully ending it would be extremely painful, and letting it end naturally will take time," Sorcha told them.

"End it," Lianna commanded, acting like she could decide for me. "We don't need her burning anything else down," she said, glancing around the ruined room.

"I should help her end it herself," Sorcha said, directing her comment mostly to Thea. "I'm her instructor for fuck's sake. It's my job to instruct. I've got a golden opportunity to do that right now."

"You're the one who caused this," Lianna argued, not allowing Thea the opportunity to speak. "I'm her bondmate, and I'm making the call. End this now!" Lianna demanded.

I looked at them as the flames emanating from my body grew larger and hotter. More fury crashed through me. Everyone was speaking for me. Something they did too often. Something I'd let them do over and over, but not anymore.

"I don't need anyone to decide for me." I cut in effortlessly.

They gaped at me as though they were surprised to hear me speak. It was insulting.

"Sorcha," I continued, "I've unlocked my magic. Teach me how to stop burning." My voice was calm, and for once so was I. It was as though the anxiety I'd always carried with me dissipated with the release of my magic.

Sorcha looked at Thea for approval, and the headmistress agreed.

"Okay," Sorcha agreed.

"But—" Lianna sputtered, then she realized she'd lost her tenuous power since I was coherent and could speak for myself.

"Leave us," Sorcha commanded. "She needs to focus."

Lianna opened her mouth like she was about to protest, but Koen had clearly had enough of her jealousy because he grabbed her arm and yanked her away from the window. The flames flickering on my skin intensified with my rage at seeing it. They disappeared from the window, but I could hear Lianna complaining as she was dragged away. I turned my focus back to myself.

There's nothing you can do for her. Focus on yourself. If she wants to be manhandled by that ass, that's her business.

Thea gave us one last glance. "If you need anything, send word."

Sorcha didn't respond, her attention fully on me.

When we were alone, Sorcha inched toward me as though she thought I might lob a fireball at her like she'd done to me so many times.

"What do I do to stop it?" I asked. My legs shook, and I was fighting to stay on my feet as exhaustion descended on me. Now that we were alone, the depth of the fatigue overwhelmed me, and I didn't know how much longer I'd last before I burned out.

"Sorcha," I whimpered, "I'm tired and scared and...and I think I'm close to burnout."

If Sorcha was worried, she didn't show it. "Relax. It's your magic. Regain control. It's been unlocked because you've freed yourself from everything holding you back. Now rein it back in. Thank your power. Don't place limitations back on your shoulders. Wish it well and release it," she said.

"Okay..." I took a deep breath and then another, thanking my power for coming to me.

When I inhaled again, the fire cooled, retreating into my body slowly at first, then as I gained confidence, the fire cooled quicker until the flames dissipated. A sheen of sweat and ash coated me, and I nearly collapsed with relief.

"Well done," Sorcha said, coming up and draping a blanket over my naked body. "You should get a shower and some sleep. You expended a large amount of magical energy. It will drain you for the next couple of days. Eat something hearty and high in calories before you go to sleep."

"Okay," I said, stepping around her.

"And Riona?"

"Yes?"

"Your magic will be volatile while you are getting the hang of it. It would be best to avoid any activities that might elicit potent feelings until you have full control over your magic."

No sex. Got it. "I don't think that will be a problem, but thanks for the heads up," I said, blushing wildly at the implication. Just when I wanted to take things to the next level with Sorcha, she tells me I can't have sex.

"You're welcome," Sorcha said.

I turned to leave, but she placed a hand on my shoulder. I looked at her, and for the first time since I'd realized she was in the room, I detected a glimmer of fear in her eyes. "Thank you for trusting me," she said, and before I could respond, she was gone.

Chapter Forty-Seven

UNLOCKED

Riona

"It's time to get down to business," Sorcha greeted as I arrived for training the following day. "Time is running out, and the queen is getting antsy."

"Right," I said, trudging into the ring. Every inch of my body was sore, and I was depleted, despite sleeping like the dead the night before.

"Since you've unlocked your magic, we will start defensive magic. Stand in front of me and close your eyes," she directed, oblivious to my discomfort.

I did as I was instructed. I rolled my shoulders and neck, then stretched my arms over my head and behind my back, trying to release the stiffness in my muscles so I'd be ready for whatever Sorcha threw at me.

"You've already demonstrated that you can produce a shield bubble large enough to offer protection to several beings at once, but now, I want to see if you can protect only yourself. I want you to picture protection for yourself. A safe place, whatever that means to you, then I want you to imagine coating your entire body in it from head to toe."

I felt silly because the first thing that popped into my mind was coating myself in sunscreen, but I did as she told me anyway. I closed my eyes and focused on the protective feelings that always produced a shield bubble. Then I focused on pulling that shield closer to me until it coated me head to toe.

"Excellent. Open your eyes."

I opened my eyes and looked down at myself. "There's nothing."

"Are you sure?" she asked. "Stop looking with your eyes."

Then I felt it. A thin layer of magic coating my skin. I grinned.

"Try to keep it up," she warned before a fireball flew at my face.

The fire bounced against my skin harmlessly and dropped to the ground where it was extinguished. Sorcha grinned, and I saw three more balls of fire flying toward me alongside a dagger. I dodged the fireballs and surprised us both when I caught the dagger midair by the blade without drawing blood.

I stared at the dagger. It had a strange blade. The handle was unremarkable, but the blade...I'd never seen anything like it. It was thick and shaped like a corkscrew. If you stabbed someone with it, you wouldn't get it back easily, nor would your victim get away easily. This knife would do severe damage, and a simple twist would eviscerate any nearby internal organs.

"Well, this is terrifying," I said, handing it to her when she approached me.

"How'd you do that?" she asked, placing the dagger in her weapon belt.

"Do what?"

"How'd you dodge those fireballs *and* catch the dagger? I didn't teach you that."

"Um, I don't know."

"Do you think you could do it again?"

I shrugged. "I'm not sure."

"Let's try. Shield up?" Sorcha asked, cocking her head.

"Yes."

Sorcha stepped back several steps before she whipped four fireballs at me in rapid succession, and then the dagger last.

Once again, I dodged the fire effortlessly and caught the dagger.

"Cool!" I said, grinning at the dagger in my hand.

But when I looked at Sorcha, the smile slipped from my face. She was frowning.

"What is it?" I asked.

"I'm not sure," she replied, staring at me for a moment longer. "Let's go again."

Sorcha and I trained for another hour, and I defended against everything she threw at me. Nothing got through my shield, and the longer we trained nothing she threw at me came close.

When we switched to sparring, I overpowered her, outran her, and outsmarted her at every turn. Every move she made, I was a step ahead. When I pinned her for the fifth time in five minutes, she yielded and decided we should start fresh the following day.

Sorcha's eyes bore through me, and my neck prickled under her scrutiny.

"What?" I asked, finally acknowledging her.

"You haven't done anything different?"

"Besides almost burning the school down? Nope. Nothing."

Sorcha's eyes lit up. "That's it!"

"What's it?" I asked.

Sorcha walked around me, assessing me, before she spoke again. "When you unlocked your magic, you unlocked everything. All of your abilities." Sorcha grinned as she faced me again. "Congratulations. You're ready."

My stomach dropped. "Ready for what?" I asked, dreading the answer.

"Meet me tomorrow. The usual time." Sorcha gathered her things and hurried back into the school, leaving me to contemplate what me being "ready" meant.

The following morning, when I walked out to meet Sorcha for training, I found Queen Nasryn, Sorcha, and Ismene all waiting outside the ring.

What now?

"Get in the ring, Riona," Sorcha said when I reached them.

"What're they doing here?" I asked without moving.

"I notified Queen Nasryn of your progress and what happened yesterday. She and Ismene wanted to see for themselves, so get in the ring." Sorcha said the last words in her best stern teacher voice, which I'd heard countless times before.

I trudged to the center of the ring, and Sorcha joined me.

"We will do the same thing we did yesterday. Your goal is to remain unharmed."

I shielded my body. I'd practiced over and over the night before, and now I could pull it up quickly and keep it up for a half hour.

"Well done," Sorcha said when she detected the shield was in place. Then, in the next instant, she was on the other side of the ring, running and hurling fireballs at me. I dodged effortlessly to the right and left, letting the fire fly past me. Then, as the last one flew at my face next to a dagger, I reached out both hands and caught the dagger in one hand and the fireball in the other. I whipped them back at Sorcha.

Surprise flashed across her face, though she dove out of the way, and each weapon missed her, but the fireball singed off the end of her braid.

She looked at me from the ground, and I expected anger, instead, a relaxed grin spread across her face. "I bet you've dreamed about having a woman fall at your feet rather than of you falling at theirs," she whispered so only I could hear.

"I'd never admit it," I whispered back, reaching down to pull her up. Clapping sounded behind us. I turned to face the Queen and Ismene. Both were beaming at Sorcha.

"Well done, Sorcha. I didn't think she had it in her, but you certainly brought it out, didn't you?" Queen Nasryn said.

Sorcha looked the queen in the eye and said, "It was Riona's doing. She's capable of anything she puts her mind to. One shouldn't forget that."

The threat was so thinly veiled I couldn't believe the queen didn't respond to it.

Queen Nasryn turned to me. "Well done, Riona. I believe you're ready for your first trial. You'll leave in two days." She glowered at Sorcha. "That'll give you both time to prepare."

"Both?" Sorcha asked.

"Yes, both of you. You'll accompany her on her quest." The queen paused before turning to me and adding, "As will Koen and Lianna. The first few tasks will be considered your graduation trials. You *all* must survive to graduate."

"You can't be serious. Lianna's pregnant. She shouldn't be traveling anywhere, let alone into other factions. It's too dangerous!"

"That's why Sorcha's accompanying you," Queen Nasryn said, gesturing toward Sorcha, who'd stepped several paces away to converse with Ismene.

"I have to agree with Riona," Sorcha said, coming back to stand beside me. "If you want this to be their graduation trial, I can't argue that.

However, as an instructor, I implore you to send more protection for them than just me. I'm good, but I can't be everywhere at once."

"No," Queen Nasryn said, offering nothing else.

"No?" Sorcha and I said together.

"Just like that?" I said.

The queen arched one eyebrow so high it disappeared into her hairline. "Just like that," she asserted. "I've decided."

"But—" I didn't have the chance to make further arguments. Power roiled through the air, and Queen Nasryn's voice echoed in my head.

Let it be known that in two days, Riona Vandeleur, Koen Trevarthen, and Lianna Hirovonen will depart from Vakmore Academy and begin their graduation trials. Sorcha Rietveld will accompany them for protection. Let it be done.

Compulsion swept over me as the queen's invasion ended, and her magic took over. The compulsion was thick and sticky, adhering to every inch of me, leaving me feeling like I desperately needed a bath. The feeling wouldn't disappear until we left Vakmore. I looked at Sorcha and could tell she was fighting to keep the disgust off her face. She glanced at me before turning to the queen.

"Your will be done, my queen," Sorcha said through gritted teeth.

I turned to the queen and bowed. "Your will be done," I whispered.

Sorcha and I turned away, the silence grew heavier with each step.

Chapter Forty-Eight

MORNING SICKNESS WOES
Lianna

Let it be known that in two days, Riona Vandeleur, Koen Trevarthen, and Lianna Hirovonen will depart from Vakmore Academy and begin their graduation trials. Sorcha Rietveld will accompany them for protection. Let it be done.

The words reverberated through my skull like a foghorn as I hunched over the toilet and retched painfully for what felt like the millionth time that day. Each wave of nausea surged from deep within, a reminder of the life growing inside me. Ophelia's teas, with their earthy fragrances and colorful labels, were a gamble. On good days, they worked wonders, soothing my upset stomach and easing the tight grip of morning sickness that clawed at my insides. But this was not one of those days.

I gripped the edges of the cold porcelain while the dim bathroom light flickered, casting dancing shadows along the stalls, mirroring the turmoil within me. My head throbbed, the dull ache intensifying with each heave, making it feel as though a jackhammer was attacking my temples. I could still taste the herbal concoction—a mix of ginger and catnip that promised relief—clinging to the back of my throat, yet it was doing nothing to assuage the storm brewing inside. I closed my eyes, wishing for the nausea to subside, praying that tomorrow might bring a more favorable outcome.

"Ew," a disgusted voice remarked from outside the stall.

I groaned inwardly, recognizing Amalie's voice. Precisely who I didn't want to deal with after hurling my guts up so publicly. I huddled over the toilet, my body convulsing as another wave of nausea surged through me, forcing me to heave again.

I didn't bother apologizing. She didn't care. She wished I'd take my morning sickness anywhere else, but it wasn't like I'd chosen the spot just like I wouldn't have chosen Cyrus's trash can earlier. He'd been gracious about it, but I was pretty sure he chucked the whole can out after class.

How the hell was I supposed to partake in the graduation trials in two days when I was this sick?

The door opened and someone else came in.

"Enter at your own risk," Amalie said from outside my door.

"For fuck's sake, Amalie, instead of tormenting the girl, why don't you return to class where you belong?" Xenryn's voice held an undercurrent of command.

I heard footsteps and someone rushed out.

"Lianna, are you alright?" Concern colored Xenryn's voice.

Gratitude that she'd made Amalie go away washed over me.

"Perfect," I muttered. My stomach calmed enough that I thought I could leave the stall without embarrassing myself. I stood, and the world wobbled a little. I closed my eyes, throwing a hand out to the wall for support. Once the world balanced again, I wiped my mouth with the back of my hand, flushed the toilet, and left the stall.

"Looks like you're leaving in two days. You need to see Ophelia before you leave so you can be at your best to help your unit with the trials."

"Looks like," I said, turning on the faucet. I splashed cool water on my face, washed my hands, and rinsed my mouth out. I glanced up into the mirror and saw Xenryn staring at me, holding out a paper towel. I turned around and took the towel from her. "Thanks."

"Go to the infirmary and get that taken care of. You're excused from your next class," Xenryn said.

"Thank you, Commander," I said with a small smile. I was happy to report to the infirmary because I genuinely felt like crap, and I needed to discuss how to manage my symptoms while on our journey.

Chapter Forty-Nine

THE JOURNEY BEGINS
Riona

Two days later, I woke at dawn, compelled by Queen Nasryn's magic. Lia's side of the bed was empty. She'd come to bed the night before with me. After my breakthrough with my magic, we'd mended our relationship at least temporarily for the sake of the quest.

"Lia?" My voice echoed slightly in the room's stillness. On cue, the sound of retching came from the bathroom, and nausea washed over me, and my instinct to flee rose like a tide. The mere thought of someone vomiting sent shivers down my spine. Hearing someone do it instantaneously triggered my flight response.

"Lia?" I tried again. "Are you okay?" I added.

More retching.

I slammed my hands over my ears, cursing myself. If I were a good partner, I'd help her and hold her hair back, but I couldn't. I brought my knees to my chest and kept my hands over my ears. Tears streamed down my face as I rocked on the bed.

A hand touched my shoulder, and I looked up at Lia. Her lips were moving, but I couldn't hear her. She tugged on one of the hands covering my ears. I dropped both hands. Her face was pale and covered in sweat, but the look of concern on her face sent me into a full-on guilt spiral. She was sick, and I was having a breakdown rather than being supportive. I wanted to be supportive, but I shrank away from her, afraid that if she were sick, she'd get me sick.

"Are you sick?" I asked, my voice an octave higher than usual.

"No, Ri, I'm pregnant..." she said. "Puking comes with the territory. Usually, you sleep through it, but I guess the queen's compulsion woke you too."

"I'm sorry," I said, shame filling me. "I'm not as good at caring for you like I should be."

"Ri," she said, taking my face in her hands. "I know you. It's okay. I've got it under control. I'm sorry you heard me."

I felt even worse that she was apologizing to me for something she had no control over.

A knock sounded at the door. Lia looked at me and smiled, though it didn't quite reach her eyes. She looked terrible. Dark circles rimmed her eyes, and her cheekbones were more pronounced than they'd been even a month before. She was losing weight. A lot of it and quickly.

"I guess it's time to get this show on the road," she said, looking vaguely green. She let my face go, and I crawled out of bed and slipped into my bathrobe. Lia opened the door. Ophelia and Thea followed her inside, both carrying packs.

Lianna whipped around, bent over the kitchen trash can, and vomited again.

I froze in the bedroom doorway, but Ophelia dropped her pack on the table and rushed to Lia's side, gathering her hair back and resting her other hand on Lia's forehead. Magic filled the room as Ophelia poured her healing magic into Lia's trembling body. Lia stopped heaving.

"Better?" Ophelia asked.

"Much. Thanks," Lia replied, then wiped her mouth on the damp cloth Thea held out before turning to me. "I'm okay. It's okay, Ri."

I was clutching the doorframe for dear life. I smiled sheepishly and pried opened my stiff knuckles, releasing the doorframe. I winced when

I saw the deep gouges my nails left in the wood. I finished entering the living room while Ophelia deftly took the soiled trash bag out of the bin, tied it closed, and stuck it in the hall.

We gathered around the table.

"Good morning," Thea said.

"Good morning," Lia and I replied almost in unison.

"I brought you some supplies that Queen Nasryn suggested." Thea held up a black unitard. "She also had these made for you," she said. "They're made from a synthetic material that repels water and retains heat or cold to protect you in all environments. The material doesn't tear or damage easily. It will also account for any growth." She directed that last bit toward Lianna, who was eyeing the suit with distaste.

"What if we don't want to wear them?" She asked.

Thea looked at her. "Queen Nasryn insisted, so if you want to take on that battle with her, you're more than welcome to, but I doubt it will do you much good," Thea said, holding the suit out to her.

Lianna took the suit, holding it away as if it might bite her.

Ophelia held the other suit out to me, and I took it. The material felt strange. It looked like spandex, but it felt like a combination of snakeskin and satin.

Thea touched the packs she and Ophelia had brought in. "These have food, medicine, camping gear, and everything you should need for your first few treks. If you run out, you're on your own, so use everything wisely. Each of you will carry one."

She opened the packs, and on top of each was a wristband. "These," she said, holding up the bands, "are your trackers and health monitors. They're also part of your first-year graduation trials. If you wish to pass, you must always keep them on."

She handed us each band and watched as we put them on.

"Excellent. Now, get dressed, gather your packs, and go downstairs to meet Sorcha and Koen. The queen expects you shortly, and we wouldn't want to disappoint Her Majesty, would we?"

Lia and I shook our heads, and Thea and Ophelia left.

Lia and I donned our suits and looked through the packs to ensure we didn't need anything else. I threw in a hairbrush, hair cream, and my toothbrush, and Lianna threw a hairbrush, toothbrush, and several medicinal-looking baggies into hers. We left the room together. I locked it and sealed it with my magic so nobody could enter the room while we were gone. Kallik and Oryn were waiting for us outside.

Kallik stepped forward, confidently leading the way as Oryn trailed closely behind, his footsteps softer. The school was alive with activity. Students milled about, their curious gazes darting toward us. We pushed through the heavy doors and emerged into the sun-drenched courtyard, a stark contrast to the dim halls we'd left.

Lush greenery surrounded us, the vibrant colors of flowers splattered across the landscape like strokes of a painter's brush. Sorcha and Koen awaited us by the old stone fountain that spilled crystal-clear water, each dressed in their own black unitard. Sorcha's eyes sparkled when she caught sight of me, and Koen leaned casually against the stone bench but threw a glare at me as we approached. Koen clenched his fists and huffed a breath. I stared him in the eye, gathered my courage.

"Here are the rules: I'm in charge. You listen to me. If you fall behind, you get left behind. I'm the only one who can break the curse, so we're doing this my way so we all survive." Every team had a designated leader, and since there were three of us who were students, I figured I might as well step into the role since the task depended on me getting where I needed to go.

Koen looked like he was about to argue, but Thea cut in. "Excellent. It looks like you have your group leader. Sorcha will protect you, but you should play to your strengths and discover where you'll most help your team," she said, directing this last bit at Koen.

Koen begrudgingly looked at me. "I'm a combat-intrinsic, so I can help with battle plans and take on that role."

"And I'm medical," Lia chirped, trying to break the tension.

I smiled at her. "Yes, you are."

"Let's get this show on the road," Sorcha said, glancing between Lianna and me with a frown.

We stepped into the whirling portal to the right of the courtyard and out the other side, directly into the Queen's foyer where Queen Nasryn was waiting, brow furrowed.

"Excellent timing," Queen Nasryn said and approached us. "We were starting to worry. Riona, here's the faerie bone dust for the first key. You'll need each key to leave your current realm. You can't pass through the portal without it. You'll also need all of the keys to enter Erebos, so don't lose them. I've opened the portal to the Hall of Realms for you.

"Only the monarch of each realm can open the portal back to the Hall of Realms. While all the kings and queens have agreed to help by opening the portals, they won't assist you further. If you get into trouble, they won't intervene."

"Why wouldn't they want to help?" I asked.

"Because they see the threat that looms if someone of another faction breaks The Mortal Curse, the realms will be under the control of the ruling power there."

"Wait...what? Why didn't I know that?" I asked. "If I succeed, you rule every realm?"

"Yes," the queen said. Her eyes brightened, and my gut clenched.

Things were falling into place. I glanced at my companions, but they averted their eyes. "Did you know this?" I asked Sorcha.

"I did."

"And you didn't tell me?"

"I couldn't," she says, inclining her head toward Queen Nasryn.

"Perfect, and what if I refuse?" I said, turning back to the queen.

"You won't. The fire burns within you now. It calls to you, and I think you'll find life won't be worth living if you don't. That fire will eat you alive until there's nothing left. I've seen it before," Queen Nasryn stated.

I threw a quizzical look at her, raising my eyebrows.

"A century ago, someone I thought would break the curse let the fire consume her rather than take on the burden of ending the curse. *You* have more to fight for." She tilted her head toward my companions. "You have something to lose."

I gaped at her as the last pieces fell into place—that voice. The voice I'd been hearing all my life was none other than Queen Nasryn. I opened my mouth to say something, to confront her, but before I could get a word out, Queen Nasryn cut me off.

"Time is of the essence. The pixie queen is expecting you and isn't nearly as generous as I am. Eat nothing you find in the pixie realm, no matter how tempting. And keep your wits about you. Pixies are conniving tricksters."

"Apparently, we aren't so different," I said, venom-coating my words.

We were herded out into the courtyard, where the bonding ceremony had changed my life not so long ago. The massive portal swirled with the Hall of Realm's brilliant, inviting prismatic colors.

"Like I said, you'll need to locate the pixie queen to pass through the realm. Do so quickly. Spend as little time in each realm as you can. The longer you stay, the more the magic of the realm will affect you. In time, if enough of that magic builds up in your blood, it will make you a prisoner—forever," Queen Nasryn said. "Good luck."

We made our way through the crowd. Cheers formed behind us as we walked up the steps to the swirling portal. I looked back over the crowd, at the hopeful faces of all who were there to see us off, then I turned away and stepped into the portal's entrance and into the Hall of Realms.

I turned to my companions behind me and looked at Sorcha. "Which is the doorway to Airestia?" I asked.

"That one," she said, pointing to a doorway filled with pastels.

Adrenaline coursed through my veins as I tightened the straps of my pack.

"It's time." I strode toward the swirling portal, its muted colors pulsating with the promise of the unknown. With a deep breath, I plunged inside, feeling the air crackle around me as the fabric of reality shifted.

The end...for now.

ACKNOWLEDGEMENTS

Let's be real. It's hard to write a novel and nearly impossible to do it alone. It takes a truly exceptional support system to reach that goal, and I am blessed to have such a system in place.

It's only fair that I credit those who have gone through the fires with me. My family.

To my wife, thank you for your never-ending love and support and for constantly encouraging me to believe in myself. That shit's exhausting. Thank you for helping me battle self-doubt and holding me every time I broke down at the immense pressure of writing a book and fighting imposter syndrome.

To my children, R and E, your continued understanding of "mom's writing time" and for respecting those pesky signs on the office door that threatened dismemberment if you interrupted me for less than bleeding or dying did not go unnoticed. Obviously, I would never, but a little humor went a long way.

To my daughter. Thank you for always making sure I have a cold Mountain Dew and making sure I eat lunch. We both know I'd probably starve without you. Thank you for your artistic input on my covers and character names.

To my son, I'll never forget your pep talk as I neared sending this book to the editor: "Mom, when have you ever failed at something truly important? Never. You've fucking got this."

To my mother, you are my rock and safe place to fall when life gets rough. Thank you for your support, especially in the months leading up to sending this book to my editor. Thank you for your encouragement and the swift kick in the butt whenever I said I couldn't do it. You're amazing and never let anyone tell you otherwise.

To my Nana. Your acknowledgment is at the beginning of this book, so you didn't have to search for it. But if for some reason you end up here at the back of the book, I reiterate: Please don't read this book. I don't want to test your unconditional love.

Thank you to the amazing alpha and beta readers team who made this possible. Alex, Alexandria, Emily, Meri, and Miranda, thank you for bearing with me and helping bring my creative vision to life with your feedback! Additionally, thank you to Samantha for always being ready for a chat and feedback.

A special shoutout to Miranda for all the handholding you've done to help this book come to life. I can never thank you enough or repay all you've done for me. Especially, answering the fifty thousand questions, even when you had your own shit to do. I am so incredibly blessed to have you in my life.

Finally, a special thanks to my editor, Brittany Ortega, for making ATOD reader friendly and for patiently and beautifully guiding me through the editing process for the first time, listening to what I was seeking, and executing it flawlessly.

ABOUT THE AUTHOR

As a child, the mythical and magical world fascinated Scylla Kairos so much that she spent much of her time pretending she was a mermaid saving damsels in distress. Of course, there were no DIDs present, so she had to make do with saving her little brother at every opportunity. Lucky for her, he was a good sport most of the time, but when he didn't want to be saved, Scylla liked to pretend she was a witch who could turn him into a toad. As she got older, she leaned into her passion and used it as an escape when she struggled with managing her mental health. This led her to writing books that feature mental health disorders and a bit of romance. Her work features LGBTQIA+ characters who battle a wide variety of mental health disorders, all while trying to survive their vicious magical worlds.

Scylla's passion for mental health has often left her wishing she was a witch with powers and a magic wand that she could wave and either cure all mental health disorders or make everyone understand the toll they take. Unfortunately for Scylla, her only means of magic lies in her pen, which she wields with chaotic energy. When Scylla isn't busy dreaming up fantasy worlds and living vicariously through her characters, she's at her home in WI with her witchy wife, their two minions of darkness and chaos (the kiddos), and their familiars, Joey the feisty feline and Cersei the sassy canine.